I0676129

Atticus

in a Skirt

TOMMI ELIZABETH POWELL

FISH HAWK PRESS | North Carolina | 2018

FISH HAWK PRESS

ATTICUS IN A SKIRT

Copyright © 2018 by Tommi Elizabeth Powell

All rights reserved. This book or any portion thereof
may not be reproduced or used in any manner
whatsoever without the express written permission of
the author except for the use of brief quotations in a
book.

This is a work of fiction. Names, characters,
places, and incidents either are the product of
the authors imagination or are used fictitiously,
and any resemblance to actual persons, living or
dead, businesses, companies, events, or locales
is entirely coincidental.

For my mother. Always.

But let justice roll on like a river, righteousness like a never-failing stream!

-Amos 5:24 (NIV)

"Paige, sweetheart." Her mother's voice, usually a warm, slow drip of spun sugar, was a shaky whisper across the miles. There was no trace of sweetness; there was just fear.

"Mom. It's four in the morning." Paige whispered back, sitting up and trying to slow the thoughts in her mind. She spoke with her parents on Sunday afternoons at 2 o'clock, not at four on a Tuesday morning. She took a deep breath and prepared for the worst.

"What's wrong?" she whispered. Paige could feel her heart beating against her ribcage. Beside her, Chris still slept. He could sleep through anything after a long shift at the hospital. She wanted to wake him so she wouldn't be alone for whatever bad news her mother was about to deliver, but her fiancé didn't like to be disturbed. She grabbed her robe and shuffled into the living room. "What's wrong?" she repeated.

"It's your father. Paige, honey, he's had a heart attack."

With those words, everything changed. With those words, the universe made herself known.

CHAPTER ONE

"Do you really have to go?" Chris asked over coffee while Paige packed. "You said it was a minor heart attack." His voice betrayed just a hint of annoyance. He didn't like the unplanned, especially when it was an inconvenience to him.

"It was a minor heart attack, but it was still a heart attack," she said, pulling blouses from the closet and tossing them on the rumpled bedsheets. "He will be in the hospital for a bit, and he'll need to take it easy once he's released. Someone has to handle his clients." Paige was irritable. She hadn't gone back to bed after the call with her mother. She'd sat in the dark until Chris woke up. She was annoyed she had to go to Merchants Town, but she was more bothered by the fact her fiancé seemed unconcerned about his soon-to-be father-in-law.

"And there's absolutely no one else who can handle this for him?"

"I've told you before, there are no other attorneys in Merchants Town. He is the only one. It's not as simple as asking someone to fill in for him."

"But what does he expect you to do? You're a corporate attorney with a career here. You can't just up and leave to go handle his affairs. What about your partner track and that case you've been slaving away over for months? Did your parents even consider your obligations here before guilting you into going home?" He asked, following her into the small kitchen.

Paige shrugged, pouring another cup of coffee from the French press. She ignored Chris when he frowned at her; he thought she drank too much coffee.

"I don't know, but there are some things that will have to be handled. Mom mentioned closing out an estate and getting an answer filed to a complaint."

"But you're a corporate attorney," he repeated. "You practice big pharma law. You handle bad drugs and products liability. Do you even know how to close an estate?"

She narrowed her eyes at him. "It has to get done and I'm an attorney. I can get it done. Are you saying I'm not capable of handling a simple estate?" she challenged.

Chris sighed and held up his hands in defeat. "I'm not saying anything of the sort. How long do you think you will have to be there?"

"No more than two weeks. I'm just shuffling things around for him. There's absolutely no reason it will take more than two weeks."

"Hmm." Chris was busy scrolling through the news on his phone. He didn't even pretend he was listening to her any longer.

Dr. Christopher LaSalle was a surgical resident at a prominent hospital in Charlotte. They'd met when Paige was in law school in Philadelphia and the relationship just made sense for both of them.

3

He was the doctor she thought best suited her aspirations, and she was the brainy brunette who could hold her own with his highly intelligent colleagues. But as brilliant as he was, he tended to be a bit self-absorbed. Paige had always been willing to forgive him that one flaw.

"You could go with me?" she offered. They'd been dating for three years and engaged for one, but he'd never been to her hometown. He had never even met her family.

"Hmm." He was still checking his phone.

"Or not," she muttered.

"What was that?" He glanced up.

"Nothing."

"So, two weeks?" he asked, putting his phone down and rejoining the conversation.

"Two weeks," she promised.

CHAPTER TWO

"Ms. Sparrow, we certainly understand why you feel obligated to go see your family, but it is really not a good time for us. As you are well aware, we are deep in discovery for the König case and depositions are scheduled for next week. Your involvement in this case is required." James A. Fitz glanced at her over the dark grey rim of his glasses. Behind him, the wall was covered with various awards he and the firm had won over the years. He didn't get those awards by having associate attorneys who expected to be able to leave at the drop of a hat.

Fitz shook his head and turned back to his computer screen with a dismissive sigh. Paige couldn't help but feel like she was disappointing her father.

"I know," she started.

"Do I need to remind you that I hand-selected you as senior associate? I personally placed you on this case. We expect to make an offer of partnership to you, Mr. Wilson, or Mr. Kennedy within the next couple of months. Do you really want to take a leave of absence for even a day with what is at stake?" He tapped his ballpoint pen on the edge of his mahogany desk for emphasis. "This is your future we're talking about."

James A. Fitz, of Fitz, Parker & Corbin, PLLC, was a no-nonsense boss. When he'd chosen Paige as his protegee, she'd been thrilled. His was a name that carried weight, that meant something, and his firm was well-known throughout the southeast. Becoming partner of a firm like Fitz, Parker & Corbin had been beyond Paige's wildest dreams when she was in law school, but an internship at the right firm led to the recommendation that got her hired. Her rapid advancement at the firm had been due solely to her own talent.

Paige never thought she'd practice pharmaceutical law, but one doesn't turn down an offer from Fitz, Parker & Corbin. She quickly learned that she loved the thrill and discovery of products liability. Representing big drug companies against bad drug claims at hefty hourly fees was exhilarating, and after the job with Fitz, Parker & Corbin had quite literally fallen into her lap, she convinced herself it was the career path she should travel. She was quickly rewarded for her hard work when Fitz hand-selected her for partner track.

The other partners, Meredith Parker and Donald Corbin, had each selected a candidate for partner track as well. Meredith had chosen Davidson Kennedy IV, a pompous Duke graduate who had previously worked for a competitor of Fitz, Parker & Corbin. Davidson had a few years more experience than Paige and a massive chip on his shoulder that she was even in the running. He wore his disdain for women as openly as the smirk on his face. How Meredith didn't find him horribly offensive had long been a mystery. Meredith, a self-proclaimed ball-buster, frequently put men in their place for lesser slights than those Davidson handed out on a regular basis to Paige and her colleagues, but Meredith never said a word to him about his behavior. Davidson was an untouchable, and he knew it. Paige hated him.

Don had chosen Paul Wilson, but everyone knew he'd never make partner. Paul was extremely intelligent, but an absolutely horrible public speaker who didn't even want to be partner. He spent his days elbows deep in discovery and drafting motions for the partners, making sure his work was done in time to be home when his children got off the school bus. With neither the necessary drive nor the public speaking skills, Paul simply wasn't a viable option for partner. But Paige was, or she had been until she'd requested two weeks leave.

"I understand what is at stake." Paige spoke slowly, pacing her words to keep her voice from betraying her nerves. "But this is my father, and he's never asked me for anything. I don't have a choice. You and I both know I've never once taken vacation since becoming employed here. I am in my office working from before the sun comes up until well after it goes down. I am committed to this firm, and I have proven that to you time and time again." Paige had Fitz's attention.

"And?" Fitz raised an eyebrow and waited for her to continue.

"And I have poured everything into this case. Trust me, I have not let my life get in the way of my work before and I'm not about to let it interfere now. As far as the depositions are concerned, I intend to leave the task in the fully capable hands of Attorney Bass. I have worked extensively with her on the König case, and I do not doubt for one second that she will be able to manage the depositions in my absence. I'd been here about as long as she has when I was given my first solo depositions for the firm, and, unlike her, I had no prior deposition experience before coming to the firm." Paige inhaled deeply and counted to five before continuing.

"I believe she is ready and even prior to this family emergency, the intention had been to allow her to lead the depositions in the König case," she continued. "This was previously discussed with all partners at the partner meeting last month." Paige's hands were shaking, but Fitz hadn't placed her on the partner track because she was such wilting wall flower. "With all due respect, sir, I have this handled."

"You better, Attorney Sparrow. Otherwise, you might as well just put a bow on the partnership and hand it to Mr. Kennedy." Fitz glanced at his watch, signaling the meeting was over.

"Two weeks," he insisted as Paige walked out of the office.

"Two weeks," she echoed back before sneaking into her office.

Paige had just settled down at her desk and was beginning to count to slow her pulse when there was a soft tap at her door. She wiped her face and took a deep breath. "Come in," she called.

"Hey!" It was Miranda Bass, the junior associate Paige was handing the depositions over to.

Miranda was just over five feet tall and a powder keg in a court room. Her explosive personality more than made up for lack of height. Prior to becoming licensed in North Carolina and moving to Charlotte, Miranda had worked as a family law associate at a boutique firm just outside of Washington DC. She'd moved to Charlotte partly because of Paige. They'd met in a study group in law school, and Paige counted her as one of her best friends. Paige didn't make friends easily, especially in law school where she was so focused on succeeded, but Miranda's persistence and sweetness had finally worn her down.

Miranda perched on the edge of Paige's desk and crossed her legs at the ankles, her hot pink kitten heels out of place in the colorless office.

"I saw you with Fitz. I could hear him getting loud. Danielle all but had a glass against the door." Miranda rolled her eyes. "She's such a gossip."

Danielle McCoy was another junior associate at the firm. She hated Paige and Miranda with a fiery passion, but the feeling was mutual. Danielle had made it clear when Paige's partner-track was announced that she found her ill-suited to be employed at one of the most prestigious firms in the southeast, let alone partner. Danielle McCoy thought she was entitled to all Paige had been offered, and she didn't hesitate to let people that Paige didn't deserve any of it. Any gossip about Paige, however insignificant it may seem, was ammunition in Danielle's clutches.

"She's insufferable." Paige groaned. "But I'm sure she'll be real excited to know I'll be out for two weeks."

"Two weeks," Miranda spat in her coffee, the green eyes that mesmerized judges and jurors alike all but leaping from her face.

"Sorry, Mir. My dad had a heart attack and I have to help with some things at his practice."

"Oh no! Is he okay?"

It was the question that no one had yet to ask, and it caused a tightness in Paige's chest. She swallowed hard and nodded. "It was a minor heart attack, but he'll be in the hospital a bit and there's…"

"No other attorney in that one-horse town you grew up in," Miranda finished her sentence with a laugh. "Please give Papa Bird my best. If I can get away, maybe I can go down this weekend and visit him."

Paige had introduced Miranda to her family at law school graduation. They'd parted ways after leaving Philadelphia, but when an opening became available at Fitz, Parker & Corbin, Paige had been delighted to see her old friend's name on the interview schedule. She'd pushed Fitz to hire the young woman, despite her background in family law and not corporate law. Paige argued that the only women on staff should not be paralegals. The firm took her words to heart and hired both Miranda and Danielle in that cycle.

Paige had taken Miranda to Merchants Town for Christmas her first year in North Carolina, and on the rare occasion the Sparrows made the trip to Charlotte to visit Paige, Miranda usually joined them for dinner. Paige's family had opened their arms and hearts to Miranda without hesitation. Miranda's family was cold and distant, and Miranda rarely made the trip to New Jersey to see them despite it being a quick flight to Newark. Paige had met her parents only once, and she'd found it difficult to believe that the bright and bubbly blonde had come from the stern individuals who'd coolly shaken her hand after law school graduation. They'd had Miranda late in life and she always seemed an inconvenient afterthought.

Miranda always compared her parents to Roger and Lillian Sparrow. She could never understand why Paige didn't go home every time the opportunity presented itself. But Paige had ghosts that she hadn't told even Miranda about, and the biggest one lived in Merchants Town.

"No, you can't come down." Paige's voice was sharp with lack of sleep and stress.

10

"Well okay then."

"The depositions," Paige explained when she saw the hurt flash across Miranda's eyes. "I'm relying on you."

"The depositions," Miranda repeated, jumping to her feet. "Oh Paige, you can't go home. I can't do those depositions by myself, and I certainly don't want to share the job with Davidson Kennedy the Jerk!"

Miranda joined Paige in her hatred of Davidson Kennedy IV. They'd taken to replacing "the fourth" in his name with "the jerk" because failure to include "the fourth" when addressing him would send him into a rage. He was too arrogant, too sure of himself, too convinced that he was better at everything. Better at being an attorney. Better at driving. Paige had once even overheard him arguing with a male junior associate that he had better aim in the bathroom. The man liked to win because winning meant he was the best. The only thing he liked more than winning was watching anyone, particularly a woman, fail. He and Danielle were cut from the same cloth, and it was no surprise to any of Paige's coworkers that the pair had started a secret relationship.

"I told Fitz you can handle it and you can. You've done depositions before, and you have the same amount of experience, if not more, that I had when I did my first solo deposition."

"Family law isn't quite the same, Paige," Miranda protested.

"We've been over this, Mir. You will be fine, and I'll be just a phone call away if needed." Paige smiled at her friend reassuringly.

"I don't know, Paige. I don't think I'm ready." Miranda fidgeted with her earrings, a sign of nerves that was one of the first things Paige had noticed about her in law school.

"You've done depositions before, Miranda." Paige repeated.

11

"Family law is an entirely different beast," Miranda pouted.

"True. But you've done depositions with me before."

"There's a big difference between sitting second chair and controlling the ship, Paige. And I'm going to be honest with you, I'm not ready to steer this thing."

"Ask Antwan to help you if it will make you more comfortable. He's extremely good at depositions, and I don't think Fitz will have any problem with you bringing him in." Paige reached out and squeezed Miranda's hand. "But you don't need anyone with you. You can do this, Mir. I promise. It's time Fitz and the rest see exactly what makes you so damn good and the König case is the perfect opportunity to show them. You'll have those plaintiffs eating out of your hand in no time; they'll forget all about the life-changing effects of Vollmonda and take whatever piddly sum we offer to settle. It's a career making case."

Fitz, Parker & Corbin were representing König Pharmaceuticals, a German company that was the subject of a class action products liability lawsuit. According to the combined complaints of forty-seven independent plaintiffs, Vollmonda, a new drug prescribed for menstrual cramps, had resulted in infertility and internal bleeding; neither were a listed side effect. The class action suit was fast on the heels of the judge's order combining the independent complaints.

Miranda and Paige spent months pouring through discovery before turning it over to the plaintiffs' attorney. By the time the discovery reached them, it had already been reviewed by a third-party servicer. Paige had to ensure there was no smoking gun in each batch. König would settle, of that Paige was certain, but the company would rather throw a little money at the problem than reveal anything showing their knowledge of the issues prior to putting the drug on the market. Paige had yet to uncover any document of concern and was in the process of inundating the plaintiffs' attorneys with box upon box full of nearly-irrelevant files. Pre-trial litigation was a chess game that Paige excelled at.

"Alleged life-changing effects," Miranda corrected. "Speaking of which, we received the box containing the emails between the researchers regarding the peer reviewed journal article. I came in early to go through them."

"Anything good?"

"Some pretty damning sexual harassment-esque conversations involving a raincoat and bratwurst, but there's nothing about hiding results of the trials. There is actually very little about the trials."

"Bratwurst?"

"Yeah, it's pretty disturbing but thankfully not relevant." Miranda winked. "Remind me to tell you about it later. It'll make you blush."

"Nothing makes me blush," Paige joked back.

"Oh, this is so fantastically offensive that it will make even you blush. Trust me."

Paige spent the next couple of hours going over questions for the upcoming depositions with Miranda and ensuring Miranda was comfortable in the role Paige was leaving her. It was about ten o'clock when Paige finally slipped her laptop into her bag and left the office. By that time, the law offices of Fitz, Parker & Corbin were fully awake and bustling. Many of the associates had been there long before the day started, and they were already on their third cup of coffee as they yelled at the interns in the discovery rooms.

Each senior associate on the partner track had been assigned a case as a final test, and they were all in various stages of litigation. The König case was close to settling; Paige would have bet it wouldn't take more than one week after the depositions to secure a settlement and put the whole thing to bed.

Davidson was taking his case to trial after settlement negotiations had failed. Five people had died over mislabeled blood thinners, and while the client didn't dispute their negligence, they did disputed the value of the lives lost. Each person who had died due to the drug's side effects had been over eighty, and as Meredith liked to say, 'the elderly aren't worth much.' The company had been willing to offer barely enough to cover the funeral expenses.

Paul was working on an answer to a complaint that the client's erectile dysfunction drug resulted in the plaintiff's husband having an affair. It was a bizarre alienation of affection case that would be readily dismissed. Paul had eagerly accepted the joke of a case when Paige and Davidson fought over having to do it. It was not a partner-making case and neither Paige nor Davidson wanted to be saddled with it. Paul eagerly snatched it up, gleefully reading snippets of the complaint to them over morning coffee.

Paul was the clear favorite among staff. Of all the attorneys at Fitz, Parker & Corbin, Paul put family first in his priorities. He didn't miss dance recitals or pee wee football games. He remembered birthdays and Administrative Assistants Day. The interns fought to work under him because of his good nature and ability to put people at ease. In comparison, the interns were terrified of Davidson, who barked orders like a drill sergeant, and they avoided Paige, who frequently snatched assigned tasks from them insisting if she wanted it done correctly, she'd do it herself.

There were only two people in that firm other than Miranda that Paige trusted. Top of the list was James Fitz, the man who had hired her and molded her into the attorney that was well-suited to be partner. Fitz was a straight shooter. He knew what he wanted in life and he'd taken it. He expected no less than perfection from his employees, and Paige craved his approval just as she'd craved that of her father when she was growing up.

Antwan Milford was the other. Like Miranda, he was a junior associate. He'd nearly been fired when he and Paige had a brief relationship, something that was heavily frowned upon at the firm because of the fear it would distract the employees. Despite their short-lived love affair, they remained good friends. He'd recently confided in Paige that he was putting his resumes in at other places. Fitz, Parker & Corbin had always been meant as a stepping stone for him, and he said it was time for him to move on. Paige would miss him, but he'd never really fit in at Fitz, Parker & Corbin. His heart was too big for corporate law, and she knew it wouldn't be long before he'd put in his notice. Selfishly, she hoped he stayed in Charlotte.

"Two weeks," Miranda reminded as Paige waited for the elevator.

"Two weeks," Paige promised.

As the elevator carried her down the thirty-three floors to the ground level, Paige tried to silence the mounting uneasiness. She'd fought hard to be on the cusp of the partnership offer at Fitz, Parker & Corbin. She'd worked herself to death that first year to prove herself. She had earned everything she had, despite what Danielle thought, but the fight wasn't over yet. Paige didn't want to go to Merchants Town and risk everything she'd worked for in Charlotte.

Paige had full faith in Miranda, but the König case was her chance to prove herself to the partners. Fitz believed in her, but Meredith remained unconvinced of her abilities. The case that Fitz had assigned to her was the chance she needed to show Meredith that her name belonged name etched in glass on the large doors that lead to the firm's office space. The case would show everyone that Paige Sparrow was ready to be partner.

And ready she was. Paige had the buy-in money already set aside, the high couture suit she intended to wear for the press release was hung in her closet, and she had already planned her response to Chris's argument that she should take his name when they married; she'd made partner as a Sparrow not a LaSalle, and a Sparrow she would stay.

"Hello. I'm Paige Lyn Sparrow of Fitz, Parker, Corbin & Sparrow," she'd practice in the mirror. This partnership meant everything to her, and her father's heart attack came at the worst possible time.

Paige breathed and counted to ten, slowing the panic attack that had become her companion since her junior year at UNC. Miranda would handle the depositions, and Paige would be back in plenty of time to negotiate the settlement, she tried to assure herself.

"Two weeks," she told her reflection as she stepped off the elevator. "Two weeks and my life will be back to normal."

The sun blinded her when she stepped out of the building and onto the sidewalk. She put on her designer sunglasses and walked the two blocks back to her apartment, her heels clicking on the sidewalk.

It was the beginning of June and the humidity of North Carolina had wrapped the morning in a wet blanket. She folded her suit jacket over her arm and made a mental note to pack the anti-humidity hairspray her salon had shipped in special for her. Humidity in Charlotte was tolerable. Humidity in Merchants Town was stifling. The humidity wasn't the only thing about Merchants Town that was stifling; Paige couldn't believe that there had once been a time she thought she'd put down her roots there. What a silly young girl she'd been, she thought.

Paige had been born and raised in Merchants Town. Her mother liked to say that she'd always been in a hurry to be an attorney because she'd been born in the lobby of her father's law office. When the contractions started, her mother made her way into town. Roger was in court so Lillian had gone to his office to wait. She'd done this song and dance twice before, and she knew they had time for him to finish his closing argument. Paige, however, had a different idea and she refused to wait. She was delivered by a fireman and Ms. Ursula Milton, her father's assistant. Paige was screaming and awaiting transport to the hospital when her father finally made it to his office from the courthouse.

"My little Atticus," he'd cooed when he first saw her. "Already in a hurry to change the world?"

Paige was their third child and second daughter. Julie was two years older. Their brother, Roger Junior, had only lived four weeks. Roger and Lillian Sparrow didn't much talk about their first born, but Paige had always thought that Roger Junior was the one who was meant to follow in Roger's footsteps and take over the practice.

Roger Sparrow was the only lawyer in Merchants Town, and his office downtown had been a bustle of activity since he'd opened it fresh out of the University of North Carolina School of Law. The first thing he'd done was hire Ms. Ursula. Roger always said that a good assistant was hard to find, and he quickly latched on to Ms. Ursula. The second thing he'd done was hang his shingle and hand out business cards at Henry's Corner Store. Word moves fast in a small town, especially when the subject is a Sparrow, and Roger had a thriving practice in a few short weeks.

The Sparrows were one of the founding families of Merchants Town. Every historical monument and moment in Merchants Town was tied to a Sparrow from even before the Carolinas split in two. It was a name that carried weight and respect.

Roger was a Sparrow by love, not birth. He'd been adopted by the Sparrow family when he was twelve. He'd been born across the state line in Virginia. His father had died in jail when he was a toddler; he had no memories of the man. His mother had left for milk when he was eight and never came back. He stayed in the house by himself for two weeks before someone called child services. After a handful of foster homes, Roger found himself in Merchants Town with the Sparrows. Despite the fact he was a gangly preteen and they'd wanted a baby, they adopted him. He'd eagerly taken their name, much to their delight, and he never once mentioned his birth surname again. He didn't much talk about his life before the Sparrows.

A wealthy family, the Sparrows provided him with every opportunity he'd been denied as a child. Roger wanted for nothing, yet he always remembered the necessity of hard work. He, better than anyone, knew that sometimes fate played a bad hand just as frequently, if not more frequently, as it played a good one. Roger had been one of the lucky ones, and he decided to devote his life to the town and the people that had saved him.

His adopted parents had both died when he was 21. His mother had died of an aneurysm and his father had a heart attack three months to the date later; it was speculated he'd died of a broken heart. Roger was their only heir and the trust they'd created when the adoption was finalized left everything in their estates to him.

Roger never forgot where he came from or how quickly life could change. There were rumors of his worth within the town, but no one would ever guess how much the Sparrow estate was worth. Roger's love language was one of service, not one of money. He wore faded suits and drove the same beat up truck he'd driven for the past fifteen years. He lived a modest life, contributing anonymously to the Merchants Town Baptist Church and Merchants Town Volunteer Fire Department, where he also served as a volunteer fireman. When a potential client with no expendable funds for legal representation showed up at his offices, he took payment in the form of labor around the house, fresh eggs and produce from local gardens, and homemade pies. He never turned a client away. Never. There was no case too big or small, no client more important than any other, for Roger Sparrow.

Paige had wanted to be just like him when she was growing up. She was certain she would follow in his footsteps, marry her high school sweetheart just as he'd married his, go to law school at his alma mater, and join him in the practice of law in the town that had defined her. But life has a way of throwing curveballs. Paige's perfectly planned life altered course her junior year of college. She broke up with her high school sweetheart when he failed to come to her rescue. With a broken heart and spirit, she turned UNC Law down and went to Philadelphia. There, in the city of brotherly love, she decided what her father did was quaint, antiquated, and not for her. Paige wanted to be an attorney that demanded respect, one that charged by the hour and who would never accept a dozen eggs as payment. She wanted to be an attorney in a field where emotional attachment was frowned upon. She was Paige Lyn Sparrow, a corporate attorney on the path to partnership with one of the most respected firms in the southeast. Roger Sparrow's 'Little Atticus' had grown up to be something, *someone*, quite different from the girl who'd grown up playing in his Merchant Town office.

Paige's phone dinged with a text message as she entered the lobby of her apartment. It was her sister.

"Have you left yet?"

"Getting ready to. Had to go to the office." She tapped back.

"Of course."

Paige knew Julie well enough to read the sarcasm in the text. "Seriously, Julie. I had to make arrangements at the office. I couldn't just drop everything and rush home."

"I'm at the hospital with Dad. If you could find time in your super busy schedule to text Mom and let her know when to expect you, that'd be swell."

"That'd be swell," Paige mimicked in her best Julie-voice. Her older sister had once been her best friend, but their conversations had grown more stilted with time and miles. Julie didn't understand the demands of Paige's job.

Like their mother, Julie had been an English teacher. Her husband, Anderson Porter, was the town pharmacist. After Avery was born, Julie decided to take the rest of the school year off. Then she got pregnant again. When Max was born, she decided to be a stay at home mom. For Julie, there was nothing that would ever be more important than family.

Paige was surprised that Julie was at the hospital. She was pregnant with triplets and had been placed on bed rest a week ago, or maybe it had been a month ago. Paige couldn't remember.

"Crap," Paige thought. "She hasn't had them yet, has she?" She flipped through her text messages and scoured through social media sites just to make sure she hadn't missed a birth announcement. Nothing. She breathed a sigh of relief.

When Paige unlocked the door to her empty apartment, she wished for the tenth time that week alone that she had a dog, a big, fluffy dog with a constantly wagging tail to greet her after a long day of work and to snuggle in bed with her when Chris worked nights or slept at his place. Unfortunately, her complex didn't allow pets and Chris was allergic anyway. There was nothing to greet her and no one to kiss goodbye before she headed east for two weeks.

"Hey, Babe. I wanted to hit up the gym before my shift, so I went to my place. Call me if you get any updates about your dad. See you when you get back. Two weeks, remember? Love you." Paige read the note she found hastily scribbled on the back of a receipt on the counter with a half-smile; the note may not have been the same as a hug, but it was something.

Paige went through her suitcase one more time to ensure she had packed all she thought she'd need. Skirts. Blouses. A black jacket and a grey one. Heels. A couple of purses. Panties and matching bras. Funky patterned leggings she slept in but pretended she worked out in. A couple of college T-shirts. After a brief pause, she slipped two novels she'd been meaning to read for the past three years into her shoulder bag. If there was any place she'd have time to read for pleasure, it would be the lazy town she'd grown up in.

Her makeup and hair products had their own suitcase and she loaded her rolling briefcase down with copies of the König deposition prep files and her laptop. She tossed the chargers for her work phone, her personal phone, and her laptop into the case and buckled it, flipping the combination to lock it. 1-9-6-0. The year *To Kill a Mockingbird* was published. The case had been a gift from her father. As embarassing as it was, she had never been able to bring herself to change the combination.

"Goodbye," Paige called to the empty apartment when she locked the door behind her. It was noon. After glancing at her hair in the rear-view mirror, she considered seeing if her stylist could fit her in for a trim before she left.

"It's only two weeks," she told herself. "Your hair can wait two weeks."

She decided to stop for lunch instead.

CHAPTER THREE

By the time Paige reached the last Starbucks before Merchants Town, it was 6 p.m. She called her mother while she waited in the drive-thru line.

"Hello, honey." Lillian answered on the first ring. "Are you close?"

"About thirty minutes away. Sorry it took so long. I had some fires to put out at work."

"Of course, honey. We know this was unexpected. We're just glad you're coming home."

"You say that like you're surprised I'm coming."

Lillian paused. "Well, honey, we did wonder. You haven't been home in eighteen months."

Paige's protest was on the tip of her tongue when she realized her mother was probably right; it had been that long. She skeptically glanced at the luggage crammed in the back of her two-seater sports car. She clearly hadn't packed enough for this guilt trip.

"Mom, work has been so…"

"I'm sorry, honey. I think we have a bad connection. We'll see you when you get here! Love you!"

"Mom? Mom?" Paige pulled the phone from her purse to see if it had disconnected from the car system. It hadn't.

"Ma'am'?" The woman at the drive thru window was trying to hand her the coffee.

"I think my mother just hung up on me!" Paige exclaimed, handing the woman her card and taking the specialty brew.

As she crossed the county line, Paige found herself stuck behind a tractor. She grumbled under her breath and tried to pass, but the driver kept pulling the tractor over the center line.

Merchants Town was a farming community, long stuck in its ways. It was a lazy town, a little over an hour from the beach, and famous for its produce and for its swamps. The town had been built around the river, and the merchants and traders used the waterways to carry their goods to the less bountiful areas in the state. Later, when the railroad was built right through the heart of town, the population grew. Hundreds of years passed, but Merchants Town was still known for its produce and timber. It was where Paige had been born, where she had been raised, and where her family still called home, but Paige had left without looking back. She couldn't remember the last time she'd been stuck behind a John Deere.

The farmer pulled over to allow Paige room to pass and she accelerated harshly, giving him a dirty look as she passed. He smiled at her and gave a friendly wave. Not five seconds later, Paige heard the sirens and saw the blue lights flashing. She glanced at her speedometer and her heart sunk.

"Evening, ma'am." The deputy tipped his hat and peered into her car. "Want to tell me where you were going in such a hurry?"

"Nowhere," she said with a sigh. "I was just trying to get past that blasted tractor."

"You passing that blasted tractor, as you call it, at the speed you decided to do so is a safety concern and against the law. You, little lady, are lucky you weren't hurt and that you didn't hurt anybody else. Clearly, you aren't from around these parts. We know how to respect our farmers and the law. License and registration, please?" He held his hand out with a growl.

"Yes, sir." Paige fumbled in her wallet for her license and handed it to him with the registration from the glove box.

"Charlotte," he said with disdain. "I should have known."

Paige looked straight ahead and kept her mouth shut.

"What brings you to Merchants Town?"

"Family."

The deputy narrowed his eyes as he looked at the license. "Are you Roger Sparrow's daughter?" he asked after a moment.

Everyone in Merchants Town knew Paige's father. They all loved him.

"I am." Paige thought she just might be able to use her father to get her out of the ticket; it wouldn't be the first time being a Sparrow had come in handy.

The deputy's face turned red. "Don't go nowhere, you hear?" he said, tapping the car door and heading back to his patrol car.

Paige drummed her fingers on the steering wheel and waited for the deputy to return. She should have known that flashy red car would be a target in Merchants Town where most residents drove sports utility vehicles and trucks. The deputy was only gone a couple of minutes when he returned with a warm smile.

25

"I'm going to let you go this time with a warning, Ms. Sparrow. You tell your father that Alan Harper hopes he's feeling better soon. Let him know the bream are biting and that I hope to see him at the river soon." He smacked the side of her car with appreciation. "As for you, if you're going to be in town for a bit, and we do hope you are, please remember to watch that lead foot of yours. I imagine it's real easy to forget how fast you're going in a car like this."

"Yes, sir. I will let my father know, and I will watch my speed while I'm here." Paige took her license and registration from his outstretched hand and eased herself back on the highway with a sigh of relief.

"Thanks, Dad," she said to herself.

When Paige finally pulled down the long drive that lead to the house of her childhood, she was surprised to see that a large farmhouse had been constructed at the neighboring property. It was set off from the road, but even at the distance, Paige could see just how beautiful it was. It sat up on a rolling hill and the slate blue siding and white trim shown in the sunlight. Rocking chairs were spread out on the wrap-around porch and there were beautiful ferns hanging down over the railings. It looked like it belonged on the cover of a magazine about southern architecture and front porch sitting.

There were several outbuildings scattered about the expansive property. Paige saw a barn and a chicken coop as well as a free-standing garage. The property had a series of fences, and one fence came all the way up to the drive. Horses and cattle stared curiously at her as she drove by. She stared back, confused. The property had once been farmland; she remembered playing in the cotton as a child. She could have sworn her father owned it. Who would he have sold family land to?

When her childhood home came into view, Paige felt an easiness settle on her bones. The porch light was on even though the sun had yet to set. Her mother was sitting on the front porch snapping green beans fresh from the garden. A blue merle Australian shepherd rested at her feet. The dog gave a low growl when Paige opened the door of the car.

"Hush now, Dory," Lillian chided the dog. "That's Paige."

The dog growled again.

"Honey, I don't know what's gotten into her. She usually loves people." Lillian placed the bowl of snapped green beans down and stretched. "Are you going to give your mother a hug, or are you just going to stand there and stare at me?"

"Is that dog going to eat me?" Paige joked, quickly covering the ground between herself and her mother and stepping into her waiting embrace. By the time Paige reached the porch, Dory had stopped growling and bounced around their feet, her rear-end wiggling with excitement.

"Told you she loved people," Lillian said as Paige scratched the dog behind the ear.

When Paige went back to the car to get her luggage, Dory happily followed her. She began to growl again as soon as Paige opened the car door.

Lillian laughed, delighted.

"The car. She hates the car."

"Silly dog," Paige said. "Do you know how much that car is worth?"

Dory didn't care. She hated that car, and she wanted it off her property. She growled the entire time Paige unloaded it.

By the time Paige had unpacked her luggage in her old bedroom, which had been turned into a guest room devoid of all remnants of childhood, Lillian had dinner on the table. There were four plates set.

"Who is joining us?" Paige asked.

"Your sister, Anderson, and the boys."

"I thought she was on bedrest?"

"She was, but you know your sister."

"Aunt Paige! Is that your car?" Avery squealed as he and Max came tearing into the house.

"It sure is," she winked at her nephews.

"It's red! Red is my favorite color," he added.

"I like green!" shouted Max, not to be outdone by his older brother.

"Holy smokes," Paige said when Julie came into view. Her sister looked like she'd swallowed at least four basketballs.

"I know. I know. Talk about looking like a beached whale. Even my maternity stuff doesn't fit anymore." Julie rubbed her distended belly with a sigh. "Thank goodness the babies are due before our beach trip in August."

Paige stood and went to her sister. "I don't think I can get my arms around you," she laughed as she awkwardly attempted a hug.

"I'm glad you're home," Julie whispered returning the hug.

Paige felt a nudge against her abdomen and stepped back in shock.

Julie laughed. "They're an active bunch. Pretty certain they're all going to be soccer players with the amount of kicking they're

28

doing." She grabbed Paige's hand and placed in firmly near her navel.

"That's absolutely amazing." Paige had never felt a baby kick before. As she removed her hand, she saw her sister's stomach moving under the thin fabric of the maternity top. "Absolutely amazing," she repeated.

"Yeah, it's pretty awesome." Julie smiled and rested her hands on top of her stomach. "As much as I'm ready for them to get here, I'm going to miss this."

"Well, this doesn't have to be your last pregnancy," Anderson said with a wink. "Right, Paige?" he asked, pulling her into a brotherly hug.

"Oh yes, yes it does." Julie laughed. "Five is more than a plenty."

"Come on. Just one more? A nice even six?"

"No, sir. This brood mare is heading out to pasture after this round." Julie smiled and kissed her husband. "But I'll never say never."

Anderson settled the boys down with their dinners. Paige was surprised to see the brightly colored cardboard boxes with toys from the fast food joint the next town over.

"We promised them if they were good while we were at the hospital, we'd get them each a kid's meal," Anderson explained. "Bribery is a great parenting tool."

"Did you bring me one?" Paige joked.

"Aunt Paige, these are for kids," Avery explained as he dipped his chicken nuggets in ketchup. "You're too old." He giggled when Paige made a show of stealing one of his fries.

Lillian dished out the summer salad she'd made with fresh strawberries and grilled chicken breasts. Anderson busied himself pouring the tea. Paige felt useless and sat back down across from her very pregnant sister.

"How's Dad?" she asked after a moment's silence.

"You know Dad. He's driving the nurses crazy and demanding we bring him his client files. His doctor has tried to explain to him that he can't hold client consultations from his hospital bed, but he's hellbent on handling his cases."

"Well, Paige is going to set him straight when she goes to see him tomorrow. Right, Paige?" Lillian didn't wait for a response. "Now let's say grace."

"Dear Heavenly Father, thank you for the food you have blessed us with and the family to share it with. Please keep Roger safe in your arms and under your protection, and let him come home to us. Amen."

CHAPTER FOUR

The next morning, Paige was up before the sun. She fumbled around in the kitchen until she found the coffee maker. Her parents weren't much on coffee, so she prayed there'd be some beans somewhere in the house. She smiled when she found the recently purchased bag that had undoubtedly been purchased because she was coming home. She hummed to herself as the coffee brewed; it may not have been French press coffee, but at least it wasn't instant.

As she passed her parents room on the way to the porch, Paige saw her mother's figure, arm outstretched over the side of the bed that was her father's. Her throat tightened and hot tears hit her eyes. She thought of Lillian's prayer before dinner. "And let him come home to us," Paige prayed softly, padding out onto the porch with Dory at her side.

She settled down on the swing, tucking her feet under her, and tapped out a message on her phone.

"Just got here. Things are going well. How's Papa Sparrow?" Miranda responded within seconds. Like Paige, she was an early riser.

"Haven't seen him yet. Going today. Apparently, he's trying to move court to his hospital room. How's it going there?"

"It's fine. Danielle had a complete fit over the fact I'm handling the depositions for you. She threw a grade A temper tantrum when Antwan told her he was helping me. Paul had to get involved before it spiraled into pure chaos." Miranda sent a laughing emoticon.

"It was bizarre, childish, and hilarious all at the same time. That woman is unhinged."

Paige pictured the scene and chuckled. She sent a laughing cat emoji and placed the phone beside her. The sun was coming up and she hadn't watched a sunrise in Merchants Town since the last summer she was home with Scotty Lewis. It had been the summer before her junior year, the summer before everything had changed. She sipped her coffee and watched as the sky quietly and proudly unfurled its colors. Across the way, a rooster crowed.

"Hey Mom," Paige began, crossing into the kitchen where Lillian was placing bacon in the pan. "Who lives next door? In that pretty farmhouse with all those animals?"

"The vet," Lillian said quickly. "Why do you ask?"

"I heard his rooster this morning."

"Ah yes, Cornflakes doesn't miss a morning."

"Cornflakes?"

Lillian smiled. "He's a funny vet."

"Sounds like it." Paige grabbed a piece of bacon from the serving dish just as Lillian removed it from the heat. "Hot! Hot! Hot!" She tossed it around in her hands.

"Well, I cooked it." Lillian winked at her youngest. "Eat as much as you'd like. We have to get it out of this house before your father comes home. Bacon isn't exactly on his new diet plan."

"I can certainly help you with that," Paige said, chewing blissfully. She didn't cook bacon at home because Chris said it was too messy.

Lillian gestured to a box on the counter. "I brought some of his files from the office. I didn't want to bombard you with them as soon as you got here, but it'd probably be good to go through them this morning. Your father is going to expect you to be prepared to discuss them when we get to the hospital. According to Ursula, these are the most pressing of the bunch. They're organized in order of priority."

Paige munched on a piece of bacon and flipped through the box. The first folder was for an estate that needed to be closed. Ursula had already prepared the document, and it just needed Roger's signature and to be filed. Paige put that in the pile to take to the hospital with her. An answer to a divorce complaint also went in that pile. The next folder was for a personal injury claim; the release needed to be signed by the client and the funds disbursed. There was a sticky note from Ursula indicating that the funds had already cleared the trust account.

"These aren't so bad," Paige told her mother. "It might not even take me two weeks to get these handled. Most of it doesn't even require an attorney."

"Oh, this is just the first box," Lillian said quickly.

"Two weeks, Mom. I can't stay any longer than that."

"I know. I know."

After breakfast, they loaded the files into Lillian's sports utility vehicle and headed to the hospital. There were no hospitals in Merchants Town. There wasn't even an emergency clinic. The closet facility was thirty minutes away.

"How is Chris?" Lillian asked as they pulled unto the main road and headed out of town.

"He's good. Busy, but good. He wanted to come with me, but he has several surgeries scheduled for the week."

"Have you set a date for the wedding?" The wedding was a touchy subject between the mother and daughter. Paige hadn't involved her mother in any part of the process. Lillian assumed it was because Paige didn't want her help, but the truth was Paige had done zero planning.

"No date as of yet. We wanted to wait until after the partnership decision at the firm."

"Do you have a dress?"

Paige laughed. "I've done nothing, Mom. Miranda bought me some wedding planner binder and it's still in the shrink-wrap." She glanced at Lillian, whose knuckles were white on the steering wheel. "Don't worry, Mom. When things start moving, and we start making plans, I am sure I will be constantly calling you for advice and help. You did such a great job with Julie's wedding; I'd be silly not to get your help."

Julie had gotten married at Merchants Town Baptist Church, but the reception had been at the Sparrow home. It had been a lovely October wedding, despite the hurricane that had been barreling down on them. When the storm shifted its track, and set its sights on Merchants Town, Lillian had somehow managed different arrangements. The final, extremely last minute product, had been perfect.

"Well, try not to get married during hurricane season."

"You got it." Paige had forgotten how easy it was to talk to her mother, how comfortable just being in her presence was. "How are you holding up?" she asked after a moment.

"Honey, I'm fine."

"Mom."

Lillian sighed. "I'm scared out of my mind," she confided. "I don't know what I'd do if something ever happened to your father."

It was a simple statement, but it rang true. Lillian and Roger were one, imagining one without the other was near impossible. Paige thought about Chris and what she would do if he suddenly wasn't there anymore. She was a little shocked when she realized it wouldn't much affect her life; she'd do exactly as she was already doing. Is it possible to be engaged to someone whose prolonged or permanent absence would have zero effect on your life, she wondered? How is that love? Or is it an independent love? That's it, she decided, her parents just had an unhealthy dependency on each other. It didn't mean they were anymore soul mates than she and Chris. Despite her attempts to convince herself otherwise, Paige knew that wasn't true. Her parents were soul mates, two parts of one whole. It was the type of love Paige was convinced she'd never know again, so she pretended it didn't exist.

"We're here," Lillian said, interrupting her thoughts.

Paige began to shift in the seat, wishing the drive could continue. She wasn't ready to see her father.

"It's okay," Lillian touched her hand. "Really. He doesn't look bad. He isn't even hooked up to any machines. It was a very minor heart attack, and he was very lucky."

"Then why is he still here?" Paige whispered as they walked through the lobby.

"They just want to keep him a couple of days for observation."

Paige could hear her father's booming laugh the moment she stepped off the elevator. At the sound, relief immediately washed over her. When they walked into his room, which was already full of flowers and balloons, he was flirting with the young female doctor. His eyes lit up when he saw Paige.

"And this, Dr. Sanjay, is my baby girl. Doesn't look much like a baby does she?"

"Hey, Daddy." Paige made her way over to the hospital bed and gently put her arms around her father. He pulled her in tight.

After he'd hugged her and kissed his wife, Roger turned back to Dr. Sanjay.

"Paige is the reason I had this heart attack, you know. Lil' and I were trying to figure out what we could do to get her to come visit and a heart attack seemed the only solution."

"Dad! You make it sound like I never come visit!" Paige was embarrassed.

"Well, you're here now. Heart attack or no heart attack." Roger winked at Dr. Sanjay.

After the doctor left, Paige spread out the files she'd pulled from the box in front of her father. All business, they went through them one by one.

"Why didn't anyone tell me Ms. Ida Creech died?" Paige asked when she handed her father the estate file. Ms. Creech had been

36

Paige's kindergarten teacher and before that, she'd taught Lillian. She lived in a small house down by the river that had been called the "honeymoon house" despite the fact Ms. Creech had never married.

"Honey, she passed away over a year ago. I could have sworn we told you."

Roger signed off on the final documents for the estate and the other documents that Paige placed in front of him. She told him which ones she'd be able to handle while she was there and which ones he needed to withdraw from or have her request a continuance.

"What about Travis?" Roger asked as he handed Paige the last document she'd brought for him to sign.

"Travis?" Paige flipped through the files she'd brought. "The name doesn't ring a bell."

"I don't think Ursula put that file in the box," Lillian explained. "She wasn't sure if you wanted Paige to..."

"Wasn't sure I wanted Paige to what?" Roger raised an eyebrow at his wife.

"Well, Paige isn't exactly a criminal law attorney."

"No. But she's a Sparrow attorney."

"And she's still in the room," Paige interrupted. "What's going on? Who is Travis?"

"I represent a young man who has been accused of rape and assault. The jury trial should start sometime next week, but we haven't even impaneled the jury yet."

Paige sucked in air through her clenched teeth. "Dad, you have to withdraw from that case and tell them find someone else. There is no way you can handle it, and there is no way I can wrap up a jury trial in one week. I have to be back in Charlotte. Back to my real job. Are there no other criminal attorneys around that you can call? I'm sure there is at least one qualified attorney who'd be willing to step in."

Roger frowned. "I'm representing Travis as a favor. The only other option would be a court appointed attorney, and you remember what they're like."

Paige did remember. They were overworked and spread out over several counties. They did the best they could with what they had, but they didn't have much to work with to begin with.

"A court appointed attorney would be fine," she lied. "At least until you're released to come back to work."

"He's a young black man. The alleged victim is white and the daughter of a sheriff's deputy." Roger held Paige's eyes. "We both know a court appointed attorney would force him to take a plea and never look back. Travis is young and bright. He's supposed to start college in August. This will destroy his life if we don't..."

"Dad. There is no 'we.' I work for Fitz, Parker & Corbin, not Sparrow Law. I am here for two weeks, no more. I can wrap up matters for you and get your pleadings drafted and filed, but a jury trial is a big commitment that I don't have the time for. You really need to see who you can unload this on."

"I am not going to unload it on anyone, Paige. This young man has been wrongfully accused and I made a commitment to him. I am asking you to help me. Dr. Sanjay has said I should be back in a courtroom in two weeks, so I just need you to handle jury selection. If I remember correctly, you're good at reading people, and we need a good jury on this case. Deputy Frank Taylor has a lot of friends in Merchants Town and his friends don't take too kindly to people like Travis."

"Dad."

"Paige, I have never asked you for anything. Not once. I need your help." Roger, an imposing figure even in a hospital gown, stared at her over the rim of his glasses. "Please?"

Lillian busied herself with tidying the flowers on the window sill.

Paige brushed her hair out of her eyes and joined her mother at the window, her arms at her sides and her back to Roger. She looked at the cards in the flowers and didn't say a word.

"Paige, this young man is going to be convicted of a crime he didn't commit. Doesn't that mean anything to you anymore?"

"This is why you called me," she turned to her mother, angrily. "Not to handle the cases you showed me last night. Ursula can manage those with one hand tied behind her back. You called me because of this jury trial."

Lillian continued to tidy the flowers.

"I asked her to call you," Roger said. "I knew you wouldn't come if you knew the truth."

"You're right. I'd have told you to immediately withdraw and tell this man to get a court appointed attorney if he can't afford one. And that is what I am telling you now."

"Paige, Travis did not harm this girl. His life will be destroyed if he is convicted."

"This isn't my problem. This isn't my case."

"Paige…"

"No, Dad. I left a very important case at a very crucial stage to come down here to help you. I've put everything on the line, including partnership, because you asked me to come. I didn't know I was being hoodwinked into a criminal jury trial. Rape?

39

Assault?" She threw her hands in the air and faced him. "What were you thinking?"

Roger chose his words carefully. "I was thinking that you are Paige Sparrow. I was thinking you still believe in justice."

"Dad..."

"I didn't plan this heart attack."

"I know you didn't plan the heart attack. But a criminal jury trial?"

"Jury selection, Paige. Just jury selection."

Paige sighed with defeat. "Okay. Jury selection."

"That's my girl." Roger beamed from the hospital bed.

"Whew. Glad that's settled. I don't know that I could have arranged these flowers for much longer," Lillian said with a smile.

"When does selection start?"

"Tomorrow."

"Dad!"

"What? You've got this, Baby Girl."

CHAPTER FIVE

The following morning, Paige selected her favorite suit and paired it with a deep burgundy blouse and pearls. She was sliding her feet into her heels, when Lillian came out of the bedroom.

"Honey, it's only six. Let me fix you breakfast. You don't have to be there until nine."

"I know. But I want to go over the file again and get some Starbucks."

"You can just get coffee here. Or at Henry's Corner Store if you'd prefer. The closest Starbucks is thirty minutes away."

Paige kissed her mother on the cheek. "I know. That's why I'm leaving at six," she said with a wink.

Dory chased the red sports car down the drive, growling the entire way. Paige laughed in the rearview mirror. "Nutty dog."

Just before nine, Paige pulled into the gravel parking lot next to the historic courthouse. Like most of the buildings downtown, the buttercream colored structure was on the state register of historic places. Unlike most of the other buildings, it still served the purpose for which it had been originally constructed.

The Merchants Town Courthouse had served as a courthouse since 1863. There was still a small cell in the basement that had been used to hold horse thieves, drunkards, and vagrants. Paige had played in the cell frequently as a child. The cell hadn't held a criminal in well over a century, but the historical society kept it in working order. Just outside the building stood a tall tree that had served as the 'hanging tree' for those sentenced to death. A total of sixty-seven men and three women had met their justice at the hanging tree. The cell, with its rusty lock and metal cot, and the large live oak just outside the doors were key tourist attractions for history buffs and ghost hunters who found themselves in Merchants Town. Paige parked her bright red car under the tree and made her way inside.

Paige was always surprised at how different court was in small towns. There wasn't a bustle of activity. There wasn't a line of folks waiting to get through the metal detector. There wasn't even a metal detector, just an officer with a wand. He waved it over Paige and lazily gestured her to pass without a word. Had she been in Charlotte, she would have been pulled aside because the wire in her bra would set it off. When the wand passed over her without so much as a beep, she wondered if the batteries were working.

She made her way to Judge Alston Fox's courtroom with her Starbucks in hand. It was easy to find; there was only one room in the building designed to hold court. There were some stares and whispers from court staff and other such busy bodies, but Paige ignored them. She sipped her Starbucks. She lined her pens up before her, just the way she liked it, and placed her blank legal pad on the table next to the thin case file she'd brought with her.

"Excuse me," a man in his mid-forties approached her. "State v. Crawley?" he asked. He knew where he was, he just didn't think she was in the right place.

Paige glanced at his suit and tie, the tapered haircut, and the cuff links in the shape of tiny fish. There was no doubt that he was the State's attorney. She stood and held her hand out. "Attorney Paige Sparrow for the defense." In her heels, she stood an inch taller than the sharp-dressed attorney.

He slowly took her hand and gave it a firm shake. "Attorney Bradley Moore." His Southern accent was a bit off, and she couldn't place where he was from.

After the pleasantries had ended and he'd gone to his table, she pulled out her phone and did a quick search. Born in New Jersey, Bradley Moore had moved to Edenton, North Carolina after attending law school at Duke University. He was currently campaigning for re-election as District Attorney. His wife, Kathleen McRay Moore, was a former beauty queen who spent her days sunning at the beach and campaigning for her husband. They had three children under the age of ten and two live-in nannies. He wasn't Merchants Town type, Paige decided; the jury would gravitate to her. She was a Sparrow, after all, not a transplant from the North.

While she was looking at her phone, a young black man awkwardly approached the defense table. He was tall and slender, with the body of a runner. His hair was cut close to his head and dark eyes peered out from a chiseled face. Even though his body showed signs of lack of sleep and fear, there was no denying how attractive he was.

He doesn't look like a rapist, Paige thought.

43

The suit was both too big and too short. It hung off his shoulders and the pants ended well above his scuffed shoes. She realized as he glanced nervously at her that it was her father's suit. Paige stood and took a quick step to him, tucking his arm in her arm like they were old friends.

"Hello Travis," she whispered. "Did Ms. Ursula explain to you about my father?"

"Yes, ma'am." His voice was soft and steady, but his hands were shaking. He was terrified.

"Okay. This is the easy part. You just sit there beside me while I ask questions. The questions won't have anything to do with the trial, but they'll help me find out who we want on the jury. I want you to look each one of them in the eye when I'm talking. Don't look down. Don't look at the table. Look everyone in the face. Do you understand?"

"Yes, ma'am."

"Now, what's going to happen is that Judge Fox is going to talk to the prospective jurors first. He will ask them if any of them have reasons they cannot serve. He will then excuse them at his discretion."

"Will I, ehh, will I have to saying anything?"

"No. And if you get scared, you squeeze my hand and keep looking up. Okay?"

"Okay. Ms. Sparrow?"

"Yes, Travis?"

"Have you heard anything about Ainsley? They won't tell me anything."

Ainsley. The alleged victim. Paige had been surprised to learn that she was still in the hospital. The police had charged Travis the night of the attack and immediately set the case for trial. For a lazy town, they'd moved quickly. Two weeks after the attack, and he was already standing trial. The victim hadn't even been released from the hospital, and they were ready to impanel a jury. The State had put a rush order on the DNA testing from the rape kit and the results had already been received. Deputy Frank Taylor clearly had friends in the system. Nothing ever moved that fast. Nothing.

"She's still in the hospital. The doctors are hoping her memory will come back, but they don't know when or even if it ever will." Paige didn't tell him that Ainsley had spent the last week in the psychiatric ward, but she had no doubts that the young woman's recent PTSD diagnosis and related memory loss would come up at trial.

"Does she remember nothing?"

"I've been told that she remembers everything but the night of the attack."

"But she's going to be okay, right?"

Paige recognized the pleading tone in his voice; it was the same tone she'd had when she'd asked her mother about her father. It was a tone of love and genuine concern.

Interesting, she thought. She could hear how much he cared for the young woman in his voice. If done correctly, it would read well for the jury.

After Judge Fox entered and all had been seated, Paige asked to approach the bench. Bradley Moore was quick on her heels when Judge Fox waved her to come forward. She hadn't seen Judge Fox since she was sixteen.

"Good morning, your Honor," she began. "As I'm sure you've heard, my father suffered a heart attack earlier this week and is currently in the hospital. We ask that you please grant my appearance in this case to serve in his stead until he is able to return to court."

"Little Paige Sparrow all grown up," Judge Fox said with a smile. "I'd heard you were practicing in Charlotte. Big pharma, is it? Roger is quite proud of you."

"Yes, your Honor. I'm just here to help my father out until he is back on his feet."

"Attorney Moore, does the State have any objections to Ms. Sparrow entering an appearance?"

"Not at all, your Honor."

"Very well. Let the voir dire begin."

As they headed back to their respective tables, Bradly touched her arm. "You're Roger's daughter?" he asked, his brow furrowing.

"Yes."

"I thought you were a school teacher."

"I'm the other one," she purred, turning on her heel, her pony tail swishing back and forth like the tail of angry cat. This was going to be fun, she thought.

Voir dire was the process of selecting individuals to serve on the jury. Paige like to think of it more as deselecting people from serving on her jury. For the Crawley case, she wanted mothers of teenage boys, young men, and people who distrusted the judicial system. She did not want racists, relatives of officers, or rape victims. Of course, the questions she'd get to ask couldn't be that straight forward. She couldn't ask a woman if she's a racist. She couldn't ask a man if he'd ever been falsely accused of a crime. Voir dire required tact, playing with words, and getting the answer to the question she didn't ask.

46

Forty members of Merchants Town sat in the court room. Of those forty, they would narrow it down to the final twelve that would then be impaneled. They would choose the twelve men and women who would decide the fate of the young man beside her. Despite the fact her father had all the confidence in her abilities, Paige had never impaneled a jury in a criminal trial. The closest she'd come was a mock trial competition in law school. She swallowed hard.

"Ladies and gentlemen, thank you for joining us today. I am glad to see so many citizens in Merchants Town still believe in their civic duty. All of you are potential jurors in the State versus Crawley case. Travis Crawley, the defendant, has been charged with the rape and aggravated assault of Ainsley Taylor. Ms. Paige Sparrow represents Mr. Crawley and Attorney Bradley Moore is here for the State."

Paige nodded in the direction of the potential jurors and squeezed Travis's hand until he looked up.

"I'll go through some questions with you. If there is any reason you are not able to serve on this jury, perhaps you know Mr. Crawley or Ms. Taylor, or perhaps you do not think you could be unbiased, or maybe you have a conflict with Ms. Sparrow or Attorney Moore. I don't care how insignificant you may think it is, you just tell me and let me decide. Do you understand?"

A chorus of "Yes, your Honor" filled the courtroom.

Paige grabbed a purple pen and smoothed down the first page of the legal pad. She always used a purple pen in jury selection. Color-coding her notes had made her more efficient and despite the raised eyebrows her rainbow pens elicited in court rooms, she wasn't going to stop using her system.

By the time Judge Fox was done with his line of questioning, he'd excused twenty-one potential jurors. Paige began to sweat. Judge Fox hadn't left much for her to work with.

Judge Fox called the first twelve to the jury box and turned to Bradley. "They're all yours, Attorney Moore."

"Thank you, your Honor." Bradley stood and straightened his tie, the fish cufflinks catching the light and throwing rainbows around the courtroom.

Paige glanced at the Merchants Town residents left after Judge Fox's excusals. There were six fishermen, possibly more, in the room. Bradley was smarter than she gave him credit for.

"Thank ya'll for coming." The 'ya'll' was forced and as fake as canned sweet tea, but the twelve seemed to be fawning over his every word.

"Now I don't see much of a reason to ask you some silly questions, but our great state of North Carolina says I have to. So, let's make it an easy one, shall we? We've all got a favorite color, right?"

Paige watched as the heads nodded, every eye trained on him.

"Now my favorite color is blue. Ms. Sparrow," he turned to her, catching her unawares. "What's your favorite color?"

She realized what he was doing almost too late. He wanted her to say any color other than blue. Then, when he questioned the potential jurors, he'd see how many he already had on his side. When put on the spot, most people will say either the first color they see or what the person before them said. It was a trick Paige had learned in law school. She glanced at Bradley's tie. It was blue.

"Blue," she said, spoiling his game.

Bradley went the through the first twelve. Nine listed blue as their favorite color. Bradley used his preemptive challenges on the remaining three. Three other candidates were brought in. All three listed blue as their favorite color when asked.

"The State approves all twelve," Bradley said with a smirk.

Judge Fox shook his head. "Well, that was an interesting voir dire. Your turn Ms. Sparrow."

Paige realized she was in a difficult spot. Bradley had set the scene and tilted the jurors in his favor by not asking anything remotely connected to the trial. It was a ballsy move that made it very clear to Paige that he didn't think it mattered who sat in the jury; he was certain that he was winning either way.

Paige stood up and felt twelve pairs of eyes on her high heels, the tailored suit that fit her curves, and the diamond on her perfectly manicured finger. She smoothed her skirt and smiled at the residents seated in the jury box.

"Well, now that we have our twelve fans of the color blue, perhaps we should ask the real question the State's attorney wanted to ask: what shade of blue?"

A few of the potential jurors smiled when they realized what Paige was getting at. Strengthened by their smiles, she continued. "We are in North Carolina and in North Carolina, you need to pick your shade of blue. Now we all know there is no love lost between the shades of blue in this state. Attorney Moore is a fan of the darker shade, but me? I'm a born, bred, and dead light blue kind of girl." She winked at the prospective jurors. "Perhaps we should be lucky this isn't basketball season."

Her comment elicited chuckles from five of the twelve. She made a mental note to keep all five. If she could make them like her, she could make them believe her. If she could make them believe her, she'd get the "not guilty" verdict. Smiles alone, however, weren't enough; Paige had to think of a question that seemed relatively harmless, like Bradley's, but meant something much more. What would her father do?

Paige took a deep breath. "I like to read. I always have. My mother taught English at the high school. I majored in English at that better shade of blue school. One of my absolute favorite authors is Harper Lee. I have read her novel countless times over the years. Have you read any of Harper Lee's few works?" She didn't reveal that there was only one novel that mattered, only one that had been published during Lee's life.

Paige shot a glance at Bradley, who was sitting up straighter, listening for the answers. Yes, he was smarter than she'd given him credit for.

Seven of the twelve said they'd read Harper Lee in high school. Of those, one stated the author and her works were inappropriate for children. The woman, in her late sixties with leathery skin and bright red nails, wrinkled her nose in disgust.

"Strike juror nine," Paige said.

The woman stared down her nose as she flounced by in an offended huff.

Paige continued with the potential jurors. Two said they had never heard of Harper Lee.

"I'm not much of a reader, ma'am," said juror twelve with an apologetic shrug. He was in his late thirties to early forties. Paige eyed him curiously. A middle-aged white male was not on her list of desired jurors; he was more likely to relate to Deputy Taylor than her young client. She glanced at his large tanned hand and saw the tell-tale tan line of the recently divorced where his ring once was. She wondered if he had children. Daughters, maybe? He smiled at her as she stared at him. His eyes were kind.

"The defense approves juror twelve," she said, surprising both herself and Bradley. She hoped he didn't have daughters.

When all was said and done, they had a jury of twelve with two alternates. There were seven women and five men. Four African Americans. One veteran. Two grandmothers. Four blue collar workers. All but two of the jurors were parents, which could work in her favor or against her; Travis may have been someone's child, but so was Ainsley.

"Attorney Moore, are you satisfied with these jurors?"

"Yes, your Honor."

"Ms. Sparrow?"

"Yes, your Honor."

"Okay, well I do believe we have our jury." Judge Fox excused the remaining individuals and turned to the selected twelve and two alternates. "Members of the jury, you have been sworn and are now impaneled to try the issue in the case of State of North Carolina versus Travis Crawley. You will sit together, hear the evidence, and render your verdict accordingly. I will see you all here tomorrow morning at 9 a.m. for opening statements."

"Your Honor," Paige stood, panic flooding through her. "If I may request that the trial not start until my father…"

"Ms. Sparrow," Judge Fox interrupted. "I'm going to stop you right there. The jury has been impaneled. You have entered an appearance in this matter. There is no reason the trial cannot begin tomorrow. I will see you then."

"Yes, your Honor," she responded through gritted teeth as Bradley smirked in her direction.

"Travis, I'm going to have Ms. Ursula get you a suit that fits. Do you think you can go by the office and meet with her today?" Paige tapped out a message to her father's assistant as she talked.

"Ma'am?"

Paige glanced up and saw the deputies approaching her client.

"You couldn't make bail?"

"No, ma'am."

She tapped another message to Ursula. "We'll take care of it. You'll be out this afternoon."

"Ms. Sparrow, I already told your father that you don't have to do that." It was the first time she'd seen him smile. "It's enough that you and Mr. Sparrow are representing me at no charge."

"Travis," she reached for the young man's hand. "I know I don't have to do it. I want to do it. I need you well-rested and well-dressed for tomorrow. I won't get either of those if you have to spend another night in jail. Let me do this for you and for your mom, okay?"

"Yes, Ms. Sparrow."

"Travis! Travis!" A woman rushed up to them, only to be grabbed by an officer. There was a stain on her blouse and her heels had chipped in several places. The silver earrings in her ears had started to turn. She was crying.

Paige nodded to the officer to release the woman.

"It's okay, Mama." Travis reached for her and pulled her to his chest. She came up to his chin.

"It's okay," he repeated. "Ms. Sparrow says she's getting me out today."

"Ms. Sparrow? Where is Mr. Sparrow?" the woman asked, eyeing Paige suspiciously.

"Hello, Ms. Crawley." Paige held out her hand.

"Call me Ciara." Travis's mother said, taking her hand.

"Hello, Ciara. I'm Paige. My father suffered a heart attack, and I've stepped in until he is well." She shook the woman's hand loosely.

"Heavens!" Ciara exclaimed. "I sure hope he's going to be okay. He's such a good man, your father."

"It was a minor heart attack, and he'll be back at this table before you know it." Paige smiled. At least, he better be, she thought.

"I thought his daughter was a teacher."

"I'm the other one."

Ciara held her eyes for a second before nodding. "I thought you lived in Charlotte?"

"I do, but I came down to help him."

"Well, I trust Roger, so I trust you. It's nice to meet you, Ms. Sparrow." Ciara's smile was the same as her son's – wide and welcoming.

"As it is to meet you, Ciara. And call me Paige, please. Now, if you'll excuse me, I need to make arrangements to get this son of yours released so he can sleep in his own bed tonight."

"Bless you, Ms. Sparrow. You are truly doing the Lord's work," Ciara said as the officers led her son away in handcuffs.

CHAPTER SIX

Paige drove straight from the courthouse to the hospital. The exchange with Ciara had left her feeling uncomfortable, and she needed to see her father. She was so afraid of failing them all.

"Trial starts tomorrow," she said after kissing her father's cheek. "What are the chances you'll be able to bust out of here by then?"

"Non-existent," Dr. Sanjay said, looking up from the chart she held. "Your father isn't going anywhere until Monday at the earliest."

"Tomorrow?" Roger propped himself up in the hospital bed. "Voir dire is already over?"

"The State's attorney wanted to play games. He didn't even ask any questions."

"And you couldn't ask any because if you did, they'd hate you for taking up their time when he didn't."

"Yep."

"They're really pushing this through." He shook his head. "Bradley Moore is no joke, Paige. I should have warned you about Slick."

"Does everyone fall for that fake southern accent he pours out? I mean, how does anyone even see past that? It's so obvious and so utterly distracting, but everyone else in the room seem to fall for it."

"He's been in the game a long time, and he's made a pretty big name for himself. People tend to forget he isn't local. You know he's running for re-election, right?"

"I saw that when I searched him online."

"It's the first time he is being challenged for the position. He's putting a lot of emphasis on this trial. He thinks he needs to put away a rapist and he'll win. It's why this thing is heading full speed ahead."

"Well, convicting the man accused of raping and nearly killing a deputy's daughter is a sure-fire way to get the votes of the boys in blue."

Roger nodded. "And that's what he is angling for. He's putting everything he has into this case."

"It sure gives a whole new meaning to a speedy trial," Paige said wryly.

"If it looks like he's not taking it seriously, look again, because he's up to something." Roger took a sip of water from the cup in front of him. "Have you had a chance to look through the discovery?"

Paige shook her head. "Briefly, but it was only supposed to be jury selection, remember?"

"Yeah, I'm sorry about that. Did you try to push it out?"

"Judge Fox nixed that before I even had the words out of my mouth."

"Alston is eager to get this over and done with. He's been working hard to keep the trial quiet and handled quickly before the media gets ahold of it. Pretty white girl, young black man from the wrong side of the tracks… the news stories write themselves these days and he wants nothing to do with it."

"Have you worked out a theory of the case?"

"Travis hasn't been the most helpful, but I have gathered that he did have a romantic relationship with the girl. A rape kit was done," Roger added. "It was a match to Travis."

"Do you think they had consensual sex and she changed her mind? That seems a mighty hard sale."

"Don't forget, Ainsley doesn't remember the night in question, and Slick has done everything and anything in his power to get this to trial before her memory comes back, assuming it ever does."

"Any chance for a continuance based on her memory loss?" A hopeful look crossed Paige's face. Judge Fox had to know that the rush to charge and convict left room open for an appeal, and Judge Fox did not like his rulings overturned.

Roger shook his head. "I tried. Slick argued that the DNA testing was more than enough evidence. Judge Fox reluctantly agreed."

"So it is what it is, and we've got to live with the cards we've been dealt?"

"You got it, but keep in mind Ainsley's silence and memory loss can work to our advantage. Her father claims he found her beaten, with her pants around her ankles. They did a rape kit at the hospital that same day, and there is no way we can challenge the positive match. But Ainsley's never once said Travis was the culprit. She's never once said she was raped."

"If she didn't name him, how did he even become a suspect?"

"A neighbor claimed to have seem him at the house earlier in the day. When he was questioned, he didn't deny being there. He was promptly arrested that same day. He voluntarily gave his DNA sample."

Paige winced. "He volunteered to give them the evidence needed to arrest him?"

Roger nodded. "He doesn't deny they had sex, and he thought if he agreed to it, they'd let him go home."

Paige shook her head. "He talked to them without you, didn't he?"

"He didn't hire me until about a week ago. By that time, this coffin already had a lot of nails in it."

"Okay, let's say she wasn't raped and the sex was entirely consensual. Did someone else beat her up after Travis left and make it look like a rape? Even I don't buy that, Dad."

"It's the best I've got. Travis won't talk to me." Roger held his hands up. "Trust me. I have tried everything to convince him that it is in the best interest of all involved that he take the stand. He refuses."

"Why'd you take the case?"

"Ursula brought the case to my attention. She's friends with his mother, Ciara. Do you remember her?"

"Should I? I met her today, but I didn't recognize her."

"She was a few years ahead of Julie in school. It was a big scandal when she got pregnant because she was in high school. The teachers and students were not kind when she started to show, and she dropped out because of the gossip. There was a lot of speculation about who the father was, but no one ever came forward and she didn't say a word. Ciara has done her best to raise that boy right, and she's done a fine job of it. She even went back and got her GED. Travis is a very bright young man. His teachers loved him in high school, and he got a full ride academic scholarship."

"He's in college right now?" Paige was puzzled. Nothing had indicated that the young man was a college student.

Roger shook his head. "He deferred for a year. He said it was to save money, but I have a feeling it was because of Ainsley. They're both supposed to start at the same school in August. He intends to be a doctor, and he has told me several times that he intends to open a practice right here in Merchants Town."

"That's an admirable goal. We all know you guys need a doctor here."

Roger nodded. "And this has the potential to derail his life entirely. I honestly don't think he hurt that girl; there's just not a single bad bone in his body. I have faith the jury will see the goodness in him, even without his testimony."

"That still doesn't tell me why you took the case."

"He's a good kid, Paige. A really good kid."

"You took this case because he's a good kid? Come on, Dad. Why did you really take the case? Was it a favor for Ursula?"

Roger looked out of the window and was silent. Paige waited.

"I took it partly because of Ursula, but that wasn't the main reason," he said after a moment. "I took the case because in a different world that could have been me. I took the case because his mother didn't go out for milk and never come back. I took the case because she didn't give up on him. And neither will I. It's a bit of bad luck that he fell in love with Deputy Frank Taylor's only daughter, but it's not something his life should be destroyed over."

"You honestly don't think he did it? Despite the DNA? Despite how her father found her?"

"No, I don't think he did it," Roger said without an ounce of doubt in his voice.

"Any ideas on how to convince a jury of his peers, one that is very much not made up of his peers, that he didn't do what he's accused of?"

Roger raised an eyebrow. "Does that mean you're staying?"

Paige gestured to Dr. Sanjay, who had reentered the room. "According to your warden here, you're not going anywhere and there's an innocent man who is about to have his entire life destroyed. And let's not forget Judge Fox has been quite clear about my presence being mandatory. Do I really have a choice?"

"That's my girl. I am so glad you're home."

Paige stopped at her father's law office on the way home from the hospital. Ursula was locking up, but she quickly unlocked the door and held it open for Paige with a smile.

"Hey, sweet child! I was wondering when you were going to come see me!" Ursula pulled Paige into a tight hug.

"Hello, Ms. Ursula. What are the chances you've got some homemade cookies floating around here?" The smell of something sweet hit her nose and her stomach growled. "I'm positively starving," she said, realizing she hadn't eaten all day.

Paige knew her odds of something delectable in the office were great; her father's assistant brought homemade baked goods into the office every single morning. They were free to clients and those who were hungry.

"No cookies today, but I did save you a mini zucchini loaf. I thought you might stop by." Ursula winked and pulled the wrapped bread from the drawer of her desk. "You may also want to know that Travis stopped by just a bit ago."

"He's out?" Paige asked, her mouth full of the moist bread. She couldn't remember the last time she'd had zucchini bread, and her taste buds danced at the taste of her childhood.

"He is. The bondsman worked quickly."

"That's a relief."

"I wish you could have seen him before all this nonsense. He doesn't even look like himself anymore. He's all skittish, like a feral cat."

"I reckon you'd be a bit skittish too if you'd been charged with rape and assault."

"I suppose you're right. He's a good kid. I'm glad you were able to get off work to come help your dad with the case. I'm sure it wasn't easy for you to get two weeks off, and I know this isn't much of a vacation for you, but we sure are glad you are here. That heart attack was an unexpected blow to all of us, and we're lucky to have you."

"Thank you, Ursula. I'm glad I can be here to help." Paige could barely squeeze the words out. The weight of what she was doing was heavy on her vocal chords. She should have stayed in Charlotte.

Paige picked up the box of case materials to take home to assist her in drafting an outline for her opening statement. She almost always went off script, feeding off opposing counsel's statements and the mood of the room, but she needed an outline to keep her from rambling away like a fool. She also had very little time to familiarize herself with the case. Her father was right, there wasn't much to go on, but there had to be something in that box she could use for her theory.

As she pulled down the long drive to her family home, a big black truck nearly ran her off the road. She was still cursing the driver when she parked and carried the box inside.

"What's wrong, sweetie?" Lillian met her at the door, an apron with embroidered chickens tied around her waist.

"That idiot vet almost drove me off the road. Does he not realize other people use that drive?"

"Oh, he knows who uses that drive, alright." Julie was in the recliner, her feet propped up. Avery and Max were coloring quietly beside her. "But he probably didn't recognize you in that car. I imagine he'd have stopped if he had."

"Why would the vet stop for me?"

Julie glanced at Lillian, who pretended she couldn't hear the conversation.

"Jules, who is the vet?"

"Scotty!" Avery piped up.

"I'm sorry. What did you say, little man?" Paige asked when she found her voice. Surely, she had misheard her nephew.

"Scotty. He's the vet. And my baseball coach. I like him. He's nice. He lets me pet the horses."

"And cows!" Max mooed. "The cows are my favorite!"

"Mom didn't tell you, did she?" The corner of Julie's mouth tilted into a half smile. "I thought for certain she'd have told you. Maybe you should have come home more often."

"Mother!"

"Yes, honey?"

"Wipe that innocent look from your face. Is Scotty Lewis our neighbor?"

"Well of course he is. Surely we told you that when your father sold him the land."

"No. You absolutely did not tell me that." Paige felt the blood drain from her face.

"Oh, well. I sure thought we did. It's been almost a year ago now. Dinner's ready!"

Scotty Lewis had been Paige's high school sweetheart, and there was time she couldn't imagine her life without him. When it came time for college, they attended Carolina. A star baseball player, he'd received a scholarship to play for the Tar Heels. Paige was at every single home game, rain or shine. In the sleepy college town, they'd plan their future and promise each other a life of dreams. Paige built her world around Scotty, and she felt safe and secure in his arms. She never trusted anyone as much as she trusted the man she'd met when they were in fifth grade.

The summer before their Junior year, they made plans to attend an off-campus party. He'd called her and told her baseball practice was running late, but he'd meet her there. He promised. Paige went to the party with a group of her girl friends. Hours passed and still no Scotty. Things started spiraling out of control. People were too loud. Too handsy. Too drunk. Paige looked for her friends to leave, but couldn't find them. She texted Scotty and asked him to come pick her up. He told her he'd be there in ten minutes. He promised. Eager to get away from the drunk frat boys, Paige told him she'd meet him outside. In the thirty minutes it took Scotty to arrive, Paige was attacked. She didn't see the man approach her from the shadows and she never saw his face, but she'd never forget how utterly alone she felt as he ignored her screams. By the time Scotty showed up, her assailant was gone and she was in tears. Scotty didn't notice that she was upset; he was too excited about the call he'd received just after practice. The call that had been the reason he'd been so late. He was being signed by a farm team for the Cleveland Indians. He was going to play in the majors.

As he excitedly told her about his news, she'd wept quietly in the passenger seat. Her Scotty hadn't been there when she needed him. He'd broken his promise. When he dropped her off, she told him never to call her again. The look on his face, how excitement had quickly melted into confusion, was something she'd never been able to forget.

Despite her demand that he never call her again, he did. Over and over again. Despite his persistence, she couldn't bring herself to talk to him. She blocked his number and retreated inside herself. Her knight had let her down by not being there, and he hadn't been there because of baseball. In Paige's mind, she decided he would always be leaving her behind for the sport he loved. Her knight, her rock, wasn't as reliable as she'd thought. Paige built up her walls and decided never to trust a man again. She would never forgive Scotty, and she'd spent years trying to forget him.

Paige was terrified at the thought of running into Scotty. For ten years, she'd made herself scarce in Merchants Town. She didn't want to see him. She didn't want to hear his voice. She had successfully avoided him for ten years, and she figured she could easily do it another ten. Why had he built his house right next to her childhood home?

"How dare he?" she screamed inside her head. How dare he buy her father's land and build his dream home, the very house they'd planned together, next door? She was running from ghosts and he was happily living the life they'd planned without her. She thought she'd explode.

"I didn't know he'd become a vet," was all she said aloud. Even as she said it, she knew it wasn't true. She'd read it in a sports magazine.

Julie nodded. "After the injury ended his baseball career, he went back to school. He'd just been hired at a practice in Raleigh when Sally and Nick were killed in the car accident. He moved back that Christmas and opened his practice the following May."

Paige vaguely remembered hearing about the death of Scotty's sister and brother-in-law. Lillian had asked if it would be okay to include Paige's name on the flowers they sent the family. It had been a tragic accident. Scotty's sister Sally and her husband had been returning from Christmas shopping in Norfolk. The driver of an 18-wheeler had lost control of his vehicle and plowed into their car. Nick had been killed instantly and Sally died the following day. But their deaths didn't explain why he'd moved back. They were his only family. With them gone, there was nothing for him in Merchants Town.

"He has Jason now," Lillian said, reading her thoughts.

"Jason?"

"Sally's son. Scotty is raising him."

"Oh." Paige couldn't think of anything else to say, so she swallowed the memories of her ghost love. If she didn't have an opening statement to prepare, she would have gotten in her car and driven to Charlotte, but she did so she didn't.

CHAPTER SEVEN

The next morning, Paige drove the thirty minutes out of her way to get a cup of specialty coffee before heading to court. The drive gave her time to think, and she practiced several different versions of her opening statement as she drove. When she passed Scotty's house, she forced herself to look the other way. She told herself that she didn't care how he was doing, what he was doing, or who he was doing it with. That part of her life was closed.

"But so was the part of your life that is Merchants Town," the voice in her head whispered mockingly. "Yet here you are. So much for closing chapters."

Paige hushed the voice by loudly presenting potential opening statements. By the time she paid for her coffee and was on her way to the courthouse, the voice was quiet and thoughts of Scotty had been replaced by thoughts of Travis and the twelve men and women would decide his fate.

When Paige walked into the courthouse, she didn't notice the jurors standing in the parking lot. They watched her park her roadster under the hanging tree, watched her step out of the car in heels that cost more than their cars, and carry her specialty coffee in one hand and her alligator skin briefcase in the other. She couldn't feel their eyes on her as she carefully made her way over the gravel; she didn't notice them at all.

Travis was waiting for her on the bench outside of the courtroom. Ursula had found him a chocolate brown suit and had paired it with a light blue shirt and darker blue tie. He looked uncomfortable and kept pulling on the tie. Ciara was sitting next to him and kept batting his hand away from the tie.

"Ms. Sparrow." Travis stood as soon as he saw Paige.

"Travis." She took his hand before turning to his mother. "Good morning, Ciara. He looks good, doesn't he?"

"A suit doesn't make him white." Ciara's voice was raw.

"No, it doesn't. And being black doesn't make him a rapist."

Paige led Travis into the courtroom and lined her pens and pad of paper in front of her. When she reached for her phone, she saw she had three missed calls. She was going to check her messages when the deputy signaled that Judge Fox was about to enter the room and they needed to stand. She silenced her phone; the messages could wait.

"All rise. This honorable court for the County of Gates is now open and sitting for the dispatch of its business. The Honorable Judge Alston Fox presiding. God save the State and this honorable court."

After everyone was seated, Judge Fox gestured to Paige and Bradley. "Are there any matters we need to discuss before we begin opening statements?"

"No, your Honor," they chimed.

"Very well. Attorney Moore, you have the floor."

66

Bradley, dressed in a dark charcoal suit with a crisp, white Oxford shirt and silver tie, stood and faced the jury. There was no denying that he was attractive. Paige found herself wondering if there were too many women on the jury.

"May it please the court and ladies and gentlemen of the jury, my name is Bradley Moore and I am counsel for the great State of North Carolina in this action. This is a simple case. A case of a man who couldn't have what he wanted, who he wanted, so he took it." He held up Ainsley's senior picture. "He took her."

Paige had seen pictures of Ainsley before, but they'd mostly been pictures taken after the attack. The picture Bradley presented to the jury was one of a happy girl, with her head slightly tilted toward the photographer and her long blonde hair falling in soft curls around her face. Her lips, a rosy pink, parted in a half-smile, as if she was about to say something funny or break into laughter.

"He took her innocence and shattered her body, leaving her broken and bloody for her loving father to find," Bradley continued. "And he will have you believe they were in love."

Paige glanced nervously at Travis, who couldn't take his eyes off the picture. The jury couldn't look away either. Paige watched as several frowned at the picture, their jaws set in firm lines. Someone had broken that beautiful girl, and they were going to hold him accountable for his actions. At least two decided Travis was guilty the moment they saw the picture of the all-American girl next door.

Bradley's fake Southern accent made it nearly impossible for Paige to pay attention to what he was saying. Paige realized he was painting a picture of a very pretty and popular girl and a guy from the wrong side of the tracks. He wasn't saying it was a black and white issue, he'd never be so bold, but every word out of his mouth insinuated it; white girls don't want black boyfriends and black men can't have white girlfriends.

Paige nearly threw up when Bradley said, "And I think we can all agree that the defendant isn't exactly Ms. Taylor's type."

She shot a glance at Travis, whose jaw twitched as he glared at Bradley. She touched his arm and leaned over. "Don't listen to him," she whispered. "Your emotions read on your face. Don't listen to him."

"This is Merchants Town," Bradley said, wrapping up his opening. The jury was eating every word as if he were serving up honey on a buttermilk biscuit.

"This is our town. Our Mayberry. We want to keep it pure and wholesome. We want to protect our innocent children from horrific crimes that leave them bloody and bruised." He leaned closer to the jurors, as if sharing a secret. "We don't need attorneys coming from Charlotte to tell us what we should believe and what is true. We know the truth; you can't take what doesn't belong to you, and no amount of pontificating by a fancy lawyer is going to change that."

Paige groaned as the jury members began to nod their heads in agreement. Her suit suddenly felt too tight about her ribcage.

"You know where the heart of Merchants Town rests – with its people. With you." Bradley continued to pull the jurors in. "I have no doubt that you will look deep into your hearts at the close of this case and justice will prevail. Ainsley Taylor, beloved daughter of Merchants Town, will be avenged because we look out for our own."

Paige needed to bring her own face in check; Bradley Moore had just labeled her an outsider and somehow managed to make the argument that her being from Charlotte made Travis guilty. And the jury loved every word of it. One woman nearly applauded when Bradley concluded his opening and headed back to his chair.

"Ms. Sparrow?" Judge Fox said after she sat for a moment.

She took a deep breath and approached the jury box.

"May it please the court and ladies and gentlemen of the jury, my name is Paige Sparrow and I am counsel for Mr. Travis Crawley in this action. Attorney Moore has made a big show about me not being from Merchants Town, about being an outsider coming in from Charlotte to make you question what you already know. This is simply not the case. I was born less than a mile from this very spot. I grew up here. I have loved here and I have lost here. I know as well as you that we look out for our own, and I shouldn't have to remind you that Mr. Crawley is one of us. He was raised here. He was educated here. He fell in love here."

As the words spilled out of Paige's mouth, she tried to make eye contact with the members of the jury. One or two smiled at her encouragingly, and for that she was grateful.

"This is not a case of man taking what he couldn't have, but the case of the wrongfully accused, the case of a man whose own victim has not named him as her perpetrator. This is a case of speculation, jumping to conclusions, and a desire to point the finger, even at the expense of justice."

As she brought her brief opening to a close, she watched the jury. A couple held her eyes and listened. They were open to what she had to say. A few stared at their nails and twirled their wedding rings. They were already bored. Three women, seated one after the

69

other, openly glared at her. She could read their faces clearly; how dare she forsake her own womankind to represent a rapist. They hated her. The realization was a punch in the gut that stole the breath from her lungs and the words from her mouth; she could barely finish the opening statement and hoped the words being vomited out of her mouth at least made coherent sentences. She'd never had such an openly hostile jury before. This was her home. These were her people. How could the jury dislike her so much already?

Paige's voice had faltered to a whisper as she reached the end of her opening. Travis squeezed her hand when she returned to the table and collapsed in the chair beside him. She could hardly hear the sounds around her due to the beating of her heart. She counted ten slow blinks. It was neither the time nor the place for a panic attack.

"Your Honor," Bradley rose to address the court. "I truly hate to do this, especially after Ms. Sparrow requested the case be continued yesterday, but my first witness was called into work and is unable to testify today. We respectfully request a continuance until Monday."

Paige summoned the courage to stand and hoped the table blocked her shaking legs from the view of the jurors. "Your Honor, I object. With all due respect, Attorney Moore can call his second witness and not waste the time of this court and these lovely jurors." She hoped her words would score points with them, but they frowned in her direction.

"Attorney Moore, who is your first witness and what was so important that he couldn't be here today? I thought I made it quite clear yesterday that I intended to get this show on the road without any unnecessary delays."

"The State's first witness is the victim's father, Deputy Frank Taylor. I have just received word that he will be unable to make it because there has been a five-car pileup just a few miles from here. There are a number of a fatalities and the helicopter is being called in from Norfolk. He is needed there presently."

Great, Paige thought. The victim's father was a heroic first responder. As if the jury needed more of a reason to hate Travis and distrust her.

Judge Fox gave a curt nod of the head. "Very well. This matter will be continued until Monday at 10 a.m."

"Thank you, your Honor. And for everyone in the courtroom, you may wish to avoid Highway 13. Deputy Taylor has advised that traffic is stopped in both directions and it's going to take some time to clear the road." Bradley smiled at the jury before turning his eyes to Paige and winking. "You're okay with the continuance, right, sweetheart?"

Paige gritted her teeth and fought the urge to bury her shoe in his crotch. She loathed being called sweetheart. Choosing a male-dominated career path came with its own issues, and the perception that she was somehow not up to par, not as intelligent, as her male counterparts infuriated her beyond measure. It was bad enough the judges referred to her as "Ms. Sparrow" and never "Attorney Sparrow." It seemed that form of respect was reserved for her male counterparts only.

"I certainly understand if you need more time to prepare your case. It doesn't bother me in the slightest." She batted her eyelashes. "You're hanging on tenterhooks, anyway, darling." Her drawl was real.

"Maybe your father will be released in time to be here so that you don't have to worry with this little issue. I imagine being here is like being a fish out of water."

"Fish out of water? Honey, this is my pond." Paige gathered her files and placed them in the alligator briefcase. "I'll see you Monday morning, dear." She winked and left him standing there, mouth agape.

"The plea is still on the table," Bradley called after he regained his composure. "We'll drop the rape if he pleads to the assault."

Paige turned on her heel and stalked up to him. In the heels she'd chosen that morning, she stood two inches taller than him.

"You can go ahead and take it off the table," she purred, forcing him to look up at her. "We're not interested in any deal."

"You might want to reconsider that stance after looking at the pictures. I'm pretty certain I know what that jury is going to think when they see that pretty girl all bruised and swollen."

Paige had seen the pictures. "I'm confident that justice will prevail," she said, trying to keep her voice from shaking.

Bradley laughed. "You're confident that justice will prevail? Clearly, you haven't been practicing law long. This has never been about justice."

"At least you're smart enough to call a spade a spade."

"Go back to Charlotte, little girl. Let your daddy handle this one. He understands how this world works." Bradley spoke through a forced smile. Any jurors witnessing the conversation would think it was a pleasant exchange between professional colleagues.

Paige gritted her teeth and smiled back. "We will see you Monday," she growled.

She was still shaking when she locked herself in the bathroom stall. She was counting and practicing her breathing techniques when she heard the door creak open.

"Can you believe her?" One voice said.

"The nerve." Another voice said.

"Who does she think she is, waltzing into our town with that ridiculous car and those hideous shoes? This isn't New York," the first voice said.

Paige looked at her heels. They were stunning, straight from the runway, and would feed a family for months. She raised her legs so her feet wouldn't show under the stall and prayed the women would hurry on their way.

"I don't care if she is Roger's daughter. She belongs here about as much as I belong on the cover of a swimsuit magazine."

The women chortled at the remark by the larger of the three.

"And does she think we're going to be impressed that she goes to Starbucks every morning? Is our coffee just not good enough for her refined palette?"

Paige peered between the cracks in the stall and watched as four members of her jury reapplied their makeup. She was terrified they could hear her heart beating.

"What do you expect from a woman who represents a rapist." The larger woman was clearly the leader of the bunch, and she'd been selected as jury forewoman. They were probably all in the same church group or book club. Paige would need the woman on her side to stand any chance in securing the not guilty verdict.

"But Attorney Moore, did you see the eyes on that man? This trial can on for weeks if I get to look at him all day," one of the women said. "He's a much better sight than Peter sitting on the couch scratching himself."

Paige breathed a sigh of relief when she heard the door close on their laughter. She counted to four hundred and seventy-two. Then she counted to two hundred and twenty-seven. When she stepped out of the stall, her hands weren't shaking anymore. She splashed water on her face, tucked her briefcase under her arm, and walked out of the rest room with her head high. The hall was empty; the jurors had all gone. There was no one to witness her struggling to get to the parking lot without breaking down.

CHAPTER EIGHT

As soon as Paige got in her car, she pressed the button for her keyless ignition and threw it in reverse, throwing bits of gravel in her wake. As soon as her phone synced to the car, she started receiving notification after notification. She had seven missed calls. Four from Miranda. One from Antwan. Two from Fitz. There were countless text messages. She listened to the voicemails as she drove.

"Call me when you get this. It's important." Miranda's voice shook in the first message.

"Paige? Please call. I'm freaking out." By the second message, Miranda was sobbing.

"Hey Paige. The shit is seriously hitting the fan here. You need to call Miranda as soon as possible, and you need to talk to her before Fitz gets ahold of you. Call her on her cell as soon as you get this message." Antwan, always the voice of steadfast reason, sounded like he was nearing his wit's end.

"Ms. Sparrow. Your presence is immediately required. If you cannot be in Charlotte by close of business today, you can consider

75

that partnership no longer an option." Fitz hesitated, as if he wanted to leave more to the message, before hanging up.

"Paige. They fired me. Please call me."

"Ms. Sparrow. There has been a meeting of the partners. If you are not in this office come Monday morning at 8 am, your employment here will be promptly terminated."

By the time her messages had cycled through the last one from Fitz, Paige's panic attack was in full force. Paige had suffered from anxiety attacks since her assault in undergrad. It always felt like she was being held under water, like she was in a snow globe that had been shaken too hard. Her heart began to race, her lungs became heavy, and she frantically clutched at the steering wheel. Her vision blurred and hearing was faint; she could barely hear Fitz's threatening message.

Paige pulled over on the side of the road and buried her face in the steering wheel, waiting for her world to settle. She'd only been gone a handful of days, and things had already fallen apart at Fitz, Parker & Corbin. What was she doing in Merchants Town? The poor kid probably didn't rape or assault anyone, but the jury already hated her. She was going to lose, and his life was going to be destroyed. She was going to let her father down. And Fitz. She didn't know what had happened at the firm in her absence, but based on his message, she had already let him down. Her dream was unraveling all because she'd promised her father two weeks and had gotten guilted into representing a rapist. Maybe the women were right. What kind of woman walks away from her career to represent a rapist?

"Alleged rapist," the voice in her head hissed.

"Rapist. Alleged rapist. It doesn't matter. The jury has already convicted him because just like he doesn't belong with Ainsley, I don't belong here." She sobbed into the leather of the steering wheel.

Paige was still talking to herself when a loud thump! shook the car. When she looked up, she was face to face with a cow. Her insurance was never going to believe that a cow had run headfirst into a parked car on the side of the road.

"Hey there, cow. Shoo. Shoo."

The cow looked at her and started grazing.

"Great," Paige muttered, unbuckling her seatbelt. "Do cows have tags like dogs?" she asked herself.

She walked up to the cow after running her hand over the front of her car. A slight dent, which would be easily repaired. She breathed heavily and turned her attention back to the cow. "Now who do you belong to?"

"I see you found my cow."

She would have recognized his voice anywhere, and his words settled on her like a homemade quilt.

"Your cow needs to look where she's going. She ran right into my parked car." Paige refused to look at him.

"Why were you parked on the side of the road?" His voice was closer. Paige kept her eyes down.

"Long story. The better question is why is your cow running loose?"

"She's half blind. I honestly have no idea how a cow that cannot see continues to find every hole in my fence." Scotty patted the cow's rump. "She's a good girl though." The cow continued to chew its cud.

"How's your dad?" Scotty asked after a moment.

"Good. He should be home soon."

"Good. I guess you'll be heading back to Charlotte when he's released?"

"Yeah." Paige thought about her voicemails. "If I still have a job, I guess."

"What do you mean if you still have a job?"

She looked at him. He was older than she remembered, but his eyes were just as blue as the day they'd met and she'd decided she would marry him. They'd been ten and he'd just moved to Merchants Town. His red hair was cut close and hid under a baseball cap, the same as it had been that August day so many years in her past. Toned and tan arms spilled out of his t-shirt and cowboy boots peaked out from the bottom of his jeans. There was a worn rope looped over his arm. She wondered if he smelled the same.

"Paige?"

She lost it the moment her name hit his lips.

"They hate me," she sobbed. "They hate me, and I think I've been fired."

"Who hates you?" Scotty reached for her, pulling her into his arms as if a decade didn't stand between them.

"The jury for this criminal trial I'm doing for Dad," she cried into his shirt, the rope rough on her face.

"Travis Crawley?"

Paige nodded. "They hate me. They hate my shoes. They hate my car. They hate me." She wiped her face on his shirt. He still smelled the same. She took a deep breath and backed away.

"Well, sweetheart, I have to agree with them on the car. This monstrosity is pretty ridiculous." Scotty kicked one of the tires. Unlike Bradley, the term of endearment on his tongue made her feel warm.

"Shut up," she said, fighting back a smile. He could always make her laugh.

"And those shoes are not the kind of shoes you walk around Merchants Town in. You have to admit that." He peered in the car. "Is that a Starbucks cup?"

"Yes," she pouted. "I don't quite see what the problem is."

"That's because you've been gone so long that you've forgotten how Merchants Town works. We love our own, but we don't trust outsiders, especially outsiders who are too good for coffee from Henry's Corner Store."

"But I'm not an outsider! I am Paige Sparrow!"

"Yes, you're Paige Sparrow. The former darling who broke her father's heart when she became a lawyer and refused to practice here."

"Ouch."

"Those that remember you are judging you pretty harshly. Those who don't remember you, think you, along with your car and shoes, simply don't belong. You have to change their perceptions of you if you want to win them over. Otherwise, you better pray your father is able to be back in that courtroom sooner rather than later."

"And how do you suppose I change their perceptions?"

"For starters, you have to stop acting like you're too good to drink the coffee in town. Seriously. The Starbucks has to go." He looked at her feet. "As do the expensive shoes." He reached into the car and pulled out her briefcase. "And this dead animal skin case." He held up the case and made a face.

"That's alligator!" she protested. "It's classy."

"Classy? It looks like you went down to the millpond and skinned one of our beloved pets." He tossed it back in the car.

"I like it," she huffed.

"Maybe you can get by with the briefcase, but at least do something about this toy car. Can't you borrow Roger's truck while you're here?"

"What is it with this town and my car? Even Mom's dog hates it."

"Dory is one smart dog."

Paige rolled her eyes. "Since you seem to be such an expert, what other suggestions do you have?"

"Show them you belong here. Remind them who you are." He shook his head at her. "I bet you haven't even been downtown yet."

"Just to court and the office." She'd intentionally avoided any risk of him or memories.

"That's what I thought. How about you come to the game tomorrow."

"The game?"

"The Little League game. There's usually a good turn out and we go to Dominic's after for pizza. Come watch Avery play. He'll love it. He's been telling me all season about his smart Aunt Paige."

"I don't know."

"Come on. You need to be seen, Paige. You need to be remembered. And this," he looked her over, "is not the Paige I remember."

She didn't tell him the Paige he remembered didn't exist anymore.

"Your blind cow is wandering off again." Paige watched as the cow slowly but happily ambled down the road.

"She tends to do that. I better get her back in the fence and fix wherever it is she's escaping from. Think about what I said. I know Avery would love to have you at the game. We both would," he added.

"I'll think about it." She watched him put the rope over the cow's neck, caressing the cow in the process. Paige never thought she'd be envious of cattle.

"What's her name?" she called as he began to lead the cow away.

Scotty laughed. "Paige."

"You named a *cow* after me?!?!"

"There was something about how she kept disappearing that reminded me of you." He winked and Paige blushed.

"Funny," she said.

"It was really good to see you. I hope I get to see you again before you leave."

"I can't believe you named a cow after me." She was still laughing when she turned the car on and headed down the drive to the house. The panic attack had long been forgotten.

Paige's phone rang the moment she put the car in park and turned the ignition off. Dory barked and bit at the car's tires while Paige fumbled for the phone; it was Miranda.

"Where have you been?" There was no greeting in Miranda's breathless voice.

"I'm sorry. I was in court. What is going on?"

"They fired me. Meredith called me in her office and told me my incompetency astounds her. Can you believe that? My incompetency astounds her. Then she fired me. No two weeks. No warning. Just 'here's a box. Get your stuff and go.' What am I going to do, Paige? I can't go home to Jersey. My parents will disown me." The words poured out in a rush.

"Slow down, Mir. What on earth happened?"

"Do you remember the discovery that we went through before you left?"

"Yeah?"

"There's an email in those thousands of pages that specifically asks what the company's liability would be for withholding information concerning the trials from the published research."

"Oh no." Paige leaned back in the seat, weighted by dread.

"They knew. They knew that blasted drug causes infertility and they buried it by paying off their scientists. Because they withheld it, they were able to push the FDA approval through. That is the correspondence that was in the discovery. That is what was missed." Miranda took several deep breaths before continuing. "The plaintiff's attorney cross referenced that email with the accounting statements and found the payoff. It's over."

"Oh no," Paige repeated. The panic attack was quickly returning.

"Fitz and Meredith are scrambling to settle before it gets worse."

"But why did they fire you? This was my case. My discovery." Paige gulped. "My fault." She thought of Fitz's message.

"Because I signed off on submitting the discovery to them. It's my signature on the box."

"Oh Mir… I am so sorry."

"The best part? I didn't even go through that box. I was swamped that day and Danielle volunteered to 'help.'" Miranda laughed, a frantic sound.

"Do you think she did it on purpose?"

"Do I think she did it on purpose?" Mir spat. "Of course she did, the venomous witch. I can't prove it, but I'm certain she did. I should have known there was a reason she would want to help me. And she made this big deal about how I'd managed to get all that discovery out and how impressed she was. She threw me under the bus, Paige. She threw me under the bus and then drove over me."

"Mir…"

"Look, I can't talk about this right now. I'm heading to Antwan's." Miranda sucked in a deep breath. "I wish you were here." She sounded so small and so very far away.

"Me too, Mir. It'll be alright. I'll be there soon, and I will fix this."

"You can't fix it," Miranda hiccupped through her tears.

"I can, and I will. I'll figure something out. I promise. I'll talk to Fitz."

"That's the other thing." Miranda was so quiet Paige could barely make out the words. "You also signed off on the box. It was the one I brought you the other morning before you left. Davidson is walking around the office crowing that the partnership is in the bag, and that they should go ahead and change the sign on the building."

Paige didn't have the heart to tell Miranda she was right; Paige had lost the partnership based on the messages from Fitz.

"It'll be okay, Mir," she soothed.

When Paige hung up with Miranda, she knew she needed to talk to Fitz. She couldn't put it off any longer. She needed to save not only her job, but Miranda's. Unlike Paige, Miranda needed the job and getting fired from Fitz, Parker & Corbin would not exactly have other employers eager to add her to their ranks.

She briefly considered driving to Charlotte. Fitz worked late; she would likely catch him in his office. She could likely beg her way into securing both her and Miranda's continued employment. Paige glanced at the file beside her and sighed. She couldn't walk away from Travis's case. She couldn't give up the weekend that she needed to, as Scotty put it, remind the town who she was. Taking Scotty's advice was her best chance at winning, and not taking it would certainly seal her and Travis's fates.

Paige fired off a quick text to Antwan while she gathered her thoughts. "Take care of her. Please?"

"You got it, Chief."

Paige breathed a bit easier knowing Antwan was there for Miranda. He was such a good friend to them both. Sometimes Paige wondered what it would have been like to have let their relationship grow. Would it have flourished or wilted? She banished the thought; she'd made her choice. They both had.

She dialed the number she was most dreading.

"I hope you're calling to say you're on your way back to the office." His voice was gruff. Paige could tell he'd been drinking.

"I can't walk away from this case. Not now. I'm sorry, Fitz."

"I put my neck out on the line for you. To get you this job. To put you on partnership track."

"I know, and I appreciate everything you've done. I am sorry I let you down, but…" Paige swallowed hard. She felt like she was being halved.

"But you're calling to tell me you won't be here on Monday?"

"I can't, Fitz. This kid is going to get convicted if I bail now. If I stay, if I fight for him, at least he has a shot." Her decision was made.

Fitz laughed. "With you beside him, he stands more than a shot. You're a damn fine attorney, Paige."

"I'm surprised to hear you say that today of all days. I spoke with Miranda."

"Yes, well, I figured you had."

"How bad is it?"

"Bad."

Paige heard the clink of ice in his glass.

"It's not her fault."

"I had to fire one of you. The partners insisted. Well, Meredith insisted."

Paige took a deep breath. "Fire me."

"What?"

"Fire me. Tell Miranda you made a mistake."

"Paige, you're one of the best attorneys we've had come through these doors in fifteen years; I'd be a fool to let you go."

"It's my fault, Fitz. I'm not there. You told me when you hired me that you expected me to always put Fitz, Parker & Corbin first and everything else second. I thought at the time I could do it, but I can't. This is my fault." The words twisted from her mouth before she could stop herself. "Just give me a good review, and let people think it was my decision. I promise I won't go to a competitor and I won't take any clients with me when I leave. Please, just call Miranda and tell her you made mistake."

He was silent.

"Please, Fitz?" she begged.

"What would you father say?"

Paige blinked in surprise. "I don't think he'll much care. I'm not certain what he has to do with any of this."

"He never told you?" Fitz laughed. "Oh Bird, you are one sneaky man."

Bird had been Roger's nickname from high school through law school.

"You know my father." It was a statement, not a question.

"Yes. I thought you knew. We used to be very close. In fact, he's the one who called me about you, asked me to give you a chance at the firm. He said your heart was set upon Charlotte, and he wanted me to watch over you."

Paige couldn't stop her mouth from falling open. Her father, the man who hated what she did and the types of clients she represented, had gotten her the very job he despised. Roger had paved the way for her to walk the path she thought she was meant to walk, and she'd had no idea.

"I'll call Miranda and tell her she's not fired, but I'm not firing you. I'll demote you back to junior, but I'm not letting you go. I won't do that to your father, and I certainly won't do it to the firm. You have a job here as long as my name is on the door. Despite what Meredith seems to think, this is still my firm. I'll handle it."

"Thank you, Fitz." She knew by 'handle it' and meant that he would handle Meredith.

"Yeah, yeah. Now get off the phone. Don't you have a trial to work on?"

Paige hung up the phone, her face still hot with the knowledge that her father had gotten her the dream job. Roger Sparrow had made her life away from Merchants Town not only possible, but an actuality. She wondered if her mom knew.

"Hey, Sunshine. You going to come in or just sit in that toy car all day?" It was as if the talk of her father had summoned him.

"Daddy!"

"Surprise!" He winked from the doorway.

"I thought Dr. Patel wasn't going to release you?"

"I presented a logical, legal reason for why she had to release me. When that didn't work, I tried bribery."

"Dad, you can't bribe your doctors." Paige shook her head with a smile. "You probably were such a pest that they were ready for you to leave."

"I am an absolute delight. A model patient if ever there was one. All of the nurses gave me a farewell party." He beamed. "We made party hats out of bedpans. It was a blast."

Paige laughed.

"Now tell me, what's this I hear about the jury hating you?" Roger held the door open for her.

Paige stared. How on earth could he possibly know that?

He waved his hand with a wink. "It's a really small town, Paige. Surely you haven't forgotten about that. Now, let's go over this file before your mother gets home and tells me I need to lie down."

"Where is Mom?"

"She's run off to grab some tasteless nonsense for my dinner. I figure we've got a good thirty minutes before she's back." He sat down across from her at the kitchen table, the box full of case materials between them.

"How was good old Slick today? Did he have the jury eating the nonsense right out of his grubby little Yankee hands?" he asked.

"Oh goodness yes. They're entirely smitten with him."

"The man could sell ice to an Eskimo. He's got a way with folks, that much is true. But he does have his kryptonite."

"Which is what, exactly?"

"You have to fluster him. Knock him down a peg or two. When things aren't going the way he wants or the way he expects, he loses that ridiculous fake accent and becomes abrasive and nasally. It breaks his façade and his argument starts to crumble. When that happens, jurors turn against him at an alarming rate."

"So how do I fluster him?"

"That's the question defense attorneys have been asking for years. It's nearly impossible to catch him off guard, because, as much as I am loathe to say it, he is really good at what he does. He is a very intelligent man who is almost always prepared for four or five different outcomes. But if you manage to take things along a path he is not prepared for, it is difficult for him to recover. That should be your strategy."

"Don't you mean our strategy?"

"I'm sorry, sweetheart. I'm not cleared for court. On that, Dr. Patel would not budge and I'm not taking any chances."

"Okay, wise one. So what about the jury hating me? Scotty suggested I make myself seen around town, remind them of who I am and whatnot."

"Oh. You saw Scotty, did you?"

"I figured you'd already know about that. Small town and all," Paige smirked.

"That tidbit is probably making the rounds as we speak. How did you run into him?"

"I ran into his cow."

"That darn cow." Roger laughed. "Paige is always showing up in the most unexpected of places. One Sunday, we were sitting in church, and she just trots past the stained-glass window. Another time, she found her way out to the baseball field and just hung around grazing in right field until the game was over. She likes to roam, but she always manages to find her way home."

CHAPTER NINE

The next morning, Paige skeptically eyed the clothes she had packed to find something suitable for a Saturday morning Little League game. Upon realizing she didn't have one single thing that would work, she picked up the phone.

"Hey, Jules. Are you home?"

"Ugh. I'm not going anywhere without a forklift, which I'm going to need if these babies don't come soon."

"Perfect. Can I borrow something to wear to the game?"

"The game? The Little League game?!?!"

"Yeah. Why do you sound so surprised?"

"Because it's you and a Little League game."

"Well Scotty sug…"

"Oh, you've seen Scotty, have you? Yes, please come over and raid my closet. You can borrow whatever you want provided you tell me all about your encounter with your past lover. I'm starved for something exciting, so if it wasn't a fiery and passionate exchange, please just embellish the details a little for me."

"Okay. I'll be over there in a minute."

Julie was stretched out on the sofa, a plate of pancakes resting on her belly, when Paige walked in.

"If you want some, you better act quick. Anderson is about ready to turn the stove off."

"Holler if you want some, Paige!" he called from the kitchen.

"I'm good, thanks," Paige yelled back.

Julie shuffled a forkful of syrup-soaked pancakes in her mouth. "The babies wanted pancakes," she said by way of explanation.

"And pancakes they got." Anderson crossed into the living room, batter on his shirt. He kissed the top of her head while she chewed. "Do you need anything else before we head out?"

"No, I'm good."

"Are you sure?"

"Positive."

"And you're not in labor?"

"I promise, I am not in labor."

"Okay, but you promise to call me if anything feels off, right? The doctors said it could happen at anytime." He looked concerned.

"I promise, love. I'll be fine," Julie reassured her husband.

Anderson nodded. "Paige, will we see you at the game? Did I hear that correctly?"

"I'll be there."

"Good." Anderson swung the bag full of gloves and bats over his shoulder. "Come on, boys! Let's go! We don't want to leave Mr. Scotty waiting!"

Paige glanced at her watch. "What time does this game start?"

"Oh, you've got plenty of time. Scotty likes the kids to come a bit early to play around."

"Aunt Paige! Are you really coming to my game?" Avery threw his arms around her waist.

"I am."

"Are you bringing Mama? She's too fat to fit behind the steering wheel." He giggled.

"No, baby. I can't go today." Julie smiled from the chair.

A cloud settled on Avery's face. "Stupid babies," he muttered.

"Avery Porter!" Anderson knelt in front of his oldest, a stern look on his face. "None of us have to go to that game today. If you want to play, you best apologize to your mother. We do not say that word in this house."

"I'm sorry." Avery's lip quivered.

"It's okay, baby." Julie pulled him into a hug, or tried; her large belly made it nearly impossible. "Your sisters will be here soon enough, and I promise that we will all go to your games."

Avery nodded and put his lips against Julie's belly. "Sorry, babies," he yelled against her skin.

Paige hid a smile behind her hand.

"Okay, bud. Why don't you go get your brother and load up." Anderson kissed Julie, quick and hard on the lips. "Please don't go into labor during his game; he'll never forgive those babies if they mess up his ball season."

Julie laughed. "I'll try my best."

Paige stood awkwardly back and watched the family life that she'd always imagined she would have before her. It was not the first time in her life that she found herself extremely jealous of her sister.

After Anderson left with the boys, Julie patted the seat next to her. "I've already pulled some jeans and a couple of shirts for you to choose from. Anderson tossed one of his ballcaps in the mix in case you wanted to go all out. You've got one hour before the game starts. Hurry up and change so you can tell me every single detail about your encounter with Scotty. And don't leave a single juicy detail out."

Paige grabbed the clothes and headed into the bathroom. She pulled on the jeans and wasn't surprised when they fit perfectly; when not pregnant, Julie was her size. The first shirt was a baggy t-shirt with the logo for the local feed store. The next shirt was a spaghetti strap striped top in garish shades of hot pink and green that Julie must have pulled from the closet as a joke; it was from their high school days. The third shirt was just a simple white tank top. She pulled it on, glad she'd at least remembered to bring her flip flops.

"You opted against the rainbow top? I thought you wanted people to see you?"

"Funny. How do you even still have that shirt?"

"I've tried to take it to some charity shops, but they always send it back with a 'thanks, but no thanks' card. I feel a bit sorry for it. I'm having three girls. At least one of them is going to have bright, funky and fun taste."

"You're going to let one of your girls wear that?" Paige raised an eyebrow. Lillian had forbidden both Paige and Julie from wearing it.

"Lord no. I was thinking it'd make a good burp cloth."

The sisters collapsed into a fit of giggles reminiscent of childhoods and sleepover. Paige laughed harder than she'd laughed in months. That was the thing about Merchants Town; she did tend to laugh longer, louder and harder there.

"So, tell me about Scotty? Was it awkward? Was it hot? Did you just want to rip his t-shirt off?"

"Jules! I'm an engaged woman!" Paige held out her hand for her sister to inspect the large diamond. No one in her family had even seen the ring except for in pictures.

"Bah. I don't believe this Dr. Chris guy exists."

At the mention of his name, Paige looked at the ring on her hand and realized she hadn't thought of Chris once since she'd been in Merchants Town. She hadn't even called him.

That's totally normal, she told herself. Chris was a busy guy who understood her busy schedule. Not calling him didn't mean anything at all. But she'd called Miranda. Several times. She'd spoken with Antwan and Fitz. She'd even called her hair dresser to set up an appointment for when she went back home to Charlotte.

Doesn't matter, Paige told herself. Her relationship with Chris was totally normal and perfect, or so she tried to convince herself.

"Gosh, Paige. I'm just joking. You look like you're about to throw up."

"My tummy just flopped over. I'm starting to wonder if the soy bacon Mom bought for Dad just doesn't agree with human consumption," she lied.

Julie scrunched her face up. "That's just gross. We have some real bacon in the kitchen if the boys didn't eat it all. The babies wanted pancakes and bacon but then filled up on pancakes."

Paige waved her hand. "I'm good, thanks. I don't want real bacon and fake bacon to battle it out in my lower intestines while I'm at the game."

"So, tell me about Scotty!"

"It was fine. It wasn't exciting at all. I hit his cow."

"You hit Paige!?"

"You knew he had a cow named after me and didn't tell me?"

"You seem to be forgetting that we weren't allowed to mention his name after…" Julie trailed off, but the unspoken words hung loud and heavy between them. 'After the rape' is what she didn't say. They'd never used that word. Not once.

Julie was the only one who knew what had happened that night, but it wasn't a topic of conversation Paige would entertain.

Paige pushed back the unpleasant thoughts. She wasn't going to let the memory bring her down.

"True," she said. "In all honesty, you'd have no idea that we hadn't spoken in years. For that matter, you'd probably have no idea that we dated from the time we were eleven until we were twenty. It was completely innocent. Better than strangers but certainly not lovers."

"It's a shame. I always thought that even after all this time, you'd somehow still wind up together. You just fit, you know?"

Julie was right; they had just fit once upon a time. Paige shrugged. "People grow up. People change."

"But you didn't change," Julie insisted. "Something horrible happened and you refused to even talk to him about it. He didn't know, Paige. He still doesn't know."

"He didn't need to know then and he doesn't need to know now." Paige was starting to remember why she and her sister had stopped talking; Julie always wanted her to report the assault, to tell Scotty what happened, to forgive him for not being there. Even after all the years, Julie wasn't going to let it go.

"It wasn't his fault, Paige."

95

"Stop." She could feel the heat slipping up her ear lobes. She knew without looking in the mirror that the tips of her ears would be red. Heat rage, Scotty had called it the first time they'd gotten into a fight. She'd never been able to mask her anger.

"I'm just saying, it's not too late." Julie reached for her sister and let forth a loud "FRAP!" from her bottom. She immediately turned scarlet.

The anger leaked out of Paige like air from a punctured balloon as she found herself shaking with laughter. "I'd like to say this is the first time I've been saved by a fart, but I did grow up with you."

"The babies," Julie said by way of excuse.

CHAPTER TEN

The grassy field that served as the parking lot for the ball games was full of SUVS and vans. The morning sun was warm and the sky a brilliant shade of blue. It was the perfect Saturday morning for a little league baseball game. Paige found a spot right next to the bleachers that just barely fit her car. She slipped Anderson's cap over her head and pulled her pony tail out of the back. She felt sixteen.

Paige scanned the bleachers and didn't immediately recognize anyone. She was looking for jurors. She wouldn't talk to them, but they needed to see her if Scotty's plan was to work. She eyed the fence line by the dugout and spotted them; two of the three moms from her jury pool. Paige looked at her toes peeking out from her flip flops. She hadn't had a chance to go to her nail salon for a couple of weeks, and the red paint was chipping slightly. She hoped the moms would notice.

"Hey, Baby Girl!" Her father waved from the bottom row of the bleachers. Several townspeople surrounded him, slapping him on the back and shaking his hand. He was a town legend, her father, and they were all relieved to see him out and about.

Paige settled herself beside him and looked for Scotty. When she caught his attention, she waved. He ran over to the fence and beckoned for her to come to him.

"I see you took my advice," he said with a wink.

"Well, sometimes you make sense," she said, noticing the moms watching them. She leaned in closer. Scotty was still the town darling and she needed the town gossip to turn in her favor.

"Once in a blue moon. It probably won't happen for another ten years. Glad you were around to see it," he joked back. "I'm digging the hat."

"I thought it fit the mood."

"Better than that damn car." He gestured to the car she'd always been so proud of. "That's probably not the best place to park it."

"Why?"

"It's not a safe place. That's why no one was parked there. It isn't really a parking spot." He laughed.

"Not safe? What's going to happen? This is Little League not the MLB. It'll be fine right where it is."

"Don't say I didn't warn you," he sing-songed as he jogged back to the dugout where ten pint-sized little ballers waited patiently. The high school baseball player turned MLB baller was back on the field where he'd caught his very first fly ball, and he was coaching Little League. The image was unexpected, but somehow it fit.

"Is that a girl?" Paige asked, sitting back down beside her father and gesturing to the first baseman.

"It sure is. That's Sloan and Peter's girl. Do you remember Sloan? I think she was in your grade."

Paige remembered her well. Sloan had always worn all black and was a photographer for the yearbook. With her thick black eye makeup and obsession with morbidity, they hadn't exactly run in the same circles.

"There's Sloan now." Roger pointed to the young woman kneeling on one knee, a large camera in her hands. She wore mom jeans and a pink baggy t-shirt with the team logo on it. It was made like a jersey, with the number 00 on the back and "MOM" written across the top. "She's a photographer for the Merchants Town Index."

The Merchants Town Index was the weekly newspaper. Paige was surprised it was still in print. By the time it was published, everyone already knew what was going on in the town.

Sloan saw them looking at her and waved. After snapping a few more shots of the team, she walked over to them.

"Glad to see you're out of the hospital, Roger." She hugged him. "Can I snag a picture for the paper?"

"Sure!" Roger beamed at the camera as Paige leaned as far the opposite way as possible without falling off the bench.

"Thanks, Roger. And don't scare us like that again!"

"Oh Sloan, we all know it was my little prank to get Paige back home." He pushed Paige forward slightly.

"Paige Sparrow! I'd heard you were back, but I didn't believe it." Sloan pulled Paige into a hug, the camera pressing into Paige's stomach. "How have you been? Your father tells us all about your big city adventures. Are you back for good?"

Paige shook her head. "Just a couple of weeks to help Dad at the practice. Dad says that's your daughter at first?"

Sloan's face lit up. "That's my Grace. When I found out I was pregnant, I was terrified I'd have a girlie girl. You remember me in high school; I didn't do dresses or dolls."

You didn't do pink either, Paige thought looking at the shirt.

"Well, I had Grace. She loves dolls and sparkles and pink, but she's a Tom boy at heart. When she was four, I found her up a tree in her tutu. She was building a fort. She's something else, that girl." Sloan's face was devoid of makeup. She watched her daughter for a moment before turning back to Paige. "What about you? Do you have any children?"

"No. Not yet."

"Yeah, I guess having a family and being a hot shot in Charlotte would be hard."

The unintended dig stung. "Well, Julie is about to have enough for both of us," Paige joked, forcing a smile.

"True. When are those sweet babies coming?"

"Any time now," Roger interjected. "My family is about to be overrun with the women. Thank goodness for Max and Avery. There's my boy now." Roger pointed to home plate, where Avery was up to bat.

"Come on, Avery!" Paige was on her feet before she realized it.

CRACK!

Avery hit the ball foul. Paige watched as it went up, up and over before landing with a satisfying crunch on her windshield. The car alarm went off and the crowd went silent.

"Everyone okay?" Scotty asked, jogging over.

"We're all fine but that little sports car has seen better days," an older man chuckled.

Scotty shot a glance to Paige, who was hiding behind her hand. Her shoulders shook with laughter.

"I told you so," he mouthed when she finally looked up.

She stuck her tongue out in response.

Paige waited until after the game was over to call a wrecker.

"Need a ride home?" Roger asked as the teams were shaking hands and the wrecker pulled in.

"Aunt Paige is going to come with us to Dominic's for pizza!" Max grabbed her hand. "Right, Aunt Paige?"

"Well, I…"

"You go ahead, Baby Girl. Your mother will kill me if I go. Enjoy a slice or two for me. Extra sausage." Roger kissed her on the cheek and headed to his truck.

"You can ride with us," Anderson said. "I just called Julie and those babies aren't coming anytime soon and she wants three slices. One for each baby."

"Okay."

When Anderson parked just off main street and Paige saw all the cars, she realized the pizzeria trip wasn't just a team affair; it was a town affair. All the little leaguers and their parents had piled into the eatery. Nearly half the town's population was there.

Dominic's was a staple in Merchants Town. It was a family business that had been in the same family since 1903. It had long been the place for first dates, birthday parties, skipping school, and drinks after work. A picture of every single homecoming court since 1972 hung on the walls, including the one of Paige and Scotty. Growing up, Paige had spent hours at Dominic's. Her first job had been waiting tables. Her first kiss had been over one of the checkered tables when she was fourteen. Her initials and Scotty's were carved in one of the old tables; she wondered if the rugged carving was still there.

Paige grabbed a table while Anderson placed the "to go" order for Julie. The children were watching with delight as the staff tossed the dough in the air, working it into shape. Dominic's was accustomed to the Saturday morning ball crown, and had prepared plenty of pepperoni and cheese pizzas already prepared when they walked in.

"Sorry about your car," Scotty said, sliding in beside her. "But I did warn you."

Paige shrugged. "It's just a car. It can be easily fixed."

"You know, when I first saw you in that car and those heels, I thought the Paige I'd known was long gone. Then I heard you laugh. You haven't changed. Not really. Not where it matters."

"I have changed, Scotty."

"I don't believe it. Look at how well you still pull off a ball cap." He whistled. "Seeing you in the stands in that hat sent me back years."

Paige felt the heat rising in her cheeks. "Things are different here. Some wise fool once told me to adapt. I did what I needed to do to adapt."

"Maybe. But this is the real you. I feel it in my bones. Look how happy you are just hanging out at Dominic's. Can you honestly tell me you are ever this happy in Charlotte?"

Paige's spine tensed at his words. This was dangerous territory.

"Of course I am," she said quickly. "Charlotte is amazing. Everything I could possibly ever want is within walking distance. As much as I love Merchants Town, it can't offer that."

"Are you sure?"

"Yes. I love Charlotte. It's home." Paige wasn't sure who she was trying to convince.

"Well, I suppose we'll have to make the most of your brief time here before you have to go back to your real world."

"Scotty!" A red-haired, green-eyed boy with pink cheeks and a snaggle toothed grin slid into the booth like he was sliding into home plate. The quickness of his actions jostled the drinks.

Scotty quickly righted the drinks before they spilt. "Watch it, buddy. We don't want to get any on Ms. Paige."

"I'm sorry," the boy chirped, grabbing a piece of pizza and running off again. Avery and Max ran off after him, their squeals fading into the sounds of laughter and talking at various tables.

"That was Jason. My nephew," Scotty explained.

"He looks like your sister."

Darkness flickered across Scotty's face. "Yeah, he does," he finally said, the light back in his eyes. "Life is funny, don't you think?

"What do you mean?"

"We spend so much time planning where life will take us, what we will be, what we will do, and in an instance, we're reminded that the universe doesn't always agree with our plans." He grabbed a piece of pizza. "The universe always gets what she wants."

"Do you ever regret it?"

"Regret what?" Scotty chewed slowly.

"Coming back. Don't you miss Raleigh?" She knew better than to ask about Cleveland. She knew how crushed he'd been when his major league dreams came to crashing halt.

"I have some regrets, but that's not one of them."

Paige was about to ask him to explore those regrets, wondering if she'd show up on that list, wanting to show up on that list, when Anderson returned to the table.

"They laughed at me. I can't believe they laughed at me." Anderson shook his head. Seeing their puzzled expressions, he explained. "Jules wants three slices of pizza, one for each baby. She wanted pickles on her first slice. Pickles and pepperoni and extra cheese."

"That is disgusting." Paige's face crinkled.

"That is your pregnant sister. Slice number two has pineapple and habaneros."

"That is certainly an interesting combination that is likely send her straight into to labor." Scotty grabbed another slice of pizza, the cheese stringing out across the table.

Paige reached out and grabbed the cheese. "Why labor?" she asked, sliding the stringy cheese in her mouth.

"Spicy foods help induce labor," he said by way of explanation, his eyes trained on her mouth.

"That makes sense. What about the third slice?" Paige asked her brother-in-law.

Anderson just shook his head. "Peanut butter as the sauce, marshmallow fluff as the cheese, and bananas."

"Now that one actually sounds good. I mean, dessert pizza is a thing."

"Maybe in Charlotte, but not in Merchants Town. I just paid the dishwasher to trot over to the Henry's Corner Store for peanut butter, marshmallow fluff, and bananas because none of the three are items typically found in a pizzeria."

"Now that is true love." Scotty stood and slapped Anderson on the back. "If those girls decide to make their appearance today, give me a call. I'll watch Max and Avery so the family can all go to the hospital."

"Thanks, man. I appreciate it."

"I hope to see you again, Paige," Scotty said with a smile that made her tingle all the way down to the tips of her exposed toes.

The pizza didn't send Julie into labor, and Saturday night was spent putting together a jigsaw puzzle while Avery and Max raced cars under the table. Julie could barely reach the table to put in her pieces so she eyeballed where the pieces should fit and handed them to Anderson to put in place. Paige was surprised that she was right more than half the time.

"You've put this puzzle of these dogs playing in the river together before, haven't you?" she accused, holding five brown pieces that clearly were part of the chocolate Labrador retrievers despite Paige not being able to find where they belonged.

"Nope," Julie shrugged. "But this pregnancy has undoubtedly improved my puzzling skills." She pointed to one of the pieces in Paige's hand. "That one goes over there."

Paige slid the puzzle piece into place with a smile.

CHAPTER ELEVEN

Paige woke up the next morning to Cornflakes crowing his head off. She borrowed one of Julie's dresses and joined her family at Merchants Town Baptist Church. The pew was just as hard on her bottom as she remembered as a child and the stained glass still turned the hair of the women in the choir purple and red. As she listened to Pastor Culpepper preach about Ruth and Naomi, she glanced around. Sloan was there. Paige assumed the man next to her was her husband. The juror with the kind eyes who had never heard of Harper Lee sat on the pew with them. Paige tried to remember if Sloan had a brother.

"But Ruth replied, 'Don't urge me to leave you or to turn back from you. Where you go I will go, and where you stay I will stay. Your people will be my people and your God my God,'" read Pastor Culpepper from the Book of Ruth. "Now Ruth wasn't blood-kin to Naomi, she was her former daughter-in-law. Both widows, the two relied heavily upon each other for survival. Ruth's devotion to Naomi is one of hard work, love and loyalty, and our Lord rewarded her just as you shall be rewarded. Remember as you leave here today that family isn't always blood and blood isn't always family. Look inside your heart and make your choices count. May God bless this, the reading of His word."

Paige mulled over Pastor Culpepper's words about family and love as the congregation stood to sing "Blest be the Tie that Binds." Paige held the worn hymnal in her hands, but she didn't need to open it. The words came naturally to her lips as soon as the music started.

After the service, the congregants, many of whom she'd known since birth, came to shake her father's hand and welcome her back.

"Just a few weeks." She smiled. "Then I have to go back to Charlotte."

Paige noticed a few congregants, ones she didn't recognize, whispering behind their hands and shooting disapproving glances her way. They turned their noses up as they passed her.

"I can't believe she is representing that boy," Paige heard one say. When he passed, she recognized the woman beside him. She was on the jury.

Paige cringed.

"Ignore them, honey," said a voice at her elbow. "You're doing a good thing. That boy didn't do a blasted thing wrong."

"Mrs. Teabout!" Paige exclaimed, pulling the white-haired woman into an embrace.

Mrs. Teabout was old as the hills and a fixture at Merchants Town Baptist Church. Widowed and childless, the church had become her family. She had to be over ninety, but she refused to tell anyone exactly how old she was. Her husband had died before Paige was born and Mrs. Teabout had never remarried. With her long white hair pulled back in a bun, thick white stockings even in the heat, sensible heels, and bird-like appearance, Mrs. Teabout hadn't aged a bit since Paige had last seen her.

"Little Sparrow, all grown up." Mrs. Teabout smiled. "Let me look at you, child."

After looking Paige over, she gave an approving nod. "You look like your mother," she said, digging through her purse. "Do you want a peppermint?"

Mrs. Teabout always had candy in that purse and, as a child, there was not a Sunday that passed that Paige didn't hug that woman and receive her candy. She took the peppermint with a smile.

"Thank you, Mrs. Teabout."

"I hope to see you again, Little Sparrow. It does this old heart wonders to see a Merchants Town child succeeding. You're doing a good thing here, and don't let anyone tell you different, you hear me? Some of these Sunday morning Christians who are so eager to be seen with their bottoms on these pews don't have a lick of the Lord in them. Let their hatred burn them from the inside, and you keep doing what you're doing. Do you hear me? Don't walk away from that boy," Mrs. Teabout commanded, her hand tight on Paige's wrist.

"I'm not going anywhere," Paige promised, popping the peppermint in her mouth.

Paige was helping Lillian make lunch after church when there was a knock at the door. With the apron still tied around her waist, she opened the door.

"Want to see something spectacular?" It was Scotty. His eyes were bright.

Paige glanced at her mother. "I've got this," Lillian said. "You two run along, but lunch will be ready in about an hour and I expect you both back here and at this table in time to say the blessing."

Paige took his outstretched hand and ran across the field with him. She felt seventeen again.

"What is it?" she asked, breathless by the time they reached his barn. He held his index finger over his lips and gestured for her to follow him.

Paige's eyes slowly adjusted to the dimness of the barn and then she saw it; standing next to the cow named after her, was a small calf on wobbly legs.

"Oh." Paige couldn't find words to explain the fullness of her being as she stood there next to the ghost of her past and watched the newborn calf figuring out its legs. She felt the heat of tears in her eyes.

"Are you okay?" Scotty whispered, his lips inches from her ear.

She nodded. "It's beautiful," she finally said.

"So are you," he whispered.

Startled, she stepped back. "Scotty," she started.

"Shhh." He placed his hand over her lips and pointed. The calf had started to nurse. It was one of the most natural and beautiful things Paige had ever seen. She leaned into Scotty and watched the calf bond with its mother.

"You know how I said the universe has her own plans and the universe always wins?" Scotty asked as they walked back across the field.

"Yeah?"

"I didn't want a cow. I had no plans of having a cow. I didn't even want to be a livestock vet." He chuckled. "But then Sally and Nick were in that accident, and I didn't want to pull Jason from the only home he knew, so I came back. I opened a practice here and hoped for the best. My first patient was a cow."

"Paige the cow was your first patient?"

"Yep. A farmer in a neighboring town gave me a call when the paint was still wet on my office sign. He said he'd ended up with a cow at auction and he wanted me to take her because she was sick. She had infectious bovine keratoconjunctivitis."

"Which is what exactly?" Paige interrupted.

"It's basically pink eye for cows. It's highly contagious and he needed her gone before she infected his herd. I told him I was a vet, not a rescuer, and offered to treat the condition. The farmer didn't want treatment; he wanted me to remove the cow or he was going to slaughter her. By the time I got the cow in the clinic, I'd already realized how severe her condition actually was. I studied keratoconjunctivitis in vet school, but I'd never seen a case this bad. I got her started on treatment and put her in one of the stalls. Thankfully, I'd had the good sense to have a barn attached to my first clinic. When I got to work the next morning, the first thing I did was go check on the cow. She wasn't there."

"How does a cow just disappear?"

"I haven't the slightest, but she'd managed to escape the barn and was hanging out in the lobby of my clinic like a puppy. I cleared up the infection, but the damage was done. She was mostly blind. I tried for weeks to rehome her, but few people wanted a blind cow. I found one farm willing to take her, but after she'd escaped the fifth time they told me I had to take her back. I brought

110

her back to the clinic and set her up in the barn. I didn't want a cow, but I didn't know what to do with her. One day, I went into the barn to check on a pig with mastitsitis that had come in and I heard it; Jason was in her stall telling her the story of how the cow jumped over the moon. I wept." Scotty paused.

"He fell in love the cow?" Paige guessed.

Scotty shook his head. "Well, we both fell in love with her. She's a really sweet cow. But I can't keep every animal I fall in love with. Paige was different. You see, Jason had stopped talking after his parents died. The cow brought him his voice back and I swore I'd never let her go. When I built this," he gestured back to his home and the barn, "I made a place for her."

"The universe always gets her way." Paige touched his hand. "Did you intend to breed her?"

Scotty nodded. "I did. She's a milk cow. I wanted to give her the chance to produce and Jason wanted a calf to take through these future farmer programs. Her blindness isn't genetic; there was no reason not to."

"That is a really sweet story. I'm glad they have you. But I do wish you'd thought of better name than Paige for your escape artist cow."

Scotty laughed. "But it's the perfect name for her. She is always leaving, but she always comes home. I guess I'd hoped you would do the same."

"There you are!" Lillian met Paige at the porch. "Your phone has been ringing off the hook." She handed Paige the device. "I'm worried something is wrong."

Paige scrolled through the missed calls. Ten of the eleven were from Chris.

"Shoot."

"Is everything okay?" Lillian asked.

"Yeah, I just forgot that I was supposed to call Chris at 12:30 today. Sundays are kind of our days," she explained, dialing his number and heading inside.

"Hey, Baby." He sounded like a stranger. "Did you forget about me?"

"Of course not, silly. Things have just been a bit crazy today. But I got to see a calf!"

"A what? We must have a bad connection. I could swear you said you saw a calf."

"Dork. I did say I saw a calf." Paige said, sitting on the bed with her feet curled up beneath her.

"Well you can go ahead and mark that off on the list of things I'd have never thought would make you excited. Are you turning into a farm girl on me now that you're back in that one-horse town?"

"Don't be ridiculous," she said, realizing she was still wearing the apron. She quickly untied it and tossed it beside her on the bed.

"I can't wait to get home," she said in a voice she didn't recognize.

"And I can't wait to have you here. It's lonely without you."

His words warmed her. She should have called him sooner.

"So how is it going?" Chris asked.

Paige started to tell him about how scared she'd been when she saw her father in the hospital, about how the jurors hated her, about the little league game. She wanted to tell him about her conversation with Fitz and how their plans for her to make partner had been derailed. She wanted to tell him about the blind cow who had her name and how the dog hated the car. She wanted to tell him that she was scared an innocent boy was going to go to jail for a very long time because she was going to fail him. She wanted to tell him about the foul ball and her windshield, about Julie's pizza toppings of choice, and about how'd she felt when she watched the calf nurse for the first time.

"It's fine. How about you?"

Chris went into a twenty-minute speech about how difficult his job was and how unhappy he was with the staff.

"I swear they are incompetent," he said of the nurses.

"Mmmhmmm," Paige murmured in sympathy. He always complained about the nurses. She'd heard all of this before.

They hung up the phone with their perfunctorily "I love you" and "you too," and Paige joined her family in the kitchen.

"How's Chris?" Lillian asked.

"He's fine, just a bit swamped at work."

"Who is Chris?" Scotty asked.

"My fiancé. Let's eat, shall we? I'm starving." Paige took Max's hand in one of her hands and Avery's in the other so her father could say the blessing. Scotty stared at her with a curious expression from across the table.

CHAPTER TWELVE

Paige woke up with the sun that Monday. She removed what was left of her nail polish and found a pair of shoes with a lower heel. She put her straightening iron away and let her hair air dry into the natural waves she worked so hard every morning to tame. She grabbed the keys to her father's truck and headed to Henry's Corner Store for coffee. She drove barefoot, the heels tucked on the seat beside her, with the windows down. She could smell the honeysuckles in the air. It was a beautiful morning.

When she walked into the courthouse, with Henry's logo on her coffee cup, she realized she was humming one of the hymns from the Sunday service. The bailiff greeted her with a smile. She remembered him from the Little League game. His son had been the catcher for one of the teams.

"Good game Saturday," she called, waving.

"Did Julie have those babies yet?" He called back. "I saw she wasn't with you guys in church and wondered."

She shook her head and laughed. "She's still at home urging them to come on out. If they're anything like her, they're going to take their sweet time."

Bradley shot her a dirty look.

"Good morning, Attorney Moore," she drawled.

"I thought your father would be here today," he barked. "I heard he was released."

"He was released from the hospital, yes, but he hasn't been cleared to return to work. My goodness, it hasn't even been a week since he had the heart attack. He is doing well, however. Thank you for your concern."

Paige sat at the defense table after hugging Travis. "How are you holding up?" She whispered in his ear.

"I'm scared."

His honesty surprised her. "Just remember, squeeze my hand whenever you get scared."

After court had been called to session, Judge Fox asked Bradley to call his first witness.

"The State calls Deputy Frank Taylor to the stand."

Paige took a deep breath and looked at Ainsley's father. Deputy Taylor was in his uniform and he cut an imposing figure. He was easily over six feet tall with his hair cut close to his head. He had the stern face of a drill sergeant. Paige tried to imagine what he was like as a father to a young girl. As he was sworn in, Paige glanced around the court room for his daughter. Paige was surprised that Ainsley was nowhere to be seen.

After introductions that were unnecessary for the well-known deputy, Bradley went straight to the heart of the State's case.

"Deputy Taylor, can you please describe what you found when you returned home from your shift on the night of the attack?"

Paige felt the objection rising in her throat and fought it back down. This jury wouldn't take to kindly to her jumping up with interruptions. She would have to pick and choose when to object. Bradley, with that knowledge close at hand, was going to play fast and loose with the rules of evidence, and she was going to have to let him.

Deputy Taylor took a deep breath before beginning. His voice was loud and clear, and his words fell through that courtroom like falling trees in a crowded forest.

"I got home around seven that evening. It had been an extremely long day as there had been a robbery not far from here, and I had to chase the suspect on foot. Thankfully, I managed to catch him before the sun set. I was tired and just wanted to see my little girl, have dinner, and go to bed. When I pulled up at the house, there were no lights on. I immediately became worried."

"Why did it immediately worry you?" Bradley interjected.

Deputy Taylor was noticeably annoyed at the interruption, but he recovered quickly. "She is a good girl. She always has dinner waiting for me when I get home from work. We eat together and talk about my day. So, when I saw the dark house, I immediately knew something was wrong. I began calling for her as soon as I pushed the door open. It was unlocked and partially ajar. Somebody had left in a hurry." Deputy Frank Taylor looked pointedly at Travis before continuing.

"I heard her before I saw her. She was whimpering, like a dog that's been struck by a car and crawled off into a ditch to die. When I walked into the kitchen, I saw her. She was on the floor, curled up on her side. Her pants were ripped and around her ankles. There was a lot of blood and at first, I couldn't tell where it was coming from." He choked back tears. "I gathered her in my arms and cleaned her up as best as I could."

"Why did you clean her up? Wouldn't that have destroyed crucial evidence that you, as an officer, would know needed to be preserved?"

Deputy Taylor nodded. This was clearly an interruption that had been planned and scripted. Bradley was going to pepper his own witness with the questions she'd been scribbling down for cross. There would be no holes left for her to make that hadn't already been made and promptly patched by the State.

"It was more important that I find where she was hurt." Deputy Taylor wiped at the tears on his face. "I needed to stop the bleeding."

Bradley pulled a handkerchief from his suit pocket, a shock of red, and handed it to Deputy Taylor. The jurors pulled tissues from pockets and purses to dab at their own eyes.

"That must have been very difficult for you, as her father, to see her like that," the smooth-talking attorney sympathized.

"Yes, sir. I see stuff like that every day in my line of work, but it's so very different when it's your own flesh and blood..." Deputy Taylor's words trailed off as he looked at the jurors. "No parent should ever have to see their daughter like that."

"Who did it?" Bradley asked. The jurors leaned forward, eyes wide.

Paige was up like a shot. "Objection! Calls for speculation."

"Withdrawn." Bradley all but winked at Paige over his shoulder before turning back to his witness.

"Do you know if Ainsley has a boyfriend?"

"No, but there were boys always calling her up and bothering her."

"Boys or just one boy?"

117

"Just one."

"Do you know who it was that always calling her up and, as you say, bothering her?"

"Yes." Deputy Taylor pointed. "Him."

"Your Honor, please let the record reflect that the witness has pointed to the defendant," Bradley addressed the court.

Judge Fox nodded to the court reporter. "So it shall reflect," he said.

Travis squeezed Paige's hand. Paige squeezed back and did not let go until it was time for her to cross exam the witness.

"You didn't allow Ainsley to date, did you, Deputy Taylor?" Paige asked, approaching the witness stand.

"No." His voice was cold and distant.

"But you don't know for certain that she wasn't dating someone?"

"Like I said, she's a good girl. She does as she's told. She wasn't dating anyone." Deputy Taylor glared at Paige. "It was against the rules."

"But you can't be certain, can you? I mean, she's a teenager." Paige gave the jurors a knowing look. "And we all know teenagers don't exactly always follow the rules."

"Objection! Ms. Sparrow is testifying." Bradley's canned sweet tea drawl was gone, and his face was red.

"Overruled, but Ms. Sparrow, please refrain from providing commentary."

"Yes, your Honor," Paige said turning back to Deputy Taylor.

"But you can't be one hundred percent certain she wasn't dating someone, can you?" she asked.

He stared at her, his eyes small and angry in his meaty face. His lip raised in a slight snarl that the jury couldn't see.

Paige took a step back. "Your Honor, please direct the witness to answer the question," she said when she found her voice. She kicked herself for responding to his physical intimidation as she did. She knew better than anyone that the jury would pick up on it. What she didn't know was if they were reading Deputy Taylor the same way she was, or if they thought she was backing down because she knew Travis was guilty.

"Deputy Taylor?" Judge Fox said after a brief moment.

"No. I reckon I can't be certain," he growled.

After Paige finished cross-examining Deputy Taylor, Bradley called the forensics specialist who had gathered and tested the DNA from the scene. Paige knew this was the most damning of evidence; she had no idea how to convince a jury that sex was consensual when there was absolutely no evidence of a relationship other than the words of the excused.

"The DNA was a match for Mr. Crawley?" Paige asked when it was her turn with the expert.

"Yes, ma'am. It was a match for the defendant."

"Was it a match for rape?"

"I'm sorry, I don't understand the question."

"Did you test it for rape?"

The expert laughed. "Ma'am. We can't test for rape."

Paige feigned surprise. "So, you can't tell me if this young man's DNA wound up in Ms. Taylor through an act of love or an act of violence?"

"No, ma'am. I can't."

"No further questions."

Bradley attempted to replace any doubt she'd placed in the jurors mind through his redirect of the expert.

"Are you positive the DNA was a match to the defendant? That the defendant's semen was found inside Ms. Ainsley Taylor, the young woman who was found bruised and bleeding on the kitchen floor by her father?"

"Yes. I am positive."

"No further questions."

Bradley called witness after witness, growing more and more flustered each time Paige opened her mouth. By the time Judge Fox called an end to the day's testimony, Bradley's face was red and he had sweat stains on his shirt.

Paige left the courthouse with her head high. She was pleased that Bradley was easily flustered during her cross-examinations, and she anticipated his frustration would only continue to grow.

As Paige was climbing into her father's truck to head to his office to meet with Travis and Ciara to discuss what to expect when the State rested, Bradley stormed over to her.

"I see what you're doing," he hissed at her through clenched teeth, forcing a smile for the jurors who were also getting in their vehicles to leave.

"I don't know what you're talking about."

"This charade. This Southern charm, aww shucks game you're playing. I see right through you, and so does the jury. You don't belong here, Ms. Sparrow."

"Bless your heart, I do believe your Yankee is showing," she cooed before shutting the truck door on his words and heading to the office.

Ursula met her at the door holding a plate of homemade muffins.

"I heard it went well today," she said. Her smile was warm and welcoming.

"How on earth have you already heard that? I just left the courthouse!" Paige grabbed a muffin and took a bite. It was blueberry, her favorite.

"You keep forgetting how fast news travels in a small town."

Paige nodded. She was tired of hearing about how quickly news spread in Merchants Town.

"Your blueberries?" she asked with her mouth full.

"Sure are. Just picked them yesterday evening. They've just started to turn, and I was able to gather just enough for the muffins. Hopefully the birds and deer don't find them any time soon."

"They're delicious." Paige reached for another muffin.

"Your shoes were also a hit today," Ursula said following her into the small conference room. "A handful of jurors were talking about how sweet it was of you to come down here to help your daddy after his heart attack. You're shifting the jurors to your side. Do you have a case to capitalize on that?" Ursula didn't mince words.

Paige nibbled on the muffin. "I need Ainsley to remember," she said. "And I need Travis to take the stand."

"He's still refusing?"

"Yep, and I have no idea why. I know he didn't do it. I know he loves that girl. I can look in his eyes and see he's telling the truth. We all know what love looks like on a person, and I'm convinced the jury would see it and believe him. They'd see the pair as star-crossed lovers who kept their relationship a secret

121

because of an overbearing father who didn't approve. But that's where things get a little iffy. What happened that night? They made love and someone beat the snot out of her after he left but before her father came home? It was still daylight out, and no one saw anything?" Paige sighed. "Who would want to hurt this girl?"

Ursula got up and locked the office door. "I ain't much on gossip, but you know I've been here my whole life. I hear things. Things I'm not permitted to discuss with anyone. What I'm about to tell you cannot leave this office, but you need to figure out how to use the information."

"What is it?"

"About eight years ago, your father represented Katie Taylor when she sought a restraining order against her husband. The judge who denied the action was one of her husband's fishing buddies."

"Who was her husband?" Paige asked.

Ursula didn't give a name, but Paige read the answer in her eyes.

"No," she said in disbelief.

"After the restraining order was denied, Katie packed her bags and ran away. Rumor has it she's somewhere in Virginia, but she certainly hasn't set foot in Merchants Town since. The only reason she didn't take Ainsley with her was because she was afraid he would kill her if she did. Katie didn't think he'd hurt Ainsley, so she left the girl behind."

"Deputy Taylor is a wife beater?"

Ursula nodded. "He put Katie in the hospital a couple of times, but she swore he'd never lay a hand on Ainsley. He loves that girl, but he's got one wicked temper."

"Such a temper that he'd hurt Travis if he found out about their relationship?"

"Hurt? He could have killed Travis and gotten away with it. I don't think he knew about the relationship until Travis was arrested."

"Okay, so that would explain why they'd keep the relationship secret. But who would have assaulted her? Could it have been a home invasion? Wrong place, wrong time? Was anything stolen from the home?"

"One of Frank's guns." Ursula riffled through some papers and handed her the report. "They haven't found it."

Paige could feel her excitement rising, but she knew pinning the actual crime on an unknown robber would be difficult if not impossible. Merchants Town was not ready to admit there could be a criminal still in their midst.

"If he won't take the stand and Ainsley can't remember, I can't show they were in a relationship and I'm pretty certain there is no one in this town who would testify as to Deputy Taylor's temper. Bradley will seek to exclude Ainsley's mom, provided I could find her to get her subpoenaed to testify."

Paige's excitement quickly faded into dread. "I don't know how I can paint this picture without his voice," she said, her voice muffled by her hands.

"Have you had a chance to look through the discovery from the phones?" Ursula hefted a box onto the conference table and searched through the file folders.

"There's nothing on Travis's phone other than calls to Ainsley's number, and that just supports what her dad was saying about him contacting her. The calls were never more than three minutes long, certainly not conversations between lovers that lasted well into the night. I went through the records twice hoping for a text message or an incoming call from her. Nothing." Paige brushed the hair out of her eyes.

"Not Travis's phone. Ainsley's. We received it from the State the day Roger had his heart attack. They had some bogus excuse as to why it was not released with the rest of the State's discovery. Roger hasn't had a chance to look at it." Ursula handed Paige the CD with the discovery saved on it. "I'll go to Henry's and get you some coffee."

Paige slipped the disc into her laptop and began going through the files from Ainsley's phone. There were a lot of text messages about college, the same college Travis was to attend. There were bubbly conversations with her new roommate about who would bring the microwave, the refrigerator, and the color scheme for the dorm room. They were both in support of pink, grey, and cream. The roommate was on the track team and was dating a football player. From the texts, Paige could sense Ainsley's excitement, but there was absolutely no mention of a boyfriend.

Paige read through some text messages between Ainsley's friends, Heather and Renee, but Bradley had already called Renee to the stand; she denied that Ainsley had a boyfriend and claimed the friends only knew Travis because he was a year older than them. Heather hadn't been called yet, but it was expected her testimony would mirror Renee's.

The social media posts were devoid of any reference of Travis. Travis and Ainsley both had accounts, but they were not even connected on the sites. There were a lot of phone calls between Ainsley and her father, the majority of which were incoming.

Deputy Taylor seemed a bit obsessive with how frequently he reached out to his daughter. Paige made a mental note of the sheer volume of his incoming calls, and continued through the files.

The photographs on the phone shed no light on any relationship. There were pictures of Ainsley and her two closest friends on a school trip to the beach, at the prom, and building houses for the church group. There were pictures of dogs and birds, and even one of a deer grazing in a field Paige recognized as Story's farm. Other than a proximity to Crawley's side of town, it served no purpose in the case. There were pictures from that winter's snow storm where the town had been blanketed under several inches. Ainsley had taken several of Merchants Town Baptist Church, with the sun shining through the stained-glass windows and hitting the brilliant white of the snow. She was a good photographer, that was certain, but there were no pictures of Travis. If they were in a relationship, it was either a ghost relationship or one hundred percent one-sided – neither boded well for Paige's client.

"Look who I found loitering outside," Ursula said, ushering Travis and Ciara into the office. "If I had known they had an appointment, I would have picked up some more coffee."

Ursula was the queen of the schedule, and she ran a tight ship. Her organizational skills were part of the reason her relationship with Roger worked so well; he couldn't schedule or remember a calendar to save his life. Unexpected clients in the office, short of an emergency, were a chaotic experience for Ursula.

"I'm sorry, Ms. Ursula. I told Travis to come by after court and forgot to put it on the calendar."

Ursula humphed. "Well, thank goodness I baked some extra muffins today." She placed the basket of blueberry muffins on the conference table and left the room.

"What's that?" Travis asked, his eyes glued to Paige's computer screen.

It was a picture of Ainsley and Heather at prom. Ainsley wore a sapphire blue ball gown with a sweetheart neckline. Her blonde hair was piled high on her head with loose ringlets framing her face. When Paige had first seen the photo, she couldn't help but wonder if Ainsley's carriage had turned into a pumpkin before she'd made it home; the resemblance to Cinderella was uncanny.

"Discovery. I'm going through the files on Ainsley's phone."

Travis nodded and touched the screen. "She was beautiful that night, like a princess." He laughed. "I told her she looked like a topper on a fancy cake."

"Were you at prom?"

"No. I saw her afterwards." His face hardened. "Why is this important? What does this have to do with my case?"

"I'm trying to find anything that will tie you and her together. Anything."

"You won't find it." He spoke softly but with certainty.

"Then I need you to take the stand."

"No."

"Travis, they need to hear from you. The jurors need to know why there isn't anything that puts the two of you together."

"I won't do it. I won't do that to Ainsley."

"You know how that will look, right? Other than your word, there is not one shred of evidence that the two of you were in a relationship. It would be hard enough to hinge the defense on your word alone, but without it, you're as good as guilty. We might want to consider taking that plea."

"I'll take the stand," Ciara spoke up from the corner. "I told him not to get involved with a white girl. I knew he was messing around with fire, but he just wouldn't listen."

"Did you know he was involved with Ainsley?"

Ciara took a deep breath. "No. I just knew it was a white girl who was a senior at the high school. He told me the girl's father wouldn't support the relationship. I told him his own mother didn't support the relationship, and he needed to end it immediately. I've told that boy repeatedly not to get involved with a white girl. They are nothing but trouble. But he didn't listen to me." She turned to her son. "And look at the fine mess you've found yourself in."

"I appreciate your willingness, Ciara, I really do, but I can't call you to the stand."

"Why not?"

"I'm going to be honest with you. Your testimony won't help him. It may actually hurt him. You can't put him in a relationship with Ainsley, just with one white girl. Your testimony would be irrelevant. Do you have any idea how many white girls are in this year's senior class? Thirty?"

"At least." Travis put his head in his hands. "Mama, I'm going to take care of it," he said when he removed his hands.

"How? How are you going to 'take care of it'? Like you've been doing so far?" Ciara started to cry. "You're supposed to be getting ready for college, not standing trial. This was not part of our plan, Travis. I will never forgive her for this. Never."

"Ciara, why don't you go join Ms. Ursula out front? I need to speak to my client alone."

Ciara gathered her purse and brushed furiously at her face. "Ms. Sparrow, I raised this boy to know that he can't rely on no one but himself in life. I don't know what he expects is going to happen with this trial, but please do what you can to get him to speak for himself because no one else is going to speak up. Everyone in this room knows he didn't do it. The only thing he's guilty of is being a damn fool."

"I can't force him to testify, but I will do what I can." Paige gave Ciara's arm a brief squeeze. "I promise."

After Ciara left, Paige sat down and continued flipping through the discovery files on her computer. The silence ticked the minutes between them.

"I'm not testifying," Travis finally said.

"And I'm not asking you to again." Paige pulled up the folder of deleted items. Her heart started beating faster as she opened it. In her experience, most people didn't know that deleted items remained in a phone's memory for a period of time after deletion. She groaned when she saw it was more of the same. Blurry pictures, text messages of no importance, and saved screenshots from various websites showing design styles for dorm rooms. Paige opened the last file and nearly fell from her seat; it was a picture of two hands, one white and one black, entwined. There was a small diamond ring on one of the white fingers.

"Travis," Paige kept her voice low.

"Yes?"

"When did you propose to Ainsley?"

His eyes went wide. "How did you..."

She turned the laptop so he could see the deleted picture.

"When did you propose to her?" she asked again.

128

"That day." His jaw twitched.

"Where is the ring now?" Paige's hands shook with excitement.

He shrugged. "I don't know. Ainsley said she was going to hide it. She was wearing it when I left."

"Travis, you have to take the stand."

He shook his head. "I'm not going to."

Frustrated, Paige slammed the lid of the laptop on the image. "Who are you protecting?" she demanded.

Her client remained silent.

"Who are you willing to go to prison for?"

Travis didn't budge.

"If you're not going to talk, you should take the plea," Paige finally said with a sigh.

"I'm not taking the plea. I didn't do anything wrong."

"So why won't you take the stand and tell the jury that?"

"Because I love her."

Paige could hardly hear him because his voice was so low, but the rawness of his words broke her heart.

"I'll see you tomorrow," Paige said, opening the conference room door and gesturing for him to leave. "The State will likely rest and we will be up. Be prepared."

"Yes, ma'am."

CHAPTER THIRTEEN

Paige was still cursing the young man and his misplaced devotion when she saw the flashing blue lights in her rear-view mirror. She glanced at the speedometer; she wasn't speeding. Confused, she pulled over to the side of the road and reached for her license and registration.

"Ms. Sparrow." It was Deputy Frank Taylor.

"Good evening, Deputy Taylor." She tried to hand him the license and registration, but he pushed it back.

"You don't belong here." His words echoed those of Bradley, but his were far more menacing.

"Excuse me?" Her heart pounded against her chest.

"Go back to Charlotte. I won't tell you again." His hand rested on the butt of the gun that rode his hip.

"Is that a threat?"

He leaned into the window, just inches from her face. "I said I won't tell you again." He smelled of whiskey and cigarette smoke.

"Is there a problem here?" Paige hadn't seen Scotty pull up behind her, but his voice covered her and made her safe.

Deputy Taylor released the butt of his gun and backed away from the truck. "I was just telling Ms. Sparrow that she should slow down. Things are a little bit different down here than they are in Charlotte."

"I think Ms. Sparrow knows exactly how things are here." Scotty stood by the truck until Deputy Taylor tipped his hat and bid his farewell.

"What was that about?" Scotty asked, leaning into the truck to get a good look at Paige. "You look like a ghost just walked over your grave."

"Nothing," she forced a smile. "He just startled me is all."

"He's been running his mouth about you all over town, and he looked like he was giving you a hard time. I'm glad I showed up when I did. I don't much care for him," Scotty said looking down the empty road. "I never have."

Paige was grateful Scotty had come to her rescue. She didn't know what Deputy Taylor would have done if he hadn't, and the thought frightened her. He was a powerful man accustomed to getting his way, and the trial of the accused attacker of his daughter was most certainly not going his way. As Paige slowed her breathing and drove home, a picture of the girl Travis loved enough to go to jail for formed in her mind.

"This is my home," she said, her hands tight on the steering wheel. "I'm not going anywhere."

Paige turned the car around and headed to the outskirts of town. She needed to warn Travis.

"Ms. Sparrow!" Ciara opened the door on the second knock, an apron around her waist and a smudge of flour on her face. "Is everything okay?"

Paige nodded, questioning whether she should have gone to the house and wondering if she was overreacting. "I just need to speak with you and Travis real quick."

Ciara opened the door wide and gestured for Paige to come in. "He's in his room reading. Give me just one second to get him. Can I get you anything?"

"No, thank you." Paige glanced around the small living room while she waited. Pictures of the family lined the walls, most were of Travis. A play pen sat in the corner, beneath the window, and a toddler eyed her curiously from it.

"Hello, little baby," Paige waved.

The toddler lifted both arms. "Up! Up!"

Paige eagerly obliged the pint-sized little girl with Ciara's eyes. When Ciara returned, with Travis a few steps behind, Paige was bouncing the girl on her hip and talking nonsense to her.

"That child has never seen a stranger," Ciara said with a laugh.

"Nah," Travis said. "Little just recognizes good people."

"I didn't know you had a sister. What's her name?"

"Sarai. But Travis calls her 'Little' because she is the spitting image of him." Ciara took the girl. "You were a bit of a surprise, weren't you?"

Sarai planted an open-mouthed kiss on her mother's cheek. "Some of our biggest mistakes give us the greatest of joys," Ciara said. "But I'm sure you didn't make the trip out here just to meet Little."

132

"No," Paige said slowly, trying to find the words. "I wanted to let you know about an incident that happened on my way home from the office. Deputy Taylor paid me a little visit."

Travis's face clouded. "Are you okay?" he asked. "Did he hurt you?"

Paige shook her head. "He just pulled me over and gave me a warning. A friend showed up and he went on his way."

"What sort of warning?" Ciara asked, sitting on the sofa with the baby on her lap.

"He told me I need to go back to Charlotte."

Travis rubbed at his eyes. "It's okay, Ms. Sparrow. I understand. We'll figure something out," he said after a moment.

"Travis. I'm not going."

The young man raised his head and met her eyes.

"I'm staying right here and representing you," Paige continued. "I don't care what Deputy Taylor says or thinks or does. I'm not going anywhere until this is over."

Both Ciara and Travis breathed a sigh of relief.

"I wanted to tell you about it because I'm concerned that he may pay you a visit. I want you to be prepared and be cautious. I do not trust that man."

Paige was interrupted by loud crash. The crunch of breaking glass was followed by the sound of tires squealing. Ciara screamed and Sarai began to cry. Travis clenched and unclenched his hands at his sides, but he didn't move from the spot where he stood.

"I think we were just paid a visit," he said, his mouth in a hard line. He walked over to Sarai's play pen and removed the large rock that had been thrown through the window. He held it up for

Paige to read the crude racial slur that had been painted in red on its face.

Paige tried to slow her heart as she looked in the play pen where Sarai had been happily playing moments before. Shards of glass covered the bottom.

"We need to call the police." Paige pulled her phone from her purse. She was convinced Deputy Taylor had followed her there and had just sent another warning.

"Why? We know who did it and he *is* the police. We can't do anything."

"You can't just ignore this," Paige exclaimed.

"We're not ignoring it, Ms. Sparrow, but there is nothing we can do. It's not the first time someone has thrown a rock at this house and it won't be the last," Ciara said calmly.

Paige was floored at how quickly the woman had composed herself.

"Why are you not outraged?" Paige looked from the rock to the window to Sarai. "Is this enough to get you to testify?" she demanded, her eyes flashing. "Will you take the stand now?"

Travis shook his head and left the room, dropping the rock on the coffee table. Paige had her answer. Ciara continued to play with Sarai, who had stopped crying. Paige picked up the rock and slipped it into her pocket.

"Is there somewhere the three of you can go for the remainder of the trial?" Paige finally asked. "It's not safe here." Paige looked out the broken window where the sun was still shining. The crime had happened in broad daylight. "I don't want any of you to spend the night here until this is resolved."

"I'm not leaving my house," Ciara said firmly.

"Mama, I think we should." Travis stood in the door way, a glass of milk in his hand. Paige could see the slightest of tremors in his fingers. "It won't be forever."

"Please?" Paige begged. "It's for your safety. Because of the conditions of Travis's release, you can't leave Merchants Town, but you need to go somewhere and you need to go now. Is there someone in town you can stay with?"

Ciara nodded. "We will go tonight," she promised.

When Paige was convinced that the Crawley family would leave that night, she headed home. She was still shaking. Roger was waiting for her when she pulled up. He had two fishing poles and a container of worms.

"Want to go down to the river with me?" he asked. "The bream are biting pretty good and your mother says I need to eat more fish. It's a win-win."

Paige wanted to run to his arms and tell him about her encounter with Deputy Taylor and the rock that was heavy in her pocket, but she stopped herself. Roger was still recovering from a heart attack and she didn't want to worry him.

"Sure, Dad. Are we taking the boat?" She tried to keep her voice steady.

"No. I figure we'll just go down to the pier and see what nibbles before the sun sets."

"Mom said you can't take the boat, didn't she?"

Roger made a face and Paige giggled. She forced her fear and anger down. She was going to enjoy the evening with her father and not get bogged down in Deputy Taylor's fear tactics.

"I'll run in to change, and we can head out." Paige raced into her room and pulled on some funky print leggings, a pair covered in bright koi fish, and a tank top. She slipped the rock out of her suit coat pocket and put it in the nightstand by the bed. She was back on the porch in less than three minutes.

"I see you dressed for the occasion," Roger said, glancing at her leggings. "If you have another pair, maybe I should give it a try," he joked.

"Stop it, Dad! "Paige laughed and took the cooler. "Let's go."

Paige was excited about heading to the river. She hadn't been fishing in over ten years. Growing up, it had been one of her favorite past times. Sundays, after church, they would load up the truck and drive the boat down to the river. She and Julie would fight over who would get to steer the boat while Roger lowered the trailer down the boat ramp. Then they would fight over who would get to sit on the live well in the boat and who had to sit on the floor. As the youngest, Paige usually lost. She'd sit on the floor of the boat as they bounced over waves to get to one of their favorite honey holes, as her father called the areas laden with fish. Afternoons after school, Roger would meet his girls as they were getting off the bus. He would already have the cane poles in the back of the truck. Crickets, worms, and minnows were his bait of choice, nothing fake for Roger Sparrow. By the time she was five, Paige could bait a hook better than she could tie her shoe.

"Here, Dad. Sit down," Paige put the cooler down on the pier and took the poles from him.

"Ya'll women need to stop fussing over me," he protested as he sat down.

They baited their hooks and tossed the lines into the water near the roots of the old Cyprus trees. The two orange corks bobbed gently in the ripples of their own making. Roger stood up and pulled two sodas from the cooler. He tossed one to Paige and settled back on his makeshift seat while she leaned against one of the posts. They were the only ones there.

"I heard today went well," he said after a moment.

Paige thought about Deputy Taylor and the sound of breaking glass. She swallowed hard.

"I think it did," she said. "Bradley was expecting and had prepared for me to attack the credibility of his experts, but he wasn't expecting me to point out the known limitations of their findings. He was sweating like a whore in church by the time we were released for the day."

"That's my girl. You know his weakness. Attack it."

"I just wish Travis would..." Paige started but stopped as her cork began to jump around. "Come on," she said softly. "Stop nibbling and bite the darn thing." When the cork took a dive, Paige jerked the pole back to set the hook. She grabbed the line and brought her catch the surface. The golden belly of the bream shown in the sunlight as she lifted it from the water.

"Want me to help you unhook him?" Roger propped his pole in one of the built-in holders on the pier and turned to her.

"Dad! Dad!" Paige yelled as his cork went down. Roger left Paige to unhook her catch and set about bringing his own in.

By the time Paige had rebaited her hook and tossed it back in the water, another fish was bringing her cork under. There was no time for discussion, and they settled into an easy silence. Within an hour, they had caught twenty fish and had only tossed back two for being too small.

"I think this is plenty enough for supper," Roger said, eyeing the cooler. "Let's get these guys home and cleaned." He smacked his lips. "How long has it been since you've had fresh fish?"

Paige thought about her favorite sushi joint back in Charlotte. "About a week."

Roger raised his eyebrows. "Fresh, cooked fish?"

Paige laughed. "A very long time."

As they were loading up the truck, Sloan's family pulled up in a muddy SUV with stick figures on the back. Paige recognized the man with them as the juror with the kind eyes.

"Hey Mr. Sparrow," Grace sang, jumping from the car and running up to him. "Did you catch anything?"

"Did we catch anything? Well, I don't know," he winked, opening the cooler. "What do you think?"

"Mama! Daddy! Look at all the fish Mr. Sparrow and Ms. Paige caught!"

"That's a pretty good haul," Peter said peering into the cooler before turning to Paige.

"I'm Peter, Sloan's husband," he said, extending his hand. "You must be Paige. Sloan told me you were in school together." Peter was gruff, with a full face beard, and his hands were hardened from manual labor. "I was going to introduce myself at church, but you were swarmed." His dimple matched Grace's.

"Nice to meet you," Paige said taking his hand.

"Peter builds houses. He's an amazing architect." Roger gave Peter a hearty slap on the back. "He designed Scotty's home."

"You're too kind, Roger." Peter gestured to the juror. "This is my brother, Kevin."

Paige nodded a greeting before turning to Grace. "What did you bring as bait?"

"Minnows," Grace said, holding up the Styrofoam container.

"Well, I don't know what their appetite is for minnows today, but they are loving some good juicy earthworms." She handed Grace the container of worms they'd been using. "Try both and let me know which they like better?"

"Mama! May I?"

"May you what, sweetheart?" Sloan rested a hand on the girl's head.

"Ms. Paige said I can use her worms and find out what the fish like better. May I have her worms?"

Sloan made a face. "You may have her worms, but I'm not baiting those hooks for you. Gross."

Paige waved goodbye and hopped in the truck next to her father. She rolled the windows down and let the afternoon sun shine on her face and the wind blow through her hair as they drove the five minutes back to the house.

"Kevin is one of your jurors, isn't he?" Roger asked.

Paige nodded.

"If he's anything like Peter, he's a good man. A nice solid choice."

"He has kind eyes," Paige turned to her father. "I honestly didn't think I'd select him, but there was something about his face."

Roger nodded. "You did good with that one, Baby Girl."

"I'm still not so sure about the other ones." She shook her head. "Those women hate me."

Roger laughed. "Stop it. They don't hate you. And the way I hear it, you're growing on them. It just takes some time."

"Travis doesn't have a lot of time left."

"Just have faith. You're doing a fine job."

Scotty was at his mailbox checking his mail when they pulled down the long road that served as their driveway.

"Want to come over for dinner?" Roger yelled through the open window. "We just caught a mess of fish that we couldn't possibly eat by ourselves!"

Scotty nodded. "Sounds delicious. We'll be over in a bit to help you clean them."

Scotty and Jason walked over to the house not long after Roger had parked the truck. Paige went inside to get the scaler and a sharp knife. She handed both to Scotty and hurried back in the house before he began chopping off heads. Dory barked excitedly about their feet, her nub of a tail a blur.

"Not going to help?" Lillian asked with a smile.

Paige shook her head with a snort. "Not on the gross part."

"Thank you for going with him. That hour with you made him the happiest man in the world. I do wish you'd come home more."

"Mom."

"I know. I know. Two weeks." Lillian held her hands up in surrender. "We'll take what we can get."

"Are you making coleslaw?" Paige peeked into the mixing bowl on the counter.

"I am. Do you want to help?" Lillian handed Paige the food processor and the cabbage to shred and they set about preparing the meal in a happy silence.

Lillian fried half the fish and baked the other half with lemon and parsley. There was fresh coleslaw, hush puppies, and snaps from the garden. A pitcher of ice cold sweet tea sat in the middle of the table with a bouquet of weeds Avery and Max had picked on the way over.

The family held hands to say the blessing and then began to feast. Paige took a fish and carefully removed the meat from the bones before placing it on Max's plate. Scotty did the same for Jason, and Anderson helped Avery. After the children were working on their food, Paige eyed her options. Her diet suggested the baked fish, but her taste buds wanted the fried.

"Just do it," Roger said with a wink.

Paige laughed and grabbed one of the fried.

"Did Paige tell you about her little incident today with Deputy Taylor?" Scotty asked taking a bite of a hush puppy.

Paige choked on the fish and reached for her glass of sweet tea.

Roger frowned. "No. What happened?"

Paige waved her hand when she'd cleared her throat. "It was nothing. I was just speeding, and he pulled me over. No big deal," she lied. Her heart started to beat faster at the reminder of the encounter.

"I don't like that man," Lillian, the woman who liked everyone, said without pause. "There's something about him that just gives me the willies."

"I've got a willie!" Max said.

Julie turned scarlet. "Anderson! Control your son."

"What do you want me to do about it, sweetheart? He is telling the truth," Anderson said with a snort.

"So, Jules, how excited are you about having three girls?" Scotty asked with a grin.

Paige watched the easy banter between her former sweetheart and her family with a tinge of jealousy. Chris would never fit in like this, she thought. Never in a million years.

CHAPTER FOURTEEN

With the sun already high in the sky, Paige hurried into town so she could stop at Henry's Corner Store before court. During the lazy evening with her family, she'd successfully pushed all thoughts of Deputy Taylor out of her mind. But the first thing she did when she woke up was look at the rock with its hateful word. He will not win, she told herself as she walked into the diner. "Not on my watch."

"Morning, honey." Barb, the waitress, said with a smile. "Has Julie had those babies yet?"

"No, ma'am. Not yet." Paige handed her cash and took the steaming cup of coffee from her. "Do you have any cinnamon?" she asked after taking a sip.

Barb reached behind the counter and pulled out a shaker. "Good call," she said. "I like mine with a little nutmeg. Just a hint of spice makes it something special."

Paige nodded. "Thank you, Barb," she called as she hurried out of the door and to the courthouse. Ursula was waiting for her with Ciara and Travis.

"Did you find somewhere in town to stay?" she whispered.

Ciara nodded. "We're fine, Ms. Sparrow. We've got some good friends in this town." She looked at Ursula. "Very good friends."

Ursula squeezed Ciara's hand without a word.

After court was called to session, Bradley began calling what seemed to be every classmate and teacher Ainsley had ever encountered at the high school. He was deadset on showing Ainsley and Travis had no interactions with each other, and he was going to drive that point home at each opportunity.

"How do you know Ms. Taylor?" Bradley asked the science teacher after she was sworn in. Mrs. Patterson had been at the high school for almost half a century. She knew everyone in Merchants Town and taught over half of them, Paige included.

"I had the privilege of having Ms. Taylor in my biology class." Mrs. Patterson nodded at the jurors. "She's a very bright student," she added.

"And do you know the defendant?" Bradley pointed at Travis.

Mrs. Patterson frowned. "Do you mean Travis Crawley? Of course I know Mr. Crawley. He was in my Advanced Placement biology class about two, three years ago now. He's going to be a doctor someday." She smiled at Travis. "God-willing and the creek doesn't rise, he'll be one right here in Merchants Town."

Paige perked up at her former teacher's words. Mrs. Patterson wasn't the witness that Bradley Moore needed her to be be.

Bradley fumbled over the next few questions, trying to salvage the testimony. Clearly, Mrs. Patterson was going off script and Paige loved every second of it.

"Did you ever see Ms. Ainsley and Mr. Crawley together?" Bradley asked.

144

"Well, I don't reckon I would, now would I? Mr. Crawley was a class ahead of Ms. Ainsley and taking rather advanced classes."

"Your Honor," Bradley protested.

"Mrs. Patterson, please just answer the question," Judge Fox said, smiling behind his hand.

"Well, if he'd ask a question properly, I would," she shot back.

"Did you ever see the defendant with Ms. Taylor?" Bradley snarled. The jurors frowned at the harshness of his tone.

"Mr. Moore, with all due respect, I have answered that question. It may not have been the answer you're over there fishing for, but it's the answer."

The jurors started laughing.

"No further questions for this witness." Bradley threw up his hands and stomped back to his seat.

"Good morning, Mrs. Patterson." Paige smiled at her former teacher. She had hated that class.

"Good morning, Ms. Sparrow. Pleasure as always."

"Mrs. Patterson, you've been at Merchants Town High for quite a few years, haven't you?"

"Honey, I taught you and your father, and I'm hoping to live long enough to teach those babies your sister is about to deliver."

"Your Honor," Bradley whined.

"Mrs. Patterson, please limit your answers to a simple 'yes' or 'no.'"

Mrs. Patterson glared at Judge Fox until he shifted his gaze elsewhere. "Yes, I have been at Merchants Town High for a very long time," she said, finally.

"You don't have time to keep up with all the relationships of your students, do you?"

Mrs. Patterson laughed. "Heavens, no. These students change their beaus as frequently as I change my under garments."

Judge Fox coughed into his hand.

"I mean, no. No, I don't have time."

"So, you wouldn't know who Ms. Taylor was dating?"

"No, I would not."

"Thank you, Mrs. Patterson. No further questions, your Honor."

Bradley tried to recover from the mess that was Mrs. Patterson's testimony by calling Heather Morris to the stand. The young brunette looked terrified.

"Hello, Ms. Morris," he began. "Can you tell the jury how you know Ms. Taylor?"

"We've been best friends since I moved here when I was six."

"And as best friends, what sort of things do you talk about?"

"Shopping. Boys. School work. Lately, we've mostly talked about college."

"Boys? You mean like who you have a crush on, who is dating whom, and things like that?" Bradley pushed.

"Yes, I suppose." Heather shifted in her seat.

"What sort of conversations did you and Ms. Taylor have about the defendant?"

"Well, I..." Heather glanced into the crowd of spectators. Paige followed her eyes and watched them land on Deputy Taylor.

"Ms. Morris?"

"We didn't have any conversations about the defendant," she said after a moment.

"Your best friend never mentioned the defendant to you? He never once came up in conversation?"

Heather shook her head. "No."

She was lying, of that Paige was certain. Paige wondered if Deputy Taylor had paid her a visit as well.

"Good morning, Ms. Morris."

"Good morning." Heather looked like she was going to throw up.

"You and Ms. Taylor shared secrets, didn't you?"

"Yes."

"Secrets you can't tell anyone?"

"Yes."

"Secrets that could hurt someone?"

Heather paused. Paige counted to five.

"Yes," the young woman finally answered.

With each answer, Heather's voice became fainter and fainter.

"And you wouldn't do anything to hurt Ms. Taylor?"

"Your Honor, is that even a question?" Bradley's chair squeaked against the floor like nails on a chalkboard as he slid it out to stand.

"I will rephrase it. You wouldn't do anything to hurt Ms. Taylor, would you?"

"No, ma'am. I wouldn't."

"No further questions."

The rest of the day was much of the same. Bradley called classmate after classmate to the stand, asking each of them if they'd ever seen Ainsley with Travis. Each testimony put the smallest of holes in Paige's argument. Paige held out hope that one would break. She was certain one would at least say they'd seen them together, but their answers parroted each other. Deputy Taylor had gotten to them all. Paige was furious. She had to remind herself

147

that they were closer to being children than they were adults. Their fear would be real. She thought about the rock in the nightstand by her bed and wondered if she would have been able to go against Deputy Taylor at that age.

After the day's session came to a close, Paige hurried to her father's truck. She didn't want to run the risk of another encounter with Deputy Taylor. As she pulled out of the parking lot, she saw him standing next to Heather and a man Paige assumed was Heather's father. Deputy Taylor shook the man's hand and gave him a hearty slap on the back. Heather looked at the gravel.

"There are definitely some dirty dealings going on here. Something is most certainly rotten in the state of Denmark," Paige whispered, referencing her mother's favorite Shakespeare play. "Now, how do I expose it without Travis?"

Paige was lost in her thoughts when she pulled into the driveway and nearly ran over Scotty.

"Paige!" He ran in front of her, frantically waving his hands. She could see Jason, Avery and Max chasing each other through the field.

"Julie is in labor," Scotty exclaimed, breathless, when she rolled down the window. "We've been trying to reach you for hours."

"Ah. My phone is still turned off from court." Paige fumbled through her purse and turned the phone on. It immediately started buzzing to alert her to all the voicemails and text messages she'd missed.

"When did she go in? Has she had them? Are Mom and Dad there?"

"Early this morning, around 9 a.m. Your mom and dad took her. Anderson closed up the pharmacy and went straight to the hospital." Scotty lowered his voice as the game of tag brought the children closer to the truck. "There are some complications. Right now, they're only letting Anderson in the room."

Paige quickly dialed her mother's number. Her hands shook.

"How is she?" she asked as soon as her mother answered.

"Oh Paige, honey. She's okay, but they've decided to send her over to another hospital about two hours away. They don't have the necessary equipment here for the labor. Your father and I are on our way there now. Anderson is riding in the ambulance with her."

"Is she going to be okay?" Paige remembered being six when Julie fell out of the tree they'd built a treehouse in. The fall had knocked her unconscious. Paige remembered trying to wake up her sister and not being able to. The ambulance had come. Convinced Julie was dead, Paige had been terrified and had hid in the cotton fields until her father found her. She couldn't shake that same feeling.

Lillian's voice caught. "They're worried about the babies."

"What's the address?" Paige fumbled through her purse for a pen. "I'll head that way now."

"No, honey. Julie doesn't want you to come. She was quite clear about that."

The words hurt. Why wouldn't her sister won't her there?

"It's not that she doesn't want you with her," Lillian explained. "She's just worried about Max and Avery. She thinks they might be too much for Scotty to handle on his own and your father and I intend to stay the night. I told her not to worry, that you'd watch the boys."

"That does make the most sense," Paige admitted. "Please tell her I love her, and I will come see her tomorrow."

"She knows, honey. Just take care of her boys for her, okay? It will be their very first night away from her and they might be scared."

Paige hung up the phone and put the truck in park.

"Are you going to the hospital?" Scotty asked, leaning in the window.

Paige shook her head. "They want me to stay here and watch the boys."

"They don't trust me?"

"With three boys under the age of six? Not in the slightest." Paige laughed. "Want to have a sleepover?"

"You're scared to be alone with Max and Avery, aren't you?"

"I haven't been around kids since I was babysitting for the Howards in high school, and they were two girls that only wanted to play dolls. I'm absolutely petrified."

"Well, let's make it an adventure for them. We can camp out under the stars. Boys like that sort of thing. You go pack a bag for yourself. Your mother has already given me overnight bags for the boys. I'll go ahead and order pizza."

Paige put the truck in drive and sped the rest of the way to the house, leaving dust in her wake. She ran inside and quickly changed, wondering what she should take with her to Scotty's. She threw some clothes in a bag and tossed the charger to her phone and laptop in. If she forgot anything, it would be no trouble for her to walk over to the house and get it.

While she was packing, her phone buzzed. It was an unknown local number.

"Ms. Sparrow?" a young woman's voice asked.

"Yes?"

"Hello. I'm Brittany Lane, Judge Fox's clerk."

"Hello, Brittany."

"Judge Fox has a family emergency and has continued the trial until Thursday. I've emailed you notice, but I'm trying to touch base with you and Attorney Moore in person since it's so last minute."

"Thank you, Brittany. I hope everything is okay with Judge Fox."

"One of his grandchildren was in a car accident, and he's heading down to Wilmington to be with family."

Paige hadn't expected the clerk to tell her what the emergency was, but then again, it was Merchants Town and there were no secrets.

"Thank you, Brittany. Please tell Judge Fox that he and his family are in my thoughts and prayers."

The phone buzzed to alert Paige to the court's email as soon as she hung up. After reviewing it to ensure that it indeed was a court document and not something Deputy Taylor and Bradley cooked up, she called Travis and let him know. The phone buzzed again as soon as she hung up. It was Miranda.

"I saw that Julie is in labor!" Miranda exclaimed as soon as Paige answered. "Are you at the hospital?"

"How could you possibly know she's in labor? I just found out myself."

"Her blog."

"Her what?"

"You don't follow your sister's blog? Oh, Paige, you're missing some fantastic gems. She has thousands of followers. This Mommy Blogger movement is legit. You seriously didn't know?"

"I had no idea." Paige laughed. It didn't surprise her; Julie had always wanted to be a writer.

"So, are you at the hospital?"

"No. I'm watching Avery and Max."

"They left you in charge of two children?"

"Well, me and Scotty."

"Scotty as in Scotty the baseball player? As in Scotty your high school sweetheart?" Miranda had limited knowledge of Scotty. She knew that Paige's high school sweetheart had played baseball professionally, but she didn't know he'd moved back to Paige's hometown unless he showed up in Julie'

"One and the same."

"This sounds like a juicy story, and I do love a juicy story about someone else's drama. I hate I'm not there for this. I'd come down, but Fitz has me drafting some interrogatories."

"Oh really?"

"Stop acting like you're surprised. I know you talked to him. I don't know what you said, but thank you."

"I just told him the truth, Mir. It wasn't your fault."

"Well, thanks. I'm glad I still have a job, and watching Danielle's face when I came to work on Monday was quite possibly the most fun I've had all month." Miranda laughed.

"I bet she was livid."

"Indeed. How's the trial coming?"

Paige groaned. "Any ideas how to get a young man to testify?"

"Why would you want to put him on the stand?"

"He didn't do it."

"Of course he didn't do it," Mir said dryly.

"Seriously, Mir. He didn't."

"Then why won't he testify?"

"I don't know. He's protecting someone. I don't know if it's the girl or the person who actually beat her. I really have no idea, and it's driving me bananas. To make matters worse, the girl's father is tampering with witnesses and threatening me."

"What do you mean he's threatening you?"

"He pulled me over on the way home from court a couple of days ago and let me know that I need to go back to Charlotte. Or else."

"Did you call the police?"

"He is the police, Mir. And I'm pretty certain he was the one who threw a rock through my client's window while I was standing in the living room. He thinks he is untouchable, and I'm half-convinced he is. Small towns are funny. Loyalties run deep here, especially with the boys in blue."

"Paige, you have to tell someone. This is serious."

"I'll be okay. It's almost over, and then I'll be back in Charlotte."

"Well, at least promise me you'll be careful. Don't make any waves that you don't have to make."

"I promise," she lied, thinking of the rock in her nightstand. Paige Sparrow intended to make some very big waves before she was done.

"If I get the interrogatories drafted, do you think your family would mind if I came down this weekend? I'd love to see the babies and you. And I simply must meet this Scotty character."

153

"Of course we wouldn't mind. We would love to have you visit."

"You sound really good, Paige. Really happy."

"It's good to be home, even for a little bit," Paige admitted.

"Okay, well I will give you a call if I'm able to get away this weekend. Keep me updated on Julie because I don't think she'll be able to update that blog fast enough."

"Of course, Mir." Paige smiled as she disconnected the phone. Miranda was right, she was happy.

Paige tossed her bag in the truck and whistled for Dory to hop in. Scotty was in the front yard trying to set up a tent when she pulled into his drive.

It was the first time she'd seen his house from the front. It was a slate blue, with white shutters and railings. Kevin had done a beautiful job with its design. It was the home of her dreams. The home of their dreams. There would be a first-floor master, with a huge soaking tub and walk in shower. Jack and Jill sinks. A massive closet. A small room across the hall that would serve as her office until it was time for a nursery. Three bedrooms upstairs for the children they'd planned on having. The Christmas tree would go in front of the large bay windows. There'd be a breakfast nook and a formal dining area. There'd be an island in the kitchen with all the counter space she could possibly want. Downstairs would be a finished basement, a man cave full of sports memorabilia where he'd have the boys over to watch the games.

"What do you think?" Scotty asked, coming up to the truck and taking her bags.

"Huh?" Paige shook the memories from her head.

"The house."

154

"It's beautiful."

"Well, come on in and let me give you the grand tour."

Inside Scotty's home was exactly as she had imagined. Natural light spilled into each and every room, just as they had designed so many years ago. The kitchen faced the west, the colors of the sunset spilling out over the counter. Paige thought of her apartment in Charlotte, with its view of downtown, and realized it had nothing on his country home.

The basement was finished, but instead of a man cave, it was a playroom and study room for Jason. There was a Jack and Jill sink in the master, but only one tooth brush sat on the counter. The formal dining table was covered with coloring books on one end and veterinary text books on the other. The room that Paige had envisioned as her office and later a nursery was Scotty's office. He'd set it up as a "patient" room. The walls were lined with cages and habitats, some empty. Some containers seemed to be strictly for bugs. Paige grimaced when she saw the habitat full of hissing cockroaches, and she started to back out of the room. A terrarium full of lush greens caught her eye and curiosity stopped her retreat.

"What's that?" Paige stepped closer.

"That is Milo." Scotty reached his hand in the enclosure and pulled out a toad with a brilliant red stomach. "The coolest fire belly toad in the world." He put the toad back in the enclosure and turned to another enclosure. "And this is Otis, Milo's bearded dragon friend."

Paige backed away from the lizard. "You don't have to bring him out. I can see him just fine from here."

Scotty ignored her and put his hand in the enclosure. The lizard lazily climbed on it, and Scotty brought him close to his chest. Paige could have sworn it winked at her.

"I didn't know you were dabbling in Herpetology. Aren't dogs, cats, and the occasional cow enough for you?"

Scotty put the lizard back in his habitat. "Milo and Otis were left at the clinic. They were in a tote on the front steps one Monday when I showed up to work. How Otis never ate Milo, I don't really know. Either way, I brought them here with the intention of finding someone to take them. After I turned down several potential adopters, I realized I wasn't going to let them go. I decided after all they'd been through, I couldn't do that to them again."

"Scotty Lewis, I'm concerned you might be an animal hoarder."

"Lover. Animal lover," he corrected.

"There's a very fine line between the two in this situation."

"Don't you listen to them, Milo and Otis. She is just some silly city lady." He looked so happy surrounded by his lizard and toad with enclosures for crickets and roaches to feed them. That had never been part of the house she had designed, but the smile on his lips made her heart quicken its pace. He'd finished growing up without her, and she was surprised and proud of the man he'd become.

"You can put your stuff in one of the guest rooms upstairs," he said, pointing up the stair case after shutting the door to the herp room. "The one in the middle is Jason's, but you can have your choice of the either of the other two. The blue room has its own bathroom so you may want that one."

"I thought we were sleeping outside?"

"Me and the boys are. I didn't think you'd want to." He stopped when he saw her pout. "You really want to sleep outside?"

"Well, yeah. We're camping out, right?"

Scotty laughed. "Paige Sparrow, when was the last time you slept outside?"

It had been a meteor shower. They'd been eighteen and madly in love. She'd convinced her parents to let her break curfew to watch the meteor shower with him. Scotty had spread a blanket out on the high school's baseball field and they'd laid under the stars, planning their lives. He was going to play for the majors. He'd get signed by a team that would be close enough to Merchants Town that they could still live there. The Braves or the Nationals. Of this he was certain. She was going to go to law school and work at her father's firm. They'd get married when after she passed the bar, and have their first of three babies by age twenty-six. He'd have won the world series by then, of course.

They'd fallen asleep under the stars, with her head on his chest. The sprinklers woke them up with a start when the sun was coming up. Her father had fumed at her, but her mother had laughed. "Don't you remember what it was like to be young and in love? It's like a shooting star, brilliant, beautiful and gone before you realize it. Let them enjoy it while it burns bright."

Paige smiled at the memory. "The meteor shower."

"We were full of dreams then, weren't we?"

"We thought we had it all figured out. Silly us."

"The universe always has her way."

"But what if…" Paige's walk into the uncharted and dangerous territory of what-ifs was cut short by the pizza delivery man and three very hungry little boys.

Paige checked in with her mother after dinner. Julie was still in labor. She was adamant that she was going to have a natural delivery of the triplets, but at least she was at a facility that could accommodate worst case scenarios. The health scare was under control, for the time being, and Julie was allowed to see family. Roger and Lillian were getting a hotel room in the city, but Anderson was staying with her. Paige didn't know how he managed to sweet talk the nurses, but they'd set up a cot by Julie's hospital bed for him.

"Kiss my boys for me," Paige heard her sister yell as she was talking to her mother.

Despite it being their first night away from home, Max and Avery thoroughly enjoyed themselves at Scotty's. They didn't know what was going on with their parents and had just been told that their mom and dad had to take a trip to get the babies. They were blissfully unaware and focused on the great adventure of a sleepover. The way they tore through Scotty's house made it clear to Paige that Scotty and Jason were indeed part of the family. The boys played catch, terrorized the miniature ponies that Dory insisted on herding, and caught fireflies well into the evening.

"I'm surprised you don't have a dog," Paige mused, watching the boys and Dory.

"What?"

"Miniature ponies. Lizards. Toads. Cows. Chickens. But no dog. I'm actually surprised that you don't have a dog."

"Maybe one day. Most of these pets just sort of happened to me. I figure I'll get a dog when it's meant to be. What about you? All you ever talked about when we were in college was moving out and getting a dog. How many times did you drag me to shelters or ask me to check out breeder websites? You wanted all of them. I figured you'd have at least five by now. What happened?"

"Law school happened. And then I got an apartment that didn't allow pets." Paige left out the part about also getting a fiancé who claimed he was allergic.

The daylight faded from the sky, and the boys started to get tired. Off in the distance, a summer storm rumbled. Scotty unfurled four sleeping bags inside the tent and tossed about ten bed pillows in. Max had Wrinkles, his stuffed dog, clutched tight to his chest. Avery and Jason shoved their respective bed toys, a stuffed dinosaur and a stuffed elephant, under the pillows hoping the other didn't see. They climbed in the tent and Dory bounded in after them, turning three times and curling up in a ball at their feet. They were asleep in less than ten minutes.

"Come here." Scotty placed a blanket on the soft grass next to the tent and lay down. "Let's look at the stars before the storm comes in."

Paige glanced nervously at the sky. "If it's going to storm, don't you think we should bring the boys inside?"

"Don't worry. It might go around us. If it doesn't, we will move the boys in."

He patted the spot on the blanket beside him again. "Come on. I won't bite. I promise."

Paige lowered herself next to him and tried to get comfortable. They weren't touching, but she could feel his closeness and the warmth washing over her. Instinctively, she shifted closer. Scotty moved his hand from under his head so that she could rest in the crook of his arm. She craved his touch.

"I'd forgotten how beautiful the moon is." The crescent moon hung over them, just a slice in the sky. Stars littered the heavens. She couldn't remember the last time she'd taken the time to actually look at the stars. "I don't get views like this in Charlotte."

"Look!" he exclaimed, pointing with his free hand to the shooting star streaking across the sky. "Make a wish."

"Another one!" Paige pointed, her hand coming to rest on his chest when she lowered it.

Scotty took her hand in his and began playing with her engagement ring, spinning it on her finger. "Do you want to know my wish?" he asked softly.

"If you tell me, it won't come true," she cautioned.

"But what if it does?"

Paige didn't answer, but she didn't remove her hand either. In silence, they watched the night sky.

"Is he good to you?" Scotty asked after a while.

"Hmm?"

"The man who gave you this?" He spun the ring again.

"Chris? Yes, he's very good to me."

"Do you love him?"

"Of course." Paige snatched her hand back and propped herself up on an elbow. "What about you?" she asked, looking at him in the light of the moon.

"What do you mean?"

"Is there someone special in your life?"

"There was. But she didn't want to be a mom and didn't want me to take Jason in after the accident. She told me I had to pick either her or the boy because she wasn't ready to be a mother. I choose him. She left. Ironically, she's married with twins." He laughed.

"Do you regret it?"

"Regret choosing Jason? Never. Family always comes first. You of all people should understand that. After her, I was a bit cautious. I didn't want to bring someone home that wasn't a forever type situation because I didn't want to hurt Jason. I quickly realized that it was just me anymore, and I had to think about him. I've dated on and off, but it's never felt like it should. You know the feeling I'm talking about."

"I do. The feeling where your heart is about to leap from your chest if you don't touch her."

"That's the one."

Paige nestled back in his arm, trying to calm her own heart.

"You're the only girl who has ever made me feel that way," he whispered after a moment of sweet silence. "Those feelings aren't lies. What went wrong?"

Paige closed her eyes and remained silent.

"Did you know that I went to Philly when you were living there for law school? I got your address from Julie. I harassed her for weeks before she finally relented. It was the very last game I played for the Majors before I shattered my wrist in that stupid jet ski accident. I must have stood outside of your apartment for three hours, just hoping to catch a glimpse of you."

"I didn't know that."

"I just don't understand why you cut me off the way you did. Did you hate baseball that much?"

"What?"

"You cut me off the second I got signed. I still don't understand it. The Majors had always been my dream, a part of our dream. Why did you walk away the minute we started to realize it?"

Paige sat up. "Scotty, you think we broke up because you made it to the Majors? You have no idea how thrilled I was for you. I watched every single game. I even bought the MLB package. I was so proud of you. I am still so very proud of you."

"Then why?"

"It's starting to rain." She felt the drops falling softly on her cheeks. "Doesn't it smell amazing?"

"Paige. Please, just tell me why."

Paige took a deep breath. "Because you weren't there when I needed you. I realized the night that you received the call that you couldn't be there for me, not how I needed you to be. I decided if I was going to have to be there for myself then I needed to let you go. Both of us needed to follow our dreams."

"What happened that night that made you have this realization? It's silly. I've always been there for you. Always. Ball wouldn't have changed that."

"It was a long time ago, Scotty. I know I was probably wrong, but what's done is done. It doesn't matter anymore."

"It matters to me."

Paige felt the tears welling in her eyes and turned her head away.

Scotty sat up. "Please, Paige," he begged. "I need to know so that maybe I can finally move on."

She knew he was right. She owed him the truth.

"The night you were signed, you were supposed to meet me at a party. While I was waiting for you, I was assaulted." The words tore from her mouth like they were barbed.

Scotty pulled her into his arms, spinning her to face him. "What do you mean?"

Paige wiped the tears and rain mixture from her face. She didn't say a word, she just looked at him.

"Paige! Why didn't you say anything? Did you report it? Does your father know? Did he…" Scotty stopped talking and wiped her tears. "I am sorry I wasn't there for you," he whispered in her hair. "I'm so sorry, Paige."

Paige's heart fluttered against her ribcage, her skin and bones barely able to contain it. She buried her face in his chest and cried while the rain fell softly around them. A crack of lightening followed by the loud boom of thunder had them quickly untangling themselves.

"Come on, boys!" Scotty yelled into the tent as it started the pour. "Let's move this camping trip inside!"

Max, Avery and Jason spilled out of the tent, giggling to hide their fear of the storm. Each one clutched their stuffed animal. Paige grabbed Scotty's hand and held it tightly as they raced inside.

CHAPTER FIFTEEN

Paige was startled awake by the chirping of her phone. She was tucked next to Scotty on the sofa and the boys were sprawled on blankets on the living room floor. Cartoons were playing on the television at a low volume. Everyone was sleeping. Paige untangled herself and tiptoed out on the porch where the sun was just beginning to rise.

"Hey, Mom," she answered. "Is everything okay? Is Julie okay?"

"Good morning, honey." Lillian sounded tired but excited. "The girls decided to make their appearance about an hour ago. After all the fuss they'd made, it was a textbook delivery with absolutely no complications. All that fuss for nothing." Lillian laughed.

"Thank goodness," Paige said. "No C-section?"

"Nope. She had them the way she wanted, and all three babies are beautiful and perfectly healthy. Julie would like for you to bring the boys and meet them today. Your father told me your case has been continued so hopefully you can come around lunch?"

"How could he possibly know the case was continued?"

"Small town, lovey. It really shouldn't come as a surprise to you anymore how fast word moves."

"Seriously. Ya'll are faster than most news networks." Paige shook her head and chuckled. "We'll be there. We'll stop on the way and pick up lunch for everyone."

"That would be fantastic. How were the boys?"

"They're great. We were going to camp out but the storm sort of thwarted those plans, so everyone is now sacked out on the living room floor."

"You camped out? Do we even have a tent?"

"Oh no, we stayed with Scotty and Jason. I figured it'd help keep them occupied."

"Well now, that sounds like a lot of fun. Bring Scotty and Jason with you to meet the babies, if they want to come."

"What did Julie and Anderson name them?"

"They haven't yet. She wants Max and Avery to help. I think she may also want her little sister there for the announcement. She is excited that you were home when they were born. You missed seeing Max and Avery until they were several months old."

"Is everything okay?" Scotty whispered from the doorway.

Paige nodded. "She had the babies. Everyone is good."

"Good." Scotty gave her a thumb's up. "I'm going to start breakfast. Scrambled eggs with cheese?"

"Yes, please."

Paige hadn't had Scotty's scrambled eggs in years. He'd read somewhere when they were much younger that every man needed at least one meal they had perfected. He'd chosen scrambled eggs. Every Saturday in high school, he could be found in the Sparrow kitchen trying out his recipes. Later, in college, his suitemates would wait patiently for a plate after a night out or a late practice. Once he'd been signed by Indians, his talent with eggs had made it in a sports magazine. Paige had the clipping somewhere. It had been one of her favorite articles because there was a picture of him holding out a plate of eggs in his ball glove.

Scotty's secret, which he'd share with anyone who asked, was adding half milk and half heavy cream mid-scramble. As much as she'd tried over the years to recreate the recipe, she failed every time.

"Oh man, would I love some of Scotty's eggs. You know he has his own chickens, right? I don't know what he feeds them, but he has the best eggs in the world."

"Okay, Mom. You and Dad find something to eat for breakfast and we will bring you lunch when we come. Love you all."

"Love you, too, sweetie."

"Real food!" Julie exclaimed from the hospital bed when Scotty and Paige walked in with bags of burgers, fries and milkshakes from the fast food place just up the road from the hospital. Her brown hair, a shade darker than Paige's with a few stray grey strands, was pulled back in a messy bun. Her cheeks were pink and her eyes were tired. She was the happiest Paige had ever seen her. "And my boys!" She held her arms open.

"Easy," Anderson cautioned as Max and Avery threw themselves on the bed to hug Julie and cover her in milkshake-sticky kisses.

"We camped outside!" Max said with a mouthful of fries.

"And there was a really big storm!" Avery added. "But I wasn't afraid. Max was. But Jason and I weren't afraid at all, were we Jason?"

Scotty's nephew shook his head and leaned into Scotty's leg. "Did you have a baby?" he whispered.

"I had three babies!" Julie held up three fingers. "Three baby girls."

"A whole litter, eh, Jason?" Scotty pushed the boy forward. "Maybe one of them will be your girlfriend," he joked.

"Ewww. I don't want a girlfriend and I certainly don't want a baby girlfriend!"

"Good plan, little man. Girls are bad news."

"Where are those babies, anyway?" Paige glanced around the room. The three bassinets were empty.

"The nurses should be bringing them in any…" Anderson's statement was cut off by three nurses entering the room, each holding a pink bundle.

"Sorry," one apologized. "They're little celebrities here. We haven't had triplets before." She handed the baby she was carrying to Paige. "You look like you need some baby snuggles," she said slyly. "But be careful. Baby fever is quite contagious." The nurse knelt until she was eye level with Jason. "Don't you want a little brother or sister?" she cooed.

No one in the room corrected her. Paige was too busy staring at the wrinkly pink face in her arms. "She's so tiny," she exclaimed, her voice full of wonder. "Are they always this tiny?"

"You must have the one Anderson calls Little Bit. She's a few ounces smaller than the other two. What color is her band?"

Paige revealed the baby's arm. "Green."

167

"Yep. That's Little Bit. Chunk over here is purple. She's the biggest. The pink one doesn't have a nickname yet. She's just pink."

"They're beautiful, Jules. You did good." Scotty winked at Anderson. "And I guess you did alright."

"Now that everyone is here, can we finally get some decisions on names? We can't call these beautiful children Little Bit, Chunk, and Pink." Lillian gestured to one of the nurses to hand her a baby.

"Okay. Okay. We promised Max and Avery that they would get to help name them, right boys?"

Max and Avery nodded their heads.

"Okay, Avery. Do you want to go first? Which baby looks most like the name you picked?"

Avery went from baby to baby, peering at their faces. "They all look the same," he grumbled. "But I guess I'll pick the one Grandma has." He went and stood by Lillian and stared at the baby. "Yep, this is the one," he said with a grin, dropping a sticky kiss on the baby's head.

"So, what's it going to be?" Roger asked.

"I forgot." He giggled, running over to Julie who whispered in his ear.

"Oh yeah! Ella Beth Porter." He sounded the name out slowly.

"That's a beautiful name. Did you pick that all by yourself?" Paige asked.

Avery just giggled. "Go on, Max. It's your turn."

Max walked up to Paige. "This one." There was no doubt in his voice. "Emma Jane."

"Am I noticing an "E" theme?" Lillian smiled at her eldest, who lay on the bed cradling the last of the triplets.

Julie just smiled. "And this one, this one is Eliza Ruth."

Paige watched as Lillian fought back tears. Ruth had been Lillian's mother's name, and Elizabeth had been her grandmother's.

"Three beautiful names for three beautiful girls," said one of the nurses. "And now that they're named, we can finish these birth certificates and make it official."

"Think you can hand Emma over for her lunch and join me for a cup of coffee in the cafeteria?" Roger looked at Paige expectantly.

"There they go," Lillian mused. "Going to talk shop, I'm sure."

Paige glanced at Scotty.

"Go ahead," he said. "We'll just hang out here with the boys for a bit and then all head back together. I imagine your folks are staying the night in town again, right?"

"We sure are. And God-willing and the creek don't rise, we will all be going home tomorrow."

Scotty took one of the babies, nestling it against his chest as Paige slipped out with her father. He was nearly more comfortable in a room full of her family than she was. She'd never realized when she cut Scotty out of her world, that her family hadn't followed her cue. He was still a very much loved part of their lives.

"He's a good guy," Roger said, reading her thoughts. "I hope you don't mind that we sort of adopted him when he moved back. He was floundering for a bit, and the only family he had left was a nephew that he had no clue how to raise. Julie took him under her wing because of Jason, but he's truly a part of the family now. I

169

suppose he has been since you first brought him home so many years ago. I didn't hesitate to sell him the land next door because he's family. I hope you don't mind."

Paige gave a quick shake of her head. "Not at all. I'm glad he's there. It's good for everyone, especially the boys."

"It's funny how the universe works, isn't it?"

"The universe always wins." Paige smiled, Scotty's words quick on her lips. "And I can think of worse neighbors."

They grabbed their coffees and headed to a table tucked in the corner. When they were certain no one could over hear them, Paige confided in her father about Deputy Taylor's threat. "I didn't want to mention it at dinner the other night because I didn't want to upset Mom, but I wasn't speeding. He pulled me over to give me a warning."

"I was afraid it was something like that. What did he say?"

"He told me to go back home."

Roger's face turned red and, remembering his heart attack, Paige quickly regretted telling him about the encounter.

"You are home," Roger seethed. "What else did he say?"

"Nothing. Scotty showed up and he told Scotty 'good afternoon,' tipped his hat to me, and got back in the cruiser. I don't know what he would have done if Scotty hadn't shown up when he did."

"Be careful, Paige. I'm not trying to scare you, but Frank Taylor is a dangerous man." Roger opened his mouth but thought better of it and took a sip of coffee inside.

"I went to Travis's house afterwards. To warn him."

"Has he been harassing them as well?"

Paige choose her words carefully. "While I was there, someone threw a rock through the window."

Roger slammed his hand on the table. "Are you sure it was him?" he asked.

Paige shook her head. "I didn't see the car. But it was in broad daylight, Dad."

"Before we went fishing?"

She nodded.

"And you didn't tell me? Paige Sparrow!"

"I didn't want to upset you."

"Paige, this isn't something you keep to yourself," Roger admonished. "Was anyone hurt?"

Paige shook her head. "They're fine. I told them they needed to stay with a friend for the rest of the trial."

"Did Ciara listen?"

"They're staying with Ursula."

Roger took a deep breath. "Good. She'll take care of them. Nobody would dare cross that woman."

"Ursula told me about his wife."

Roger stared at Paige long and hard. "It's not just his wife," he said finally.

"Ainsley?" she asked in a breathless whisper.

Roger took another sip of his coffee. His hand was shaking. "There have been rumors, but they're mostly whispers. There is no proof and she isn't talking."

"Dad. Do you think Travis beat this girl?"

"No." He looked Paige squarely in the eye. "I know for a fact he didn't beat her."

"Did Travis tell you that Deputy Taylor hits her?" Paige asked, the pieces of the puzzle finally coming together in her head.

"Under the bonds of attorney client privilege, yes."

"How do I get him to take the stand and tell the jury?"

"You won't."

"But it's the only way."

"You have to find another way."

Paige felt her eyes go hot. "I can't, Daddy," she whispered.

Roger reached across the table and squeezed her hand. "Yes, you can, Baby Girl. It's the reason you're the only one I trusted to take over this case. If anyone can get the truth out, it's you."

"I don't know how if he won't take the stand."

"Ainsley was released from the hospital today." Roger said the words casually. "I've heard Slick is calling her to the stand at the close of the State's case."

"Great. So, I get to cross exam someone with no memory of the events that serve as the basis for the trial? Someone who is still bruised from the encounter?"

"Memory is a funny thing. Sometimes we tell the world we don't remember because we fear voicing the truth will make it hurt even worse. So, we hide the truth and pretend. We have all worn that lie before, and we all know how it hurts. Help her see that she needs to voice it so she can start to heal."

"You think she remembers."

"I think she's terrified of her father, and I think she has a reason to be."

Later that night, as she lay in Scotty's guest bedroom with him sleeping in the large bed on the first floor and the boys sprawled on blankets in front of the TV for another sleepover, Paige thought about what her father had said.

"We have all worn that lie before." His words played on repeat in her head.

Did he know? Had Julie shared the bits and pieces of a night Paige longed to forget with their father? Bits and pieces that Paige had reluctantly told Julie six months after the incident when the anxiety attacks were at their worse and Paige had turned to drinking.

Paige wiped at her face. "He was talking about Ainsley," she chided herself. "This isn't about you."

"What isn't about you?"

Paige jerked the sheets up to her throat, eyes wide. Scotty was leaning in the door frame holding two steaming mugs, a bemused expression on his face.

"Nothing," Paige muttered when her heart rate slowed down. "How long have you been standing there?"

"Just long enough to catch the tail end of that conversation. I heard you puttering around up here and figured you might like some tea." He held out one of the mugs. "It'll help you sleep."

"Thanks," she took the mug.

"Well, I guess I'll head back down." He lingered in the doorway.

"Wait." The words were out of her mouth before Paige could stop them.

Scotty turned slowly, his face cast in the light of the moon. There was a twitch in his jaw, a hesitation in his eyes.

"Just until we finish the tea?" she asked.

"Okay, but only like your parents made us do in high school."

173

Paige laughed at the memory. When they'd dated in high school, Roger and Lillian had been less than thrilled about the two of them hanging out in Paige's bedroom alone. They insisted one be under the covers and one be over the covers and that the lights stay on and the door stay opened.

Paige propped herself up on the pillows and patted the area on the bed beside her, mimicking his gesture from the night before. "We can even leave the door open," she grinned.

"What's keeping you up tonight? The case?" he asked after he settled beside her.

"Yeah. Travis didn't do it, Scotty."

"How do you know?"

"Just a feeling. Maybe it's the look in his eyes when he talks about her. You can't fake a love like that."

"Is that what you and Roger were talking about today?"

"Yes. Travis refuses to take the stand. I don't understand it. It's the only way to save himself and he is adamantly refusing." Paige took a sip of tea and shook her head. "If I understood why he was so adamant about it, maybe I could convince him otherwise, but I'm at a loss as to why he won't save himself."

"Maybe it's not about saving himself."

"That's what Dad said, but I can't understand that mentality."

"You don't understand love?"

Paige snorted. "You think this is about love? Love isn't about sacrificing yourself. A conviction will destroy this young man's life. End of story. There will be no redemption for him, no life for him. I would do anything to save myself if I were in his shoes."

"Including destroying the one you love?"

"Why does anyone have to be destroyed except for the person who beat Ainsley? Why wouldn't both of them want that to happen?"

"Maybe Ainsley loves whomever attacked her."

"She loves this mystery person who beat the snot out of her?" Paige shook her head. "No way. The best theory I have is it was a robbery go wrong. Deputy Taylor's gun is missing, after all."

"You're not listening to what's not being said."

"That makes zero sense, Scotty."

He took a deep breath and held her gaze. "Maybe she loves her attacker because she has no other choice."

Paige's mouth fell open. "You know," she accused.

He nodded, a pained look crossing his brow. "I hear things, and it sounds like you've heard those same things."

"So why hasn't anyone done anything?" Paige exploded.

"Because we can't. We don't have the proof, and Ainsley will never speak out against her father."

"Okay, then why is Travis standing trial for something every last person in this town knows he didn't do?"

"That's one hundred percent because of Bradley Moore. He is up for re-election in November, and this is the first time that he is running opposed. Frank Taylor is one of his biggest supporters and has promised the support of the entire Merchants Town police force if he puts Travis away. This case has been made a top priority in order to have a conviction well before the polls open this fall."

"But what about justice?"

"Slick doesn't care about justice, only wins. Travis was the easiest target. He didn't think anyone would care about the young black man."

"Well, what about the jury? They're so quick to condemn Travis, but it sounds like they've probably heard the rumors about Deputy Taylor."

"I'm sure they have heard the gossip and they likely have their own suspicions, but it's much easier to believe that a young black man raped and beat a pretty blonde girl than it is to believe that the young black man and that pretty blonde girl are in love. It's much easier to believe that Travis put her in the hospital, not her father."

"Dad said I need to question Ainsley. Bradley is putting her on the stand. Assumingly, he is going to establish she has no memory of the night and ask that she be excused from further questioning. I can't let that happen."

"Tread carefully, Paige. I know her. I've known her for a couple of years. I coached her in softball last season when I helped out with the high school team. She is a very smart young woman, but she startles easily. If you come at her with too much force, she will retreat into a shell you won't be able to bring her back from. She may already be there."

"Do you think I should do it?"

"Do what? Question her?"

"Yeah. Should I put her on the stand?"

"Do you remember that fawn that we found our Freshman year? It had been hit just off Franklin Street?"

"I'd forgotten all about Bambi."

"I couldn't get near her. Every time I moved in her direction, she'd scramble away, dragging her broken leg with her."

"But she let me," Paige said proudly.

"That's right. She let you. Approach Ainsley the same way you did that fawn, slowly and reassuringly. If anyone can get her to reveal the truth, it's you."

"That's exactly what Dad said!"

"He's a smart man."

Paige took another sip of her tea, now cold. She didn't want to finish it because she knew he'd leave when she was done. Scotty's cup was already on the nightstand by the bed. "Maybe you can help me."

"How so?"

"Pretend to be me and I'll pretend to be Ainsley. Ask me questions about the attack."

"I don't want to do that." Scotty shifted uncomfortably.

"Why not?"

"Because, it doesn't feel right. I'm not an attorney."

"Please?"

Scotty sighed. "Did your father hit you?" he asked gruffly.

"I can see why that fawn wouldn't let you anywhere near it; you're about as delicate as a bull in china shop." Paige laughed.

"I warned you."

"You're right. This is a bad idea. I'm just trying to figure out how best to approach the questions."

"Well," he started, taking her empty cup and placing it beside his. "How would you want to be asked? What would make you tell your story?"

"My story?" Paige knew what he meant, but she wanted him to say it.

"About that night."

"I don't talk about it," she said, realizing even as the words came from her mouth what her subconscious had been trying to tell her ever since her conversation with her father; she had to put herself in Ainsley's shoes. No, Paige hadn't been abused by her father and an innocent man's life wasn't destroyed by her silence, but there was a night that had left Paige scarred that she refused to talk about.

"You don't have to tell me. You don't have to tell anyone. But think about it. You need to find a way to show Ainsley why she should talk. Show her what the stakes are. Her silence will destroy an innocent man's life."

"All I destroyed was us." Paige felt her lip quiver.

"Stop. You didn't destroy us. I'm still here. You're still here. We're just different. You destroyed nothing."

"I just wonder…"

"Paige, that isn't a wise game to play. We can't change the past. The things that happened to us, the choices we made, made us. I hate that you ever had to make them, but the choices made you who you are. They made you the very woman who is going to save a man's life. You just have to have a little faith in yourself."

Paige smiled. "Why are you always so good to me?"

"Because you're you."

Paige leaned closer to him until their lips touched with a question. Scotty deepened the kiss, his hand on her lower back, fitting her against him. The moment broke when they heard crying from downstairs.

"It's Jason," Scotty said, jumping up. "He still has nightmares." He gathered the cups and hurried from the room. "See you in the morning," he called over his shoulder.

Paige touched her lips, wondering what would have happened had Jason not cried out. It was a mistake, of that she was certain, and it would never happen again, but it was the sweetest of mistakes. He tasted like memories and happiness. He tasted like home.

CHAPTER SIXTEEN

Paige awoke to the sound of children playing and Dory barking outside of the window. Cornflakes was crowing. She stretched and glanced at her phone. It was after nine. She hadn't slept past six in years. She hurriedly threw on some jeans and raced downstairs. Scotty was in the kitchen reading the paper and sipping coffee.

"Morning, sunshine."

"Why didn't you wake me? Why aren't the kids in school? Why aren't you at work? And why does your rooster not crow at sunrise?" She fired off question after question while fumbling around the coffee pot.

"Because you needed your sleep. Because school is out for the summer. Because I took the day off. And Cornflakes has never been the best at telling time."

Paige took a sip of coffee and breathed. "Oh, that's good. You can do that? Take a day off?"

"Sure. I'm the boss. My assistant can handle things today. I usually take off this time of year to spend time with Jason anyway. I only go in for emergencies."

"Must be nice." She took another sip of coffee, starting to feel human. "You have an assistant?"

"Yep. You might want to sit down for this one," he said with a smirk. "I have six employees. Two vet techs, one veterinarian, two receptionists, and one groomer."

"Fancy. It sounds like you've employed half of Merchants Town." She eyed the empty frying pan. "So, am I getting eggs again this morning?"

"Sorry, lady. Breakfast is eight sharp. You slept through it."

"Drat," Paige pouted as her phone rang.

"Your fiancé?" Scotty asked, not taking his eyes from the paper.

"The office," Paige responded, pushing the twinge of guilt that hit her from her mind. "I need to take this if only to ensure I still have a job."

Paige stepped out on the porch, coffee in hand.

"Hey, Mir. What's up?"

"Hey, I figured I'd let you know that they announced that the Jerk is partner today."

"I figured it was only a matter of time after my screw up."

"After our screw up," Miranda corrected. "I'm really sorry about that. I forgot to ask what Chis had to say about it."

"About what?"

"About you being pulled from partner track and demoted. Weren't you waiting for the partnership to set a date for the wedding?"

"Oh, he's fine with it."

"Paige Sparrow! You haven't told him, have you?"

"I've been a little busy."

"A little busy with that hunky vet?"

"What? Don't be silly."

"I saw the pictures."

"Pictures?"

"Of him holding one of the triplets. You took him to the hospital to see Julie."

"Good lord. My sister's blog must be the only way anyone anywhere gets any information."

"It's useful information. You didn't tell me that the vet is hot. Maybe I should get a dog if all vets look like him."

"I didn't really think about it."

"Liar."

"Stop it. He's my past and that is where he will stay," Paige said with a laugh.

There was a faint cough from behind her. Paige spun around just in time to see Scotty's retreating back. Well, she thought, at least there will be no unrealistic expectations after last night.

"So, when do you think you'll be home? Everyone at work is asking, but my reasons are purely selfish. You simply can't miss Antwan's going away party!"

"Going away party? Surely, he hasn't been fired?"

"No, he wasn't fired, but he did quit. Meredith told him she didn't want or need his two weeks notice. And we both know that Antwan has been chomping at the bit to move on. The best looking man in Charlotte is going to be heading to the Triangle," Miranda said with a sigh. "We're celebrating Saturday, so I won't be able to come see Julie and the babies this weekend."

"The Triangle! That's amazing. Did he get the job with the General Assembly?"

182

"Better. He's going to be working for one of the law clinics there, I just don't remember which. But I do know he will be teaching a few law classes as part of the gig."

"Oh… sweet Antwan. Can you imagine having a law professor that looked like him? Talk about eye candy. Those kids are going to eat him up."

"Uh huh." Miranda was one of the few employees at Fitz, Parker & Corbin that knew about Paige's brief affair with the handsome attorney. "You know my thoughts on that matter."

"Mir, attorneys should never become involved with other attorneys, especially those that work at the same firm."

"I guess you're right. But a vet, now a vet would be a perfect pairing for an attorney," Miranda hinted. She'd never been found of Chris.

"Or a doctor," Paige joked back and their laughter echoed across the miles.

"Do you think the trial will be over in time for the going away party? Or that you can at least slip away to come back, if only for Saturday? It won't be the same without you, and I know Antwan wants to tell you goodbye."

"I honestly don't know. If we hadn't been delayed for two days, I'd say sure. I really thought the State would have rested by now, but I know of at least one more witness they intend to call. I have very few witnesses to call since my client refuses to take the stand," Paige fumed. "And I don't know how deliberations will go. I'm going to move for a directed verdict, but in researching Judge Fox, he never grants them."

"But more likely than not, the trial will be over?"

"Yeah. If anything, it'll just be deliberations."

"What's your read on the jury so far?"

"They like me now, but I don't know if they like my client. If they could just hear him talk about Ainsley, all of this would be over. I don't know why I can't get him to talk."

"Well, let me know me know how it goes. Your trial is the one thing Julie doesn't blog about."

"Of course. I'll call you when I get back Saturday," Paige said walking back into Scotty's kitchen. He was back at the table reading the paper. A plate of eggs sat in front of the seat across from him.

"I made you eggs," he gestured without looking up. "They're probably cold by now."

"That's okay. "Paige ignored the chill in his voice and eased herself into the chair across from him.

"I take it you're going back to Charlotte on Saturday?" He still wasn't looking at her.

"Yeah, one of my good friends is having a going away party."

"Maybe the trial will be over by then and you can go back for good."

Paige recoiled as if she'd been kicked.

Scotty glanced at her. "I'm sure you're eager to get back to your life, your friends, your fiancé."

"I guess I am."

Paige finished her eggs in silence, gathered up Max and Avery despite their protests, and returned to her parents' home to await her family without another word to Scotty. Merchants Town Motors called as Roger and Lillian were pulling in the drive; Paige's car was ready to be picked up.

CHAPTER SEVENTEEN

Paige was at Henry's Corner Store when it opened Thursday morning. She sat at the counter and buried her head in her hands.

"Morning, honey," Barb said. "You look like you could use some coffee."

Paige lowered her hands and smiled. "Thanks, Barb."

Barb fixed the coffee to Paige's liking without asking. Even though Paige had only been going there a short time, the sixty-year-old woman had memorized Paige's preferences. She even tapped a bit of cinnamon over the top.

"Do you want to talk about it?"

"Have you ever felt like you were being split in two?" Paige asked after a minute.

"When I had those big-headed sons of mine I was certain I was being ripped in half, but I don't think that's what you're talking about."

Paige laughed. "No, it's not."

"Honey, you're only one person. Your heart is only one heart. You will not split. You will not break. Whatever ails you, whatever is pulling at you, is likely because you're stubborn."

"What?"

"Your heart is pulling you in one direction but you're holding on to something else, trying to force yourself down a path you don't belong. That's what creates that feeling of being ripped in half. Stop being so darn stubborn and listen to your heart."

"My heart has a history making really bad decisions."

"I don't believe that for a second. The heart follows truth and truth is never wrong. It may not always be pretty and it may not always be what you want it to be, but it's never wrong. Just let go of whatever isn't in your heart, whatever isn't true. You'll feel better. I promise."

"Thanks, Barb."

Barb winked and handed Paige a to-go cup of coffee. "Now go win that trial."

After court was called to session, Bradley called a forensics specialist to the stand. He was trying to get information gathered from Ainsley's phone introduced as evidence. Paige suspected he wanted to admit the text to an unknown number that simply read: "He is mad. I am afraid of him." After Bradley had tendered the man as an expert in the field, he pulled out the binder of information printed off the phone.

"Did you use the process you just outlined for our dear jury to access information on Ainsley Taylor's phone?"

"I did. I followed all standard procedures and protocols and provided this hard copy to your office."

"Does this hard copy contain every text message, picture, and downloaded item accessible on that phone?"

"It does. It also includes incoming and outcoming call logs and cached social media posts."

"I have marked this State's Exhibit M." Bradley handed the expert a page pulled from the binder. "Was this gathered through that process?"

"Your Honor," Paige said, standing.

"Yes, Ms. Sparrow?"

"I have reviewed the binder. I have reviewed Mr. Hartley's resume and relevant experience. I have no intentions of challenging his skill or the process. I request that the court take judicial notice that every item in that binder was properly processed and all information accessible was properly pulled by Mr. Hartley."

"You're not going to challenge these documents?" Judge Fox raised an eyebrow.

"No, your Honor. Obviously, some of the items in that binder are irrelevant and I would challenge them on those grounds should Attorney Moore attempt to enter them, but as far as establishing that these items were pulled from Ainsley Taylor's phone, I think it's in the best interest of this court and out of consideration to the jury that we just take judicial notice. Mr. Hartley is a very intelligent and respectable man. I do not doubt his work."

Judge Fox glanced at Bradley, who was opening and closing his mouth like a fish. "Do you have any objections, Attorney Moore?"

"Well, no, I don't guess I do." He shook his head in disbelief. "Your Honor, as Ms. Sparrow has already admitted that these were pulled from Ms. Taylor's phone, I would like to admit what has already been marked as State's Exhibit M into evidence."

"Objection, your Honor." Paige stood with a smile. Bradley had underestimated her again.

"Your Honor, Ms. Sparrow has already moved the court to take judicial notice of the information in this binder. She cannot now object to it."

"Your Honor, I moved the court to take judicial notice that the information was pulled from Ms. Taylor's phone. That is simply one piece of the puzzle in laying the foundation to have this entered into evidence. If Attorney Moore wishes to have it admitted, he should lay the proper foundation."

Paige knew Bradley couldn't lay the proper foundation without Ainsley. No one had been able to determine who Ainsley had texted, so the recipient couldn't be called to the stand. The number had been a disposable phone, a dead end. Paige had her suspicions who the recipient was, but she had no proof that it was Ainsley's mother. Shy of Ainsley, there was no one who could testify as to the meaning behind the text. There was no one who could say with any knowledge who the "he" referred to.

"I agree, Ms. Sparrow. Objection sustained."

"I guess I have no further questions for Mr. Hartley." Bradley was flustered. There was no trace of a southern accent anymore.

"You guess?" Judge Fox frowned.

"I have no further questions for this witness, your Honor."

"Thank you. Ms. Sparrow?"

"I have no questions for this witness, but I would like to thank him for his time."

"Well that was easy. Attorney Moore, who will you be calling next?"

"Your Honor, I would like to request a brief recess to allow my witness time to appear."

"Attorney Moore, why isn't your witness already present?"

"Your Honor, I intend to call Ms. Ainsley Taylor to the stand. She is currently at home having just been released from the hospital. I did not anticipate her presence would be required at this stage."

Travis squeezed Paige's hand. Hard.

"At this stage? Attorney Moore, I do hope you're about ready to rest."

"I am, your Honor. She is my last witness."

"Very well then. Recess granted." Judge Fox turned to the jurors. "Who is hungry? How about some barbeque from Mitch's?"

The jurors eagerly responded. Mitch's was famous for its barbeque, eastern North Carolina style. It frequently made the list of top barbeque joints in North Carolina. There was no barbeque like it in Charlotte. Paige felt her stomach growl.

"Ya'll write down your orders and give them to the bailiff. We will recess for lunch, give these hard-working men and women who are doing us a favor by sitting on this jury a good meal, and resume around 2 o'clock. Any objections, Ms. Sparrow?"

"No, your Honor. But can I put in an order for hush puppies?"

The jury laughed. Bradley fumed.

Paige fired off a quick text to Ursula and by the time she and Travis made it the law office, barbeque sandwiches, piled high with a sweet cole slaw, were waiting for them. A basket of hushpuppies sat in the middle of the conference room table. Roger was already eating a sandwich when they walked in.

"Don't tell your mother," he begged, savoring each bite of a food that was certainly not on his approved diet.

"Why are they putting Ainsley on the stand?" Travis asked, picking at the plate Ursula sat before him.

"Because they need her."

"But she doesn't remember. What could they possibly need her for? She doesn't remember anything." Travis coughed and pretended to cover his mouth while wiping his eyes.

"Let's just see how it plays out, son." Roger pushed the basket of hush puppies toward the young man. "Now you better eat some of these before Mrs. Sparrow comes in here and yells at you for making me eat them all."

Travis laughed, a pure and sweet sound. "Yes, sir."

They didn't talk about the case during lunch. They all knew it was nearing its natural close and there were no guarantees as to the outcome. Paige didn't ask Travis to testify. Instead, she directed the conversation to the fall and Travis's plans for college.

"I'll be the first one in my family to go. They're all rooting for me."

"Family is very important," Roger stated. "As you may know, my family wasn't the best. I was adopted when I was twelve. Ended up being pretty lucky as the Sparrows moved heaven and earth for me. Some families you are born into and some you make, but either way, you need a support network."

"Absolutely," Paige agreed. "I wouldn't be where I am today without my mom and dad."

"Yeah, my mom is pretty awesome. I just want to make her proud and be a good role model for Little."

"I think all children want to make their parents proud." Roger grabbed another hush puppy. "Your mother is very proud of you,

190

Travis. Very." He accentuated his words by pointing with the hush puppy.

"She's pretty mad at me right now."

"She's scared."

"I just wish she'd trust me."

"Your mother hasn't had a lot of things go right in her life. You were one of the few things that did. She trusts you, but she's just terrified right now."

"You know, I'm not really scared."

"What?" Paige's hand started to shake. Didn't he realize what was at stake?

"I was at first, but not now. I still believe in truth and things happening the way they should. I trust you, Ms. Sparrow."

Paige wanted to tell the young man that his trust was misplaced, and he had a better chance of directing the truth if he would only take the stand and tell the jury what she could so plainly see, but she knew it was not a battle she'd win. There was so much she wanted to tell him, but she wanted him to enjoy the meal. If the afternoon went south, it would likely be a long time before he'd be able to enjoy hush puppies and laugh.

After lunch, they entered the court room together, Travis between the two Sparrows. Roger shook Travis's hand, hugged Paige, and took a seat with the spectators.

Judge Fox called the court to session and Bradley called Ainsley to the stand. A silence fell over the room as the large wooden doors opened and the young woman was led forward, a sheriff's deputy at each side. She looked only at the floor. Her face was a devastating shade of a purplish green, her lip still swollen. Travis set at the edge of his seat, his entire body electric at the sight of her. Paige grabbed his hand and held on tight. She was half afraid he'd leap from his seat and run to the young woman.

As Ainsley was sworn in, she lifted her head. There was a gasp from the jury box as they saw the extent of her injuries. They'd seen the pictures, and the pictures had been quite graphic, but there was something about seeing how small Ainsley was. She looked twelve. She looked scared. Paige watched as the jurors glanced from Ainsley to Travis and back again. She knew what was going in their heads. They were trying to picture this woman loving that man. Trying to see if his hands, so large and smooth and strong, had broken her or held her.

"Hello Ms. Taylor." Bradley's voice was soft and smooth. "How are you feeling?"

"I'm okay." She was shaking. Paige could barely hear her.

"I know this is difficult for you, and I am truly sorry for making you go through this, but it is important for justice that you be here today. Do you understand?"

"Yes, sir." Ainsley looked at her hands.

"Do you know why you are here today?"

"Yes, sir."

"Can you tell the jury why you are here?" He prodded.

"I was beaten," she said after a minute.

Paige noticed she didn't say she was raped.

"Now your doctors have already testified that you suffered memory loss from the attack. Is that true?"

"Yes, sir."

"Can you tell us who did this to you?"

Ainsley's shoulders started shaking. Paige clutched Travis's hand for all she was worth, and held her breath.

"Honey, can you?"

Ainsley shook her head. "I can't," she sobbed.

Bradley handed her his handkerchief. "Your Honor, further questioning is clearly fruitless. We ask that the witness be released."

Paige stood, putting one hand firmly on Travis's shoulder. "Your Honor, I have no objections to a recess until tomorrow, but my client is entitled to a cross examination of this witness."

"But she can't remember anything!" Bradley huffed.

"My client is entitled, Attorney Moore. Justice requires it."

"Very well." Judge Fox turned to Ainsley. "Young lady, do you think you could continue just a little longer today?"

Ainsley shook her head, her blond hair flying about her face.

"Let the record reflect that the witness has indicated a need to stop for the day. With no objections from counsel, we will resume tomorrow. I do expect that Ms. Taylor will be prepared tomorrow and I further expect that the questioning will not take long, considering." Judge Fox pounded the gavel, dismissing court.

Deputy Taylor pushed from the crowd and helped Ainsley from the stand. As they passed Travis, he shielded her with his body. "Don't you dare look at her!" he hissed at Travis.

Paige squeezed the young man's hand and prayed he could control his emotions long enough for Ainsley and her father to leave the courtroom. Travis watched their retreating backs until the doors closed behind them.

"Do you have to do that?" Travis turned to Paige, his eyes flashing.

"Do what?"

"Question her. Can't you see this is killing her?" He wrung his hands.

"Travis," Paige said firmly. "You have to stop thinking about her. Focus on you. For once, focus on you. You're the one on trial and as your attorney, I'm going to take all steps necessary to protect your rights."

"Maybe I need a new attorney," he spat.

Paige glanced at the jurors, several of whom were watching the exchange. She forced a smile and placed a hand on his arm.

"Judge Fox won't let me withdraw," she said lowly. "And you wouldn't want me to withdraw anyway. You're mad, I get it. I really do. But I need you to look at me like you don't want to rip my head off, and I need you to do it right now. Do you remember just a few hours ago when you told me you trusted me? Trust me now," she pleaded.

His jaw twitched. "Every day this trial drags on, she's in his house. Every day since she was released from the hospital, she's being attacked. His words always hit harder than his hands."

"You want to be convicted?" The realization hit her like a bullet.

"I want her to be free." Travis put his hand over hers and smiled for the jury. "I want her not to hurt anymore and I'll do anything to make sure that happens. Anything. Including going to jail. Do not hurt her anymore. Promise me?"

"I promise," Paige lied.

When Paige stepped out of the courthouse doors, she was immediately approached by a swarm of smartly dressed men and women. The gravel lot was full of news vans, microphones, and reporters. The media circus had finally gotten wind of the trial, and Judge Fox was going to be furious.

"Attorney Sparrow," one reporter called to her. "Is it true you intend to question the victim?"

"No comment." Paige hurried to the truck.

"Why would you put her through such an ordeal? Our sources say she has no memory of the event in question."

"No comment." Paige pushed the microphone out her face.

"But we have just one question," another reporter insisted.

"No comment," Paige repeated, closing the door on the woman's question. She picked up her phone and fired off a text to Travis advising him not to speak to the media. She wished she'd known they'd been crouching outside the doors. Had she, she would have walked her client to his car with their heads held high.

"Judge Fox is going to be livid," Roger said, slamming the passenger door on the same reporter's face. "Thank goodness he had the foresight to ban all media from his courtroom." Roger counted the vans. "This is ridiculous. Did you tell Travis and his mother not to talk to them?"

Paige nodded. "Look," she gestured with a tilt of her head to where Bradley stood in the middle of the group of reporters, strutting like a proud peacock. "Ten bucks says I can tell you who tipped the media off."

"Slick is worried. Very worried." Roger shook his head. "If Judge Fox sees that man giving an interview about this trial, there will be hell to pay tomorrow. He is taking one risky gamble."

Paige pulled out of the parking lot and headed to Merchants Town Motors to pick up her car.

"See you at home, sweetie," Roger said, kissing her on the cheek before sliding over to the driver's seat of his truck. He waved to the mechanics as he pulled away.

"Good afternoon, Ms. Sparrow. This sure is one fancy ride you've got here." A mechanic with the name Fred sewn on the front pocket of his shirt wiped his hands on his pants as she approached. "I hope you don't mind, but a bunch of the boys wanted their picture taken with it." He shrugged. "I wouldn't let them drive it though. Just in the lot to park it," he assured her.

Paige laughed. "It's fine. They could have driven it."

"No, ma'am. Can't give 'em a taste of the fancy stuff or they'll stop wanting to work on a Ford." He shook her hand and handed her the keys.

"There is nothing wrong with a Ford," Paige said, reaching for her wallet. "How much do I owe you?"

Fred held up his hand. "No charge. Your insurance covered it. We went ahead and fixed the dent in the front as well. What'd you hit?"

"A cow," she laughed.

"Bet that was the first time this car saw cattle."

"You've got that right," she chuckled. "Thank you for all you've done."

"Any time, Ms. Sparrow."

Paige opened the convertible top and began the drive back to her parents' house with the wind in her hair. As she turned down the private road they shared with Julie's family and Scotty, she saw a large brown object. She slammed on the brakes and hopped out of the car.

"Whatcha' doing, Paige?" she asked the cow named after her. "Don't you have a baby you should be taking care of?"

Paige the cow mooed at her and continued chewing the wild flowers growing on the side of the road.

"Come on, Mama Cow," Paige cooed, running her hands over the warm brown hide before pushing against her. "You don't want to leave your baby all alone." Paige the cow took a step forward, guided by Paige's hand. "Silly cow. Looks like I'm leading you home. A real see and eye human, I suppose. Maybe I should consider a new career if this whole attorney thing doesn't work out."

Paige gently led the cow to Scotty's, stepping over holes and cow patties in her high heels and nearly breaking an ankle before slipping her shoes off and continuing barefoot. As they neared the fence, the calf began mooing loudly and pacing back and forth by the fence. Paige the cow took off at a trot, straight to the fence.

"Slow down, you silly cow!" Paige yelled, running behind her. "You're going to hurt yourself."

Paige the cow did not slow down. As she neared the fence, the cow rose as gracefully as a deer and sailed over the top of the five-foot tall fence. After landing with a soft thump, she mooed in Paige's direction before returning to chewing her cud while the calf nursed.

Paige was still staring open mouthed when she heard someone walk up behind her.

"Why are staring at my cows?"

"Huh?"

"I saw your car on the side of the road. I thought you'd wrecked or broken down. Or had another run in with Deputy

Taylor. I've looked everywhere for you, called your phone at least ten times, and I broke into your parents' house. And here you are at my house, staring at my cows like you've never seen cattle before." Scotty was mad. His eyes turned almost grey when he was mad.

"She jumps." Paige walked up to the fence and touched the top rail. "It has to be at least five feet and she cleared it like it was one." Paige started laughing.

"What?" Scotty's face began to break into a smile as Paige's laughter proved to be contagious.

"Your cow is a jumper! And the form on her! Paige the cow, I give that jump a ten!" Paige held up all ten of her fingers before collapsing against the fence with laughter. When she looked back, Scotty was on his phone.

"Checking to see if they have an open room in the looney bin on the other side of the river," he joked. "Actually, I had to let your father know to call off the cavalry." He rested his arms on the railing and watched the calf nurse. "So, Paige the cow is a jumper?"

"Yep. Saw it with my own eyes."

"Well, that explains why I never saw where the fence was compromised. This has been driving me crazy for ages. I just assumed she was pushing the gate open and then closing it behind her. She's a pretty smart cow. A jumper." He laughed. "Did she clear it?"

"It was close, but she cleared it."

"I'll have my guy come out and add another foot to the fence this afternoon. Silly cow."

"Smart cow," Paige corrected.

"She does live up to her name sake, that's for sure."

"Uncle Scotty!" Jason yelled from the back porch, holding something white and fluffy. "I love him!"

Paige stared at Scotty wide-eyed. "You didn't!"

"I did. Jason picked him out this morning."

Paige raced barefoot to the porch to see the puppy that Jason was holding in his lap. Jason giggled as the dog put two large paws on his shoulders and licked his face. It was the sweetest sound.

"Look, Aunt Paige!" Jason chirped with delight. "Meet my puppy!"

"That is a very pretty puppy, Jason. Did you pick him out yourself?"

"I did! And I wasn't scared at all. His mama is real big, but she's not scary. You want to hold him?" The little boy looked up, his eyes reminding her so much of Scotty it nearly took her breath, and grinned a gap-toothed grin.

Paige dropped her shoes and sat cross-legged next to Jason. The fluffy white dog wiggled its way onto her lap.

"He looks like a marshmallow!" she exclaimed, inhaling the sweet smell of puppy breath.

Jason let loose another giggle. "He's not a marshmallow, silly. He's Vern and he's the best dog in the whole wide world."

"Well, hello there Mr. Vern." Paige took one of the big paws in her hand and shook it. "Ever so nice to meet you." The puppy licked her nose and wriggled free to chase Jason, who screamed with sheer joy.

"So, Dr. Lewis," she said, turning to Scotty. "I don't think this puppy came about the same way as Milo, Otis, and Paige the Cow."

"It's Jason's birthday next week. I asked him what he wanted. He said a puppy."

"I said a big, fluffy puppy!" Jason corrected from across the yard.

"Yes, buddy, you did."

"And you just happened upon this fella?"

"Not exactly. I've worked with the breeder for a couple of years. This particular litter was sired by the top winning Great Pyrenees from about fifteen years ago. The breeder was quite pleased with my results, and I was quite pleased with the temperaments of her dogs. She told me awhile back that if I ever wanted a puppy, to just give her a call. So I did."

"How is that even possible? The sire must be ancient!"

"Well," Scotty squatted and rubbed the top of Vern's head as the puppy stopped to lap water from the stainless steel dish. "The sire has passed on but his semen was collected several years ago and frozen. The breeder went through three vials and five other vets before it worked."

"Invitro?" Paige's face crinkled. "Doesn't that require a specialist or something?"

Scotty held out his hand. "Hello. I'm Dr. Scotty Lewis, board-certified reproduction specialist."

Paige's mouth fell open. "Shut up. Seriously?"

"Seriously. I'm the only one in about a hundred miles. It's pretty much all I practice in anymore. Matty handles everything else at the clinic."

"Matty?"

"Dr. Mathilda Greene. She's the other vet at the clinic I was telling you about. My assistant."

"Ah. I had no idea."

"I'm realizing that." He laughed. "You really don't know anything about me, do you?"

"I guess in my mind, you're still the gum chewing leftie who took us to the State Championships twice. I always forget how smart you are."

"Uncle Scotty is super smart," Jason piped up. "Can I go play with Vern some more?"

"Sure, buddy. Remember, if he potties outside, you tell him he's a good boy, okay?"

"Okay." Jason ran off, Vern close on his heels.

"You look surprised. Is it really that hard to believe?" Scotty asked.

"I just… I don't know what to say."

"You didn't expect someone to be successful in Merchants Town or you didn't expect me to be successful?"

"No, that's not it." Paige couldn't explain it. She'd spent years telling herself that shutting Scotty out of her life was the best course of action. She needed a reliable man, like a successful doctor, to further her goals. She needed someone like Chris. Yet there was Scotty, a highly successful doctor, albeit one that treated animals and not humans, right before her. Chris couldn't be bothered to come see her family, yet Scotty drove her to the hospital to meet her nieces. Scotty willingly watched her nephews whereas Chris had never even met them. Chris tasted like the life she thought she wanted. Scotty tasted like the life she was meant to have. Barb's words ran through her head: "Stop being stubborn."

"Scotty," she started, rising to her feet.

A horn sounded from the front yard.

"That'll be Matty. We're taking Jason to Norfolk for a baseball game," he explained. "Do you want a ride to your car?"

"No." Paige was flustered. "I'll walk. Have fun."

"If I don't see you before you leave, have a safe drive back home," he called over his shoulder as he went to round up Jason and put Vern away.

Paige snuck around the side of the house, hoping to catch a glimpse of Matty. She wanted to see what the woman he let hang around his nephew looked like. She was pretty; even from a distance, Paige couldn't deny that. Matty had an exotic look, with dark, almost black curls that cascaded down her back. She was wearing a simple pink tank top and jeans, that looked painted on each and every curve. She didn't look like any vet Paige had seen.

"Hey, you must be Paige!" Matty called, waving her over after spying her lurking.

Paige briefly considered pretending she didn't hear her, but it was pretty obvious she did. She took a deep breath and walked over to the woman.

"Hi," she said, holding out one hand and realizing she was still holding her shoes in the other.

"Hi!" Matty's lips were painted a sweetheart shade of pink and they parted into a brilliant white smile. Her eyes were that shocking shade of blue that Paige had only seen on a Siberian Husky.

"Paige was just leaving," Scotty said, jogging over to them. "Paige the Cow got out again and Paige the human came to her rescue, and solved the riddle of our escape artist in the process."

"Really? We've been trying to figure that out for ages! Do tell!"

The pronouns they used floated around Paige's head. We. Our. How had Paige missed that Scotty was involved? How had her family not told her? It was Merchants Town. Scotty Lewis dating the raven-haired beauty who worked for him should be front page news, or at least worthy of Julie's blog. Paige thought about the night under the stars. Scotty had said there wasn't anyone. Did he just not want her to know about Matty?

She realized as she had the conversation with herself that Matty was expecting her to explain the great mystery. "She jumps it," Paige offered.

"Like the cow over the moon." Matty laughed. Paige wanted to hate her, but she couldn't. In another universe, they'd be friends.

"Exactly." Paige smiled.

"Paige walked her back over this way after finding her down the drive. Hence the bare feet. I offered her a ride back to her car, but she said she'd rather walk." Scotty loaded Jason in Matty's SUV and turned to them expectantly. "Offer still stands," he told Paige, "but we have to go or we're going to be late for the game."

"Jump in. It's not a problem at all." Matty tossed Scotty the keys. "He hates my driving," she said over her shoulder as Paige buckled in beside Jason.

Matty and Scotty. Scotty and Matty. It was almost too disgustingly cute to be real.

Paige sat in silence for the three minutes it took to reach her car.

"It was nice meeting you," Matty called through the open window as Scotty drove away. "I hope to see you again."

Paige started her car and slowly drove to the home where she'd grown up. She wiped at her face. "Stop being silly," she chided herself. "You're engaged to a handsome, respectable surgeon who loves you. Why does it matter if your high school sweetheart is dating a hot vet?"

"When did you start talking to yourself?" Julie was standing on the porch, a bemused expression on her face.

"I just met Matty."

"She's great, isn't she? How Scotty convinced her to move down here after she graduated, I have no idea, but they make one heck of a great team."

"Yeah, I guess they do."

"You want to come in and help feed the girls?"

Paige couldn't think of anything she wanted more than to hold one of those babies. She'd always said that puppies and babies were the best therapy for a bad day, and she'd been without both for far too long.

After dinner, Roger turned on the news and the entire family watched Bradley's interview. He talked about the case, he talked about the upcoming election, and he talked about the attorney who'd come down from Charlotte to represent the accused. He didn't mince words; he wanted everyone to know that Paige didn't belong there. His interview carried the same tones as his opening statement.

"He's just a blowhard," Julie said. "Don't listen to him."

Despite her family's assurances, Paige couldn't get his words out of her head. "Ms. Paige Sparrow belongs in Charlotte, not in this great town," he'd said. "We need to heal after this tragic attack on one of our own, and Ms. Sparrow is insisting that healing not be allowed."

"We don't need healing," Paige grumbled to herself. "We need justice."

Later that night, long after Julie's family had left for their own home to make their own memories of the first night the babies were home, Paige's phone rang. It was a blocked number.

"Hello?"

"Go home."

"Excuse me?"

"Go home or you'll regret it."

"Who is this?"

"Those are three beautiful little girls," the voice growled. "If you love them, you'll go home."

Paige was shaking when she hung up the phone. This was the second time Deputy Frank Taylor had threatened her, but it was the first time he'd threatened her family. She took the rock from the nightstand and traced the letters of hate. She thought about how Ciara and Travis had quickly recovered from the incident, how Ciara had said it wasn't the first time a rock had been thrown at their house. She put the rock in her briefcase. Paige would finish the trial and go home. Not because she was afraid of Deputy Taylor, though she was, but because Charlotte was her home. It was where her life was. But she would finish what she started. Paige was going to cause waves, and no amount of rocks or threats would stop her.

CHAPTER EIGHTEEN

Paige started her Friday morning at Henry's Corner Store. Barb was behind the counter waiting with a fresh mug of coffee and a smile. As soon as she walked in, Paige noticed Deputy Taylor sitting at a corner booth with Bradley. She forced a smile in their direction.

"There's a lot of people here this morning," she said, sliding onto an empty stool at the counter.

Barb nodded. "The trial." She pointed to several tables were reporters were furiously scribbling on notepads. "The vultures need their coffee."

Paige made a face. "But it's got to be good for business," she offered.

Barb snorted. "These reporters are walking twigs. They live on nicotine and black coffee. I'm about one day away from telling them refills aren't free. I'd fall over dead if one of them actually ordered something from the menu, but they're all 'gluten-free' and 'vegan.' No wonder they're so small, the poor dears can't eat anything."

"Hopefully the trial will be over and they'll be on their way soon. I do enjoy my free refills." Paige winked and held her nearly empty mug out.

"I guess you'll be heading back to Charlotte when it's over," Barb said, topping the coffee off.

"It's my home." Paige shrugged. "It's where I belong."

"Hogwash. Your home is here. You just live in Charlotte."

"I think there are some here that would disagree."

"You're a Sparrow. I don't care where on the four corners of God's earth you wind up, Merchants Town is your home. I told your mother the day you left that you'd be back; it's in your blood. Just don't wait too long to figure that out."

Paige wished Barb was right. She wanted Merchants Town to be her home. She wanted that family unit she'd grown up with around. But that wasn't what Chris signed up for. He'd hate it, and he'd hate her for asking him to move to a sleepy town. For not the first time since she'd returned, she wished she had made different choices, responded differently to the curve balls life tossed her way. She'd ran when she should have fought, but she wasn't going to run again. She couldn't fix her life, but she could fix Travis's.

Paige reached into her briefcase and removed the rock. It was cool in her hand as she walked to the table. Bradley looked up, surprised to see her standing there. Deputy Taylor's face began to darken.

"Mornin', Ms. Sparrow," Bradley said after swallowing the mouthful of pancakes.

Paige nodded her head in his direction before turning to Deputy Taylor. His sausage fingers gripped the mug in front of him.

"Good morning, Deputy Taylor," she said sweetly.

The diner fell silent save for the scratching of pens on paper from the table of reporters.

"Ms. Sparrow," he growled.

"I'd like to make a police report."

"Then you should probably go to the station."

Paige shook her head. "No, I wanted to make this report directly with you."

Deputy Taylor raised an eyebrow.

"Ms. Sparrow, this isn't exactly the appropriate time or place." Bradley wiped his hands. "We're preparing for the trial."

Paige nodded. "Yes, I can see that, but this is important." She had the attention of everyone in the diner. Her heart began to flutter, but she refused to back down.

Deputy Taylor laughed, a harsh, ugly sound. "Very well. Go ahead, Ms. Sparrow. Please share what is so important."

"Thank you, Deputy Taylor. I do appreciate your concern for the citizens of Merchants Town. The other day, I was at my client's house. We were conversing in his living room, and this was thrown through the window." She dropped the rock on the table with a thud.

"Is this a joke?" Bradley asked, his eyes on the red paint.

"Oh, not at all, Mr. Moore."

All eyes were on Paige and the rock. One of the reporters began to scribble furiously on his notepad.

"This rock was thrown through a window over a child's play pen. That child could have been injured," Paige continued.

Deputy Taylor's eyes narrowed as he glared at Paige. He did not look at the rock.

"And I wondered who in this great town that I was born and raised in would have such hate in their hearts that they would throw a rock through the window of someone's home. Who in this town would take the time to paint such a hateful message on a rock?" Paige shook her head. "This isn't the town I know and love. Our citizens wouldn't do this."

"I'm sure it was just some teenagers out for a thrill. Acting out on a dare or some nonsense like that." Deputy Taylor had yet to look at the rock.

"Maybe, but I do hope you use all the resources at your disposal to hold the culprit accountable for his actions. People like that just don't belong here." Paige walked out of Henry's Corner Store with her head high and the whispers of the reporters in her wake. She could feel the waves.

At the courthouse, the air vibrated with electric energy. More media vans sat in the parking lot, and reporters had been swarming at the windows and doors all morning. A decision was expected soon.

"Before I call this court to session, I want to make it very clear that I do not want anyone in this room to speak to the circus of reporters outside. I thought I'd made that very clear when I'd banned the media from my courtroom, so imagine my surprise last night during the evening news when this case was the top story. I don't want to sequester this jury, but I will if I hear one more peep from those reporters about my case. I will sequester them in a heartbeat." Judge Fox looked at the jurors. "Do ya'll want to be sequestered?"

The jurors shook their heads.

"That's what I thought. No more interviews." Judge Fox glared at Bradley. "Am I understood?"

Everyone in the room nodded in agreement. Bradley kept his eyes on the floor.

"Good. This court is now in session. Attorney Moore, you have the floor."

Paige held Travis's hand as Bradley called Ainsley to the stand. He asked her how she was feeling.

The young woman kept her eyes down and murmured a barely audible response.

"I move the court that judicial notice be taken that due to her memory loss, she has no personal knowledge of the events in question."

Paige stood. "I object. As stated yesterday, Mr. Crawley has constitutional rights. We will not be waiving them."

"Sustained."

"I have no further questions," Bradley said, taking a seat.

"Your witness, Ms. Sparrow."

Paige took a deep breath. She caught her father's eye off to the side and he nodded at her reassuringly. She smoothed her skirt and approached Ainsley.

"Good morning, Ms. Taylor."

"Good morning."

"Before we begin, I want you to know that I understand how difficult this must be for you. I myself was the victim of an assault when I was not much older than you. It isn't easy to talk about it, even now. My heart goes out to you, Ms. Taylor. It truly does. As women, we…"

"Objection, your Honor. Attorney Sparrow is testifying."
Bradley stood, huffing as he interrupted her.

"Your Honor, we are not disputing that something horrible
happened to Ms. Taylor. I want her to know that she is not on trial.
Even though this is a cross examination, I want her to know that I
understand how painful this truly is and I want to make her as
comfortable as possible."

"Very well, Ms. Sparrow. I appreciate your concern for the
witness. I think your intentions have been made, so I do ask that
you please stick to your questions and refrain from personal
narratives."

"Yes, your Honor." Paige returned Judge Fox's smile before
turning her attention back to Ainsley.

"You know Mr. Crawley, right?"

"Yes, ma'am."

"You went to high school with him?"

"Yes, ma'am."

"You had classes with him?"

"No, ma'am. He's a year older than me."

"But you know him?"

"Yes, ma'am."

"And you've known him for a long time?"

"Since I was twelve."

"You are friends?"

Ainsley looked at her hands.

"Let me rephrase. You were friendly toward each other in
school?"

"Yes, ma'am."

"Did he have your telephone number?"

"Yes, ma'am."

"Did he bother you with texts and phone calls?"

Ainsley darted a frightened look at her father and then looked back at her hands.

"I withdraw the question," Paige said quickly, remembering the fawn.

"Your doctors say that you don't remember what happened," Paige said softly.

"That is correct."

Paige walked over to the table and flipped through her binder.

"What are you doing?" Travis hissed.

"Trust me," she whispered. She found what she was looking for and returned to the witness box.

"Ms. Ainsley, I'm showing you what has been marked as Defense Exhibit A."

"Objection!" Bradley was on his feet like a shot.

"On what grounds?" Judge Fox peered over his glasses.

"Lack of foundation," he huffed.

"Your Honor, if I'm not mistaken we did take judicial notice and if you would allow me, the rest of the foundation will be laid with Ms. Taylor."

"She's got you there, Attorney Moore. Carry on, Ms. Sparrow." Paige could have sworn he smiled.

"Ms. Ainsley, I am showing you, again, what has been marked as Defense Exhibit A. Do you recognize it?"

"Objection!"

Both Judge Fox and Paige looked at Bradley expectantly.

"It's already been established the girl has no memory of the events."

"The girl, as you call her, is a young woman who can answer the question. Ms. Taylor, if you please?" Judge Fox nodded reassuringly at Ainsley.

"May I?" Her voice shook as she reached for the photograph.

"Of course." Paige handed her the blown-up photograph showing the clasped hands and the engagement ring. She positioned herself in front of Ainsley, effectively blocking the young woman's view of her father.

"This is ridiculous!" Bradley was on his feet again.

"Give her a minute, please, your Honor?"

"Ms. Sparrow, she has had a minute. Either she recognizes it, or she doesn't."

"I do."

Paige could hardly hear her. Even Judge Fox leaned over.

Ainsley cleared her throat. "I do recognize it," she said a bit louder.

"You took this picture, didn't you?"

"Yes, ma'am."

Relief flooded through Paige. "Do you remember when?" she asked.

"That day."

"By that day, do you mean the day of the attack?"

"Yes." Ainsley's eyes quickly darted to find her father in the crowd. Paige could feel her retreating.

"It's okay," Paige soothed. "I just want to talk about the picture."

Ainsley relaxed.

"It's a picture of you, isn't it?"

"Yes."

"And Travis?"

"Yes."

"You're holding hands?"

"Yes."

"Your Honor, at this time I would like to admit this photograph into evidence."

Judge Fox gestured to Bradley, who was already standing. "Let's hear it, Attorney Moore."

"Objection. Irrelevant."

"This picture, taken the very day of the attack, shows the relationship between Mr. Crawley and Ms. Taylor. A relationship that Attorney Moore has argued for days does not exist. I find it very relevant."

"I do as well, Ms. Sparrow. Objection overruled. Evidence is admitted."

"Thank you, your Honor. I do have copies if I may submit them to the jury?"

Bradley fish mouthed but no words came out.

"You may."

Paige gathered up the copies and walked over to the jury box. She handed the stack to the jury forewoman. The woman who had been so vocal about her distrust of Paige smiled with a nod as she took them.

"You're wearing a ring in the photo, right?" Paige asked Ainsley.

"Yes."

"Who gave you that ring?"

"Travis."

"Did he say anything when he gave you the ring?"

"Yes."

"What did he say?"

"He asked me to marry him."

"This is preposterous. You are leading my daughter down a vicious path. These are all lies." Deputy Taylor's face was red, and his meaty hands pushed against the deputies blocking his path.

"Attorney Moore, you best do something. Now!" He bellowed.

Bradley shuffled his files around and didn't look up.

"Order! I will have order in my court!" Judge Fox banged his gavel and glared.

Ainsley winced with each smack of the wood on wood.

"Deputy Taylor, another outburst from you and I will remove you from my court. Do we have an understanding?"

"Yes," the man growled.

"Yes, what?" Judge Fox roared.

"Yes, sir."

After Deputy Taylor was subdued, Paige turned back to Ainsley.

"Look at me. Just me," she told the young woman. "You said yes?"

"Yes."

"Where's the ring?"

"I don't know." Ainsley began to cry. "He took it."

"Who took it?" Paige asked.

Ainsley shook her head.

"Your Honor, clearly we've reached a point in Ainsley's timeline that she doesn't remember. This line of questioning must immediately stop." Bradley was on his feet, his face red. The words squeezed from his mouth as if someone had their hands tight on his windpipe.

"Ms. Sparrow?"

"I will stop if Ainsley wants to stop." Paige took another gamble. So far, Ainsley hadn't let her down. Scotty would say she was batting a thousand.

"Young lady, do you wish to stop?" Judge Fox's voice was warm.

"No, sir," Ainsley said, her chin quivering when she lifted her head to meet his eyes. "I do not want to stop."

Brave girl, thought Paige.

"Carry on, Ms. Sparrow."

"After Travis asked you to marry him, what did you do?"

"Objection!"

"Attorney Moore, if you're going to tell me you're objecting because she doesn't remember..." Judge Fox let his unspoken threat hang in the air.

Bradley paused for a moment. "Calls for narrative," he finally said.

"Please reword the question, Ms. Sparrow, and remember that you are cross-examining this witness."

"He didn't force you to have sexual intercourse, did he?"

"No."

"But you made love that day?"

"Yes."

"Lies!" Deputy Taylor was on his feet again. His eyes were small in his face.

"This is truly your last warning, Deputy Taylor. If you cannot control yourself, please leave. As a father myself, I understand this

216

line of questioning may be difficult for you. But I will not tolerate another outburst. If you interrupt my courtroom again, I will hold you in contempt and you can spend the night in a jail cell. I trust that's clear."

Deputy Taylor sat down. Paige could feel the heat of his gaze on her back as she faced Ainsley.

"Did Travis ever force himself on you?"

"No."

"Did he ever make you do something you did not want to do?"

"No."

"Does he love you?"

Ainsley looked past Paige and met Travis's eyes for the first time since she'd been in the court room. "Not as much as I love him."

Two of the jurors openly gasped.

"Now Ainsley, I know sometimes the ones we love can hurt us the most. Has Travis ever hurt you?"

Ainsley wiped her eyes. "No."

"He didn't hit you that night, did he?"

"No."

"Has he ever hit you?"

"No."

"Do you remember what happened that night?" Paige held her breath and waited.

Ainsley looked at her father and sat in silence.

"Don't look at your father, look at me. Do you remember what happened that night?" she asked again.

Ainsley nodded her head.

"Stop lying!" Frank Taylor was on his feet, spittle flying from his mouth as he bellowed at his daughter. "You will regret this," he snarled at Paige.

As Paige turned to confront him, she saw an unknown woman sitting near the exit and chewing on her fingernails. Paige was certain it was Ainsley's mom, and if Deputy Taylor was escorted out, he would pass right by her.

"Your Honor," Ainsley looked to Judge Fox, her eyes wide. "Please let my father stay." Her eyes darted between Deputy Taylor and her mother.

"Very well, Ms. Taylor. But your father must learn to behave himself," Judge Fox sighed. "Please continue," he told Paige, his face still red with rage.

"Ainsley, I need you to respond out loud. Can you do that for me?" Paige's voice was soft, like vanilla ice cream melting over an apple pie fresh from the oven. This was the voice that the fawn let approach it.

"Yes."

"I'm going to ask you the same question again, and I want you to look at me. Just me. Do you remember what happened that night?" Paige's voice was low and steady. This was the voice of her father.

Ainsley looked Paige straight in the eyes. "Yes."

"Travis didn't hurt you, did he?"

"No."

The jury began to twitter with excitement.

From where she sat just behind her son, Ciara broke down into sobs. "Thank you, Jesus. Thank you," she said over and over.

"Your Honor," Bradley stood. "In light of this new information, the State moves to dismiss all charges against Travis Crawley."

"I think that's probably a wise move, Attorney Moore. Ms. Sparrow, I would assume you do not have any objections?"

Paige looked at the brave woman before her and then at her own father, who simply nodded his approval.

"I'm not finished questioning this witness."

Judge Fox looked surprised, but he didn't stop her.

Paige breathed deeply. Time to make more waves, she thought.

"You know who hit you, don't you, Ainsley?" she asked softly.

"Yes." Ainsley's voice was louder, stronger, more sure of itself than it had been all morning. She held a shaking finger out and pointed at her father

"You lying whore!" Deputy Taylor roared. "You just wait until I get my hands on you. I'll beat the slut out of you for good this time! No child of mine is going to spread her legs for a nigger!!" With his hand on his gun, Deputy Frank Taylor stormed the stand.

Paige planted her feet and stood in front of Ainsley as chaos ensued. Bradley Moore cowered under the prosecutor's table, and the bailiff quickly sprung to action and ushered Judge Fox out of the room. The jurors screamed and ducked low in the box. Kevin covered several of the women with his own body. Without hesitation, Travis unfolded his long legs and stood between Paige and Deputy Taylor.

The scene play out before Paige as if in slow motion. Frank stopped in front of Travis and unholstered his gun, his face twisted into a smiling grimace. Only seconds had passed since the outburst, but it felt like hours. The only sound Paige could hear was that of her own beating heart. She blinked as Frank raised the gun. When she opened her eyes, Frank was on the floor, pinned by a deputy, and being handcuffed. Only then did Paige breathe.

"Thank you," Ainsley was at Paige's side, squeezing her hand as they watched his coworkers escort Deputy Taylor from the courthouse.

"Thank you for believing in Travis. For believing in us," Ainsley whispered in a rush. "I didn't realize I was brave until you told me I was." The young girl shook with fear, anger, and relief. "Thank you."

Travis pulled Ainsley into his arms, kissing every bruise on her face. "I'm sorry," he said against her skin. "I'm sorry."

"It was time for the truth." Ainsley leaned into his chest.

"I told you I trusted you," Travis said, squeezing Paige's hand one last time before turning back to Ainsley.

Ciara joined the throng standing around and Paige watched as the woman tentatively approached Ainsley, the young woman who had nearly destroyed her son's life. Paige couldn't hear the words exchanged between the two, but both women began to cry and embraced.

Ainsley's mother made her way from the back of the room.

"I'm so sorry, baby." The tears streamed down her face as she looked at her daughter for the first time in years. "I should have taken you with me. I should never have left you with that monster."

Ainsley stepped from Ciara's embrace and pulled her mother into her arms. "It's okay, Mama. It's over now. It's all over."

Judge Fox attempted to restore order after the threat was extinguished and Deputy Taylor was removed from the room, but no one was listening to him. He finally threw up his hands with a laugh.

"Case dismissed," he yelled, banging his gavel.

"Attorney Sparrow," he said, coming to stand by Paige. "I've never called you Attorney Sparrow until now and for that I do apologize. Attorney Sparrow has always been your father, but you are your father's daughter and well deserving of the respect that name brings. It was a pleasure and an honor to have you in my court room, Attorney Sparrow, and I hope you return one day."

"So do I," Roger said, joining the conversation. "But I'd prefer she never have a gun pointed in her direction again."

Roger pulled Paige into a strong hug. "I'm so proud of you, Baby Girl," he whispered in her ear. "So very proud."

"Come on, Dad. Let's go home," Paige said when she finally found her voice.

CHAPTER NINETEEN

"Do you really have to go back tomorrow?" Lillian asked, mixing the cake batter and pouring it into the cake pan.

"I do. Antwan is having his farewell party and I promised Miranda I would go." Paige ran her finger around the rim of the discarded bowl and licked the sweet batter off her finger. "And I have to figure out what is going on at work."

"Did coming here really mess up the partner track?"

Paige nodded with a shrug. "But it's okay. I'm not really sure I want to be partner at a big pharma firm anyway. Being here and representing Travis reminded me how much I enjoy representing people as opposed to businesses."

"There's always a space for you at Sparrow Law," Roger interjected from the living room where he was watching the news report on the trial. "Just say the word. The sign is even still around here somewhere. And after this," he pointed to the TV screen, "you're a bit of a local celebrity."

Puzzled, Paige asked Lillian about the sign.

"You never saw it?" Lillian wiped her hands on her apron and walked into the garage, gesturing for Paige to follow. She reached between the deep freezer and the wall and pulled out a rustic wooden sign covered in dust. In big script letters, the words "Sparrow & Sparrow, Attorneys at Law" were burned into the wood.

"He had it made before you took the bar, but then you went to Charlotte so…" Lillian sighed and slid the sign back in its spot. "So, it's been here ever since."

"What are you ladies doing?" Roger asked from the doorway.

"Just getting some rolls," Lillian yelled as she pulled a bag of frozen yeast rolls from the freezer.

"Grab some extra. Scotty and Jason are here."

Paige wiped the tears from her face before following her mother out of the garage. She'd never fully realized how much she'd hurt her family when she'd turned her back on Merchants Town.

"Congratulations, Paige!" Scotty said as soon as he saw her. "Your face is plastered on every TV screen in Merchants Town. Shoot, you're probably on every screen in North Carolina. Good job getting Ainsley to talk. You're one hell of an attorney."

"Thanks," she said, wondering where Matty was.

"I'm proud of you, Sis," Julie said over the celebratory dinner. "This whole town let that girl down. We all knew what was happening, and we were powerless to stop it. When Dad got sick, I worried about what would happen to Travis and Ainsley. But then you stayed. I know it messed up things for you in Charlotte, but you saved a life and you gave those two kids a shot at something real together."

"I just did what anybody would do," Paige blushed, brushing off the comment and wondering when the last time Julie had complimented her was.

"No, you didn't." Anderson shifted Emma to his other arm and pulled the pouting Max into his lap. "Don't sell yourself short. What you did was pretty amazing."

"Dad would have done the same thing."

"I'd like to think I could have gotten the case dismissed after questioning Ainsley on the stand, but I know I wouldn't have gotten her to open up the way you did. At my best, I'd have been able to poke holes in Slick's argument. You, however, blew his argument to shreds. Frank Taylor being arrested at the close is certainly something I never expected to happen. How on earth did you get her to turn on her father?"

Paige shrugged. "I received some pretty wise advice from an old friend." She smiled at Scotty. "He reminded who I was."

CHAPTER TWENTY

The following morning, after her goodbyes, Paige slowly loaded her bags into the red car. Dory raced around the yard, barking at the vehicle and snarling at its tires. After the car was loaded, Paige slipped into the garage and grabbed the sign. It barely fit in the trunk, but it fit. As she passed Scotty's house on her way down the road, she slowed down. He and Jason were in the yard playing with Vern. Paige started to turn into his driveway, but she changed her mind when she saw Matty's SUV parked by the barn. She beeped her horn and waved before heading down the road. If she had looked in the rear-view mirror, she'd have seen Scotty trying to flag her down, but she never looked back.

When she arrived in Charlotte, Paige unloaded the car and set about cleaning up the sign. When it glistened, she propped it up against the wall. She sent Chris a message to let him know she was home, but she knew he was likely in surgery. She turned the televisions on in the living room and the bedroom to combat the loneliness she was feeling. She missed the constant noise of Merchants Town, the way people just walked in and out of their neighbor's homes. She realized sitting on the floor looking at the sign that she didn't even know who her neighbors were.

"I'm so glad you could make it," Miranda exclaimed hours later when Paige showed up at the bar for Antwan's party.

"Did that girl's father really point a gun at you?" Antwan asked, wrapping his strong arms around her and kissing her cheek.

"How'd you know that?" She laughed. "Do you read my sister's blog, too?"

"Sweetheart, that case and Deputy Frank Taylor's reaction is national news. You put that little town on the map. I'm pretty certain you're going to get inundated with requests for interviews. You're a celebrity."

Paige shook her head. "I'm no celebrity. Travis never should have been charged to begin with."

Antwan nodded, a brief pained expression flashing across his dark eyes. "It happens."

"And that love story between Ainsley and Travis. How sweet is that?" Miranda gushed. "Someone has even started an online campaign to raise money for their wedding."

"What?" Paige laughed.

"Oh yes. I've already donated a couple hundred dollars to the cause."

"Well, they do need a new engagement ring," Paige said before turning the conversation to Antwan's new job. "Are you excited?"

"Yes. More than you have any idea. I was little annoyed that Meredith told me she didn't want me to stay for two weeks, but now I'm so ready to get out of Charlotte. And I'm ready to actually start helping people. That's why I became an attorney to begin with, to help people. Let's be honest, how did you feel when Travis walked out of the courtroom a free man? We don't feel like that representing the clients we do here."

Antwan was right. Paige had settled many a successful case for Fitz, Parker & Corbin, but she'd never closed a file feeling the way she did after representing Travis.

"Didn't we all become attorneys to help people?" Miranda took a swig of her beer and glanced around the table. "To challenge the perception of attorneys as money hungry bottom feeders?"

"Speak for yourself. I became an attorney for the chicks," Paul joked as his wife punched him in the arm.

"Who invited her?" Miranda asked as Danielle sashayed onto the outdoor courtyard, a wine glass in hand.

"I did." Antwan raised his hand to get Danielle's attention. "We're all in this together, Mir. We've got to look out for each other."

"I see you got that guy off," Danielle said as she approached the table. "Criminal work is a far cry from big pharma law." She made a face. "I wouldn't touch it with a ten-foot pole. I wonder what Fitz thinks of your new-found fame."

"Fitz is quite pleased."

None of the group had seen Fitz approach the table from the shadows. He winked at Paige. "And I know her father is quite proud." He squeezed Paige's shoulder in a fatherly way. "Good job, Paige. I expected no less from you."

"Mr. Fitz." Antwan stood and extended his hand. "I want to thank you for all you've done for me."

Fitz took his hand. "Mr. Milford, there are no thanks needed. You are a talented attorney and we are going to miss you, but I think you're going where you need to be. When you run for

President, just invite me and Mrs. Fitz to the White House for Christmas one year. She's been dying to see those Christmas lights."

Antwan laughed. "Deal."

"I'm not going to interrupt your fun by having the boss around. I just wanted to stop by and let you know that you will be missed. I also wanted to let you know that the firm is picking up the tab tonight, so enjoy yourselves. You've earned it. All of you." He turned to Paige. "As for you, Ms. Sparrow, I fully expect to see you back in your office come Monday morning."

"Yes, sir. I will be there with bells on."

Fitz nodded and glanced around the table of attorneys and paralegals. "Where is Mr. Kennedy?"

"He couldn't make it," Danielle responded.

"Hmm. Well I'm sure he would be here if he could. It's important to support your colleagues." Fitz finished his beer and gave Antwan one last handshake. "I am very proud of you, young man," he said.

After Fitz left, several others followed suit.

"We have to get home to the kids," Paul explained. "Keep in touch, Antwan. Don't ever hesitate to give me a call if you need anything. We're really going to miss you. Fitz, Parker & Corbin just won't be the same without you."

Danielle left not long after, having received a text that made her blush. She didn't even tell Antwan goodbye.

"I'm sure that was Davidson," Miranda smirked. "They think they're being so secretive with that relationship."

"Well, I hope she knows what she's doing." Antwan took a sip of beer and glanced at Paige. "We all know how work place

228

relationships at Fitz, Parker & Corbin play out. Meredith will fire her in a heartbeat to protect Davidson if this thing continues."

"At some point, you have to make the decision between your relationship and your job." Paige gestured to the waitress for another round. "It wasn't an easy choice."

"I know. I ruined you for all men, didn't I?" Antwan joked.

Paige and Miranda laughed.

"Things always work out in the end. Someone once told me the universe always wins. Clearly the universe didn't have us in the cards."

"And the universe picked Chris for you?" Miranda made a face. "Where is he, anyway? Have you even seen him or heard from him since you've been back?"

"Mir, I just got back a few hours ago and he's working. He's a…"

"very busy man," Antwan and Mir finished the excuse for her, rolling their eyes.

It was late when Paige hailed the cab to take her back to the apartment. Chris was there, but fast asleep. Paige quietly took a shower and climbed into bed beside him. She felt like she was sharing a bed with a stranger.

"Good morning, beautiful," he greeted her when she stumbled into the kitchen hours later. He handed her a mug of coffee. "Figured you might need that after your little party last night."

"Hey," she smiled, taking the mug and inhaling the smell of pressed coffee. "I missed you."

"I missed you, too. You wouldn't believe the week I had." Chris launched into an in-depth discussion of his week at the hospital. Paige tuned him out somewhere between "emergency appendectomy" and one of the orderlies slipping in vomit and spilling a urine sample on him.

"And I had to deliver a baby Thursday night because the neonatal ward was swamped." He shuddered. "Oh, how I hate obstetrics."

"Julie had her babies."

"That's great. And they've hired a new administrator who has no idea what she's doing. It's such a pain."

"My case was dismissed."

"Uh huh," he continued, unphased. "I'm supposed to present information on our department to her, but I just don't think she'll ever understand it."

"I had a gun pulled on me."

"That's great. I mean, do you have any idea how difficult it is to explain something to someone who refuses to listen to what you're saying? This woman acts like she knows everything. It's so frustrating."

Paige raised an eyebrow. "Yep. It's pretty frustrating."

"Oh, I've been meaning to ask you what is with that thing you brought home? I stubbed my toe on it when I came in last night." Chris pointed to the rustic wooden sign. "Is it a joke or something?"

"It's just something my dad had made a long time ago."

"It's not staying there, right? I mean, it doesn't really match the décor. It's just a little 'folksy,' don't you think?"

"I'll move it."

Chris laughed. "I should have figured your father had something to do with it. Does he even know you at all? I mean, that's a weird gift. It's like the time he gave you that first edition novel. It would have been worth a mint had he not scribbled some nonsense in it."

Chris meant the first edition *To Kill a Mockingbird* Roger had sent Paige several Christmases ago. He'd inscribed it: "To my Little Atticus in a Skirt – may you never forget who you are and where you belong." Paige had stuffed the book in a box in her closet after receiving it.

"I said I'll move it," she snapped.

"Thanks, Babe. I'll see you when I get back." Chris grabbed his bag and headed to the door.

"You're leaving?"

"Did I forget to tell you I have a conference in Philly? It's only a couple of days. I will be back Tuesday night." He looked at her face. "I did forget to tell you. I'm sorry, Paige. It was a bit weird with you not being here, and then things kind of slipped away from me. I would have mentioned last night, but you were out so late and I was just too exhausted to wait up. I'll make it up to you when I come back. I promise." He strode forward and planted a kiss on her forehead. "I love you."

"Love you, too," she said, fighting back tears.

Paige sat at the small dining room table and ate cold cereal in silence, looking at the sign. She'd wanted her name on a sign for so long, and her father had done it for her years ago.

After she finished her breakfast and washed the bowl, Paige pulled a box from her closet. She'd forgotten about the book until Chris had mentioned it. She remembered being embarrassed by it, by how Chris had responded when she'd received it in the mail that December.

Paige sat on the floor, cross-legged and opened the box of memories. On top, was the book. She traced the inscription and smiled. Her father knew who she was better than anyone else. Better even than her sometimes. Under the book was a photo album. All the memories of Scotty that she'd tried to forget after the night he hadn't come to her rescue were neatly packaged in the album. There was a picture of her holding the fawn with the broken leg. A picture of the two of them at a Carolina basketball game, arms entwined, their smiles from a Carolina victory frozen in time. There was a picture of her drinking from the Old Well before classes started. Pictures she'd taken of baseball practice. Pictures of leaves changing on Stadium Drive and kisses under the Davey Popular. Pictures from prom. Pictures from homecoming. Pictures from the State Championships. Pictures from the river that ran just south of Merchants Town, the one the high schoolers skipped school to skinny dip in. Picture after picture, and she was smiling in them all. Under the picture album, was a stack of clippings from sports magazines. The one with Scotty's egg recipe was just under the article after he was injured. Beneath the clippings was a worn baseball jersey with LEWIS written across the top. She'd slept in that jersey nearly every night until they broke up. She'd forgotten she'd put in the box. She held the worn fabric to her nose; it smelled of the past and the perfume she'd worn religiously her Freshman and Sophomore years of college. She slipped it over her head and continued through the box. As she reached the bottom, she wiped her face.

"This is Paige Sparrow," she said aloud. "This box." Her voice echoed through the cold apartment.

Paige spent the rest of the morning reading Julie's blog. The years she'd been absent from Merchants Town and her family unfolded before her. There was the time Avery broke his arm trying to fly. Max's first word – "puppy." A post about Sally's car crash and Scotty's return. Pictures from Little League games. Stories of postpartum depression and miscarriages. Christmases without Paige. A post from when Anderson opened the pharmacy in the downtown location. Merchants Town Baptist Church revival messages. Bible verses.

Julie's writing was full of faith, heart, and hope. One of the later posts detailed the publishing contract she'd been offered based on her writing. Paige wasn't surprised that a publishing company latched on to what Julie had created. Her sister was an extremely talented writer. How was it that Paige had no idea?

The last post was about Paige and titled "My Sister, the Prodigal Daughter." Written earlier in the week, the post detailed Paige's absence from Merchants Town and the warm welcome she'd received upon returning. Paige wept as she read about how angry Julie was when she returned and was treated like a queen, and how happy Julie had been that Paige was there to meet the triplets. Julie wrote about how close they'd been as children and how an unfortunate event drove them apart.

It drove Paige away from everything and everyone. I know a hint of what changed her world, but that is not my truth to tell. I can say that she is home, and my heart is now full. Oh how we pray she'll stay. She is so much a part of us, of this town. I wish she could see that.

Julie concluded the entry by quoting from the prodigal son parable:

It was fitting to celebrate and be glad, for this your brother was dead, and is alive; he was lost, and is found. Luke 15:32

Paige was engulfed in the warmth of her sister's words when her phone buzzed.

"Hello?" she answered without looking at the display screen to see who was calling her.

"Hey, Baby. I just wanted to let you know that I made it to Philly safely and just checked in at the hotel. I'm getting ready to head down the street for some lunch. Do you remember that cheesesteak place we ate at for our first date?"

Paige laughed. "Of course I do. We were covered in ooey gooey goodness within moments of taking the first bite."

It had been small counter-front soda shop with limited seating outside. They had ordered their food and sat on the curb, thighs touching, laughing at the mess and each other. They'd been introduced through mutual friends, and it had taken weeks for them to be able to schedule a date. Exasperated with how difficult it was to find a time to take Paige on a proper first date, Chris had surprised her with a quick bite to eat.

"I thought I might go there for a late lunch."

"Sounds yummy."

"It won't be the same without you."

"I'm sure it will taste just as good."

"Maybe, but I won't be nervously waiting for a pretty girl to finish her hoagie so I can kiss her this time."

"It's a good memory," she said after a bit.

"I want to be honest with you, Paige. I feel bad about leaving the way I did. I know I didn't tell you I was going to Philly. I honestly wasn't sure if the trial would be over and if you'd be back, and I wanted to avoid a scene."

Paige sat in silence.

"I'm not here for a conference. I'm here for a job interview," Chris confessed.

"You want to move back to Pennsylvania?" Paige padded to the kitchen and made herself another cup of coffee.

"I'm seriously thinking about it. The position just sort of fell in my lap. I promise I wasn't looking for openings, but one of my former colleagues gave me a call because she thought I'd be interested. I'd be surgical lead. I'd be able to work a more compatible schedule, and I'd get to teach some classes at the medical school. It is the ideal job for me. For us."

"How long have you been thinking about it?"

"I applied four months ago."

"Oh." Paige's stomach dropped.

"Paige, I know you're on partnership track at Fitz, Parker & Corbin and that a move to Pennsylvania isn't really what you want, but I feel like we could have a life there. A good one. One different from two strangers passing in the night. We can finally start a family."

Paige realized as the words poured out of his mouth that she still hadn't told him that she had lost the partnership track and been demoted.

"Don't worry about the partnership, Chris. I didn't make it. They announced it while I was in Merchants Town."

"Baby, I am so sorry. But maybe it's a good thing. Now there's nothing standing in our way.

"This is what you've always wanted?" she asked, knowing the answer.

"Yes, but I want it with you."

"Then kill it at the interview. I have faith in you."

After she hung up the phone, she glanced at the time. It was just after 1:00 pm; Julie would be home from church. She pressed the button and waited.

"Hey, Sis. Is everything okay?"

Paige never called her sister. "Yeah, I was just checking in on you and the babies."

"They're good. They were perfect angels at church this morning, except for Ella. She was really fussy. Pastor Culpepper took her from Dad and bounced her around while he preached from the pulpit. Put her right to sleep."

"I don't know what that says about his sermon," Paige chuckled.

"How was Antwan's going away party?"

"It was good. I'm going to miss him."

"Raleigh isn't that far from Charlotte. I'm sure you'll keep in touch."

Paige knew what 'keep in touch' meant. It meant Christmas cards for a few years and finally just following each other on social media. "Maybe," she said.

"How is Chris? I figured the two of you would be doing something fun today. Doesn't he usually have Sundays off?"

"He's at a job interview in Philadelphia." The words fell like seven bricks from her mouth.

Julie was silent.

"Are you still there?" Paige asked after a while.

236

"Yeah, I just… Do you want to move back to Philly?"

"No." Paige didn't hesitate. She didn't have to think about it.

"Have you told him that?"

"No."

"Is that Aunt Paige?" A small voice asked.

"Yes, Avery. Do you want to tell her 'hello'?"

"Uh huh."

There was a clattering sound of the phone being dropped and then Avery was on the line. "Hey Aunt Paige!"

"Hey, Little Man."

"My last baseball game is Saturday. Are you gonna come watch it?"

Paige felt her heart swell.

"Avery, honey, Aunt Paige is a very busy lady and she lives very far away. She might not be able to come," Paige heard Julie explaining.

"I'll try," Paige said. "I will try my very best."

"Promise?"

"Pinky promise," Paige said extending her pinkie even though her young nephew couldn't see her.

"Don't make him promises you can't keep," Julie warned when she took the phone back. "He doesn't understand."

"I told him I will try, and I will."

"Okay. We'd love to see you before the girls are walking."

Paige laughed. "They're only a week old, Jules."

"So this Philly thing," Julie started, returning to the conversation that had been interrupted by an excited little boy. "What are you going to do?"

"I don't know. I guess I'll see what happens with the interview and go from there." Paige spun the sparkling engagement ring around on her finger. "It just makes me angry that he was plotting this for months without consulting me even once. But I guess I can't hold it against him. You have to make sacrifices for love, right?"

"Some. But never your happiness. And moving to Philly is a big deal that he should have consulted you about before applying. Are you even licensed to practice in Philadelphia?"

"No, but..."

"Paige, don't sacrifice your happiness. It's not worth it."

"When did you get so smart?"

"Oh, I was born this way."

"Funny. When you asked Anderson to move to Merchants Town after college, how'd that go?"

"I didn't ask him."

"What?"

"I didn't ask him," Julie repeated. "The day he proposed, he told me that he'd seen my heart and knew my heart was in Merchants Town. He asked if there was room for him here."

"That's disgustingly sweet."

"In all honesty, I think he fell in love the town long before he fell in love with me. I'm pretty certain he'd still be running the pharmacy here even if I'd declined the proposal."

"Can you imagine how awkward it would be to live somewhere like Merchants Town where you'd be constantly running into a past love?"

"You mean like you and Scotty?"

Paige hadn't meant that, but it was true. The fear of running into Scotty and memories of him were what had kept her away from her home for so many years.

"I guess it's not as bad as it sounds," she said before remembering the dull ache she felt when she saw Scotty with Matty. "But it's still pretty bad."

"Eh. I think you did just fine." Julie started laughing. "We actually had a bet that the two of you would get back together while you were here. I lost."

"You guys bet on me?"

"Indeed. When you showed up to the hospital with him and Jason in tow, I was ready to dance my victory dance. I guess that fiancé of yours must be something pretty special, especially if you're considering going back to Pennsylvania."

"Chris is pretty special. He's a great doctor and a good guy, but…" Paige stopped herself. "Sorry you lost the bet, but Chris wasn't the only one standing in the way."

"What do you mean?"

"Matty. Scotty seems pretty happy with his beautiful partner." Paige rolled her eyes.

"What are you talking about? Scotty isn't dating Matty! They're…Stop it! Stop it this instance. Avery Porter! I will not tell you again!"

"Everything okay?"

"These kids. I've got to go before someone breaks something. Love you."

"Love you, too." Paige hung up the phone wondering when the last time she told her sister she loved her was.

CHAPTER TWENTY-ONE

Monday came and Paige found herself at the office before anyone else, even Fitz. She sat at her desk and went through her emails, grumbling when she reached the announcement about Davidson. Meredith had sent it to the entire firm, gushing about his many accolades. According to the announcement, Davidson was the "clear choice" for the direction the firm was taken. Paige stuck her tongue out at the screen and deleted the message. She was still going through her emails when Miranda popped her head in to see if she wanted anything for lunch.

"No, thank you," Paige said, glancing up. "I'm going to try and finish getting through these emails, and then I'm probably going to head home."

Miranda's eyes widened and a smile tugged at the corners of her lips. "Paige Sparrow is leaving work early? Ok, spill. What have you done with the real Paige and when should we expect her back?"

"Funny. There are just some things I have to get done before I can get back in the groove here. I'm not even supposed to be here. Two weeks, remember?"

"Well, Fitz saw you Saturday and I'm pretty certain he commanded you be here today. So those two weeks are out."

"I don't think he'll mind. These interviews are good for the firm."

"Interviews?"

Paige gestured to her computer screen. "They found me," she said, with a laugh.

"Paige! These are national newspapers!" Miranda grabbed the mouse and scrolled. "And networks! You're going to be on television?"

"Maybe. I have to talk to Travis and Ainsley. Their story isn't mine to tell."

"What does Chris think about all the attention you're getting?"

Paige took her mouse back and continued to go through the emails, forwarding the interview requests to her personal email to address from home. She didn't want Meredith breathing down her neck about her using Fitz, Parker & Corbin time for it. She didn't answer Miranda's question.

"He doesn't know? How could he not know? Your name has been all over the news."

"I guess he doesn't watch the news."

"And you didn't tell him?"

"I didn't really have time. He left Sunday morning for Philadelphia."

"What's he doing there?"

Paige hesitated before meeting Miranda's eyes. "A job interview."

"Oh, Paige. No."

"Yep."

"Are you moving back to Pennsylvania?"

"I don't know."

"You can't." Miranda started to cry. "You just can't."

"He hasn't gotten the job yet, Mir."

"But he will. We both know it. He's brilliant." Miranda reached for a tissue and blew her nose.

Paige didn't say anything.

"Have you told him you don't want to move back to Philadelphia?"

Paige shook her head. "We'll cross that bridge when we get to it."

"But you don't want to move back. Do you?"

Paige shook her head again.

"This is the worst news ever and now I have to go eat my feelings. You sure you can't come with me for a quick lunch at Wasabi? Surely you need some sushi in your life."

"That does sound amazing. Merchants Town doesn't exactly have a sushi restaurant, but I really need to finish these emails and head out. Sorry."

"It's okay. But soon?"

"Absolutely. And Mir?"

"Yeah?" Miranda stopped in the doorway.

"Please don't say anything about his job interview. I don't want Fitz to hear it from anyone but me."

"My lips are sealed."

Paige slipped out of the office around 4pm. No one noticed her leave. Everyone, including the receptionist, had their eyes focused on their computer screens. The office was quiet save for the frantic tapping on keyboards. It was a far cry from Ursula's booming presence at Sparrow Law.

Paige swung by Wasabi to pick up some rolls and pot stickers to take home and ate in front of the television. The local news had picked up the trial and had pulled her picture from Fitz, Parker & Corbin's website. She had declined their interview earlier in the day, but they had interviewed Meredith. When Meredith began to gush about how the firm had fully supported Paige's trip home to help her ailing father, Paige turned the channel. She contemplated calling the station and granting them the interview, if only to tell them she'd lost partnership track to go, but she cared for Fitz too much.

When she was full, Paige powered up her laptop and visited Julie's blog to see if there was a new post. There wasn't. She refreshed the page ten times over the span of the next two hours. When she was convinced there wouldn't be an update, she ran herself a bath and poured in Lavender bath salts that someone had given her as a present years ago and she'd never had the chance to use. She lowered herself into the steaming water and closed her eyes. She wondered what Scotty was doing.

"Stop being so darn stubborn and listen to your heart." Barb's voice was so clear in her head, Paige opened her eyes, half surprised to find the waitress was not in her apartment.

When the water had cooled, Paige stepped out of the tub and dried herself off. She knew what she had to do. She called Fitz and told him she was taking Tuesday off to handle some things, but she needed to speak with him when she came in on Wednesday. He didn't protest. He just quietly said he'd mark her on his calendar first thing Wednesday morning. With her plan formulated, Paige slept better in that apartment than she ever had.

She woke early, as was her habit, but she didn't put on a suit and heels. Paige pulled on jeans and an old T-shirt depicting her high school mascot. She pulled her hair back in a ponytail, grabbed her purse, and jumped in the car. She was waiting at the dealership when they opened.

"I want to trade this in," she told the sales representative who met her at the door.

He looked from her to the shiny red sports car. "Do you want a newer model?"

"No. I'm thinking I need something a little more..." Paige couldn't think of the word.

"Flashier?"

"No."

"Faster?"

"No, no that. Bigger."

"We have a few four door sports cars, but not many. Follow me."

"No, I'm not looking for a sports car. I'm thinking maybe a sports utility?"

The sales representative took a step back. "Are you sure?"

"Positive."

"Ah yes. I suppose we must all trade in our toys and get a family car at some point."

Paige didn't comment.

The sales representative led her over to the SUVs. "Any color preference? We do have red."

"No. Not red." She eyed the rows of colored vehicles until she saw it. Black on black. "That one." She pointed.

"Okay, I'll go get the keys so we can test drive it."

"I don't need to."

"You don't want to test drive it? A Ford drives quite a bit differently from your car. You may want to at least…"

Paige waved him off. "I grew up with Fords. I think I'll be fine."

"Okay then. Let's go in and complete the paperwork. I'll have someone clean it up and give you a full tank of gas before you go."

Paige followed him inside and walked out forty-five minutes later holding the keys to her new vehicle. She watched as an employee drove her red car around back and felt the slightest ping of guilt. Chris had loved that car. She'd only gotten it because he'd picked it out.

"He'll get over it," she told herself. "If he wants a flashy red sports car, he can go buy one for himself. I don't need one anymore."

Her next stop was a storage facility that advertised boxes of all sizes. She loaded her new car down with packing boxes, bubble wrap, and packing tape. Her heart started to beat faster as she headed to her apartment to pack up her life. She had made her decision. Paige Sparrow was finally listening to her heart.

CHAPTER TWENTY-TWO

Paige walked to the office before the sun was up. When she reached the entrance to the building, she turned and walked to Starbucks. Once there, she sat at a table in the corner and enjoyed the coffee that couldn't compare to Barb's at Henry's Corner Store. Thirty minutes later, she stood in front of the entrance again.

"It's now or never," she said, scanning the badge that granted her entry. Her heels echoed off the walls as she walked to the elevators and punched the buttons. When she stepped off, Fitz was waiting for her with a cup of coffee.

"You're coming to tell me you're quitting, aren't you?" he said by way of greeting.

She sipped the coffee and counted the seconds. "I'm sorry."

"I figured this day would come." Fitz sighed. "What is it about that town?" He led her into his office and closed the door behind them.

"What do you mean?" Paige asked, sitting on the hard leather chair across from his large mahogany desk.

"When your father and I were in law school, we had plans of opening our own firm." Fitz rummaged through the top desk drawer and handed Paige a picture. It was her father and a much younger Fitz holding a sign that read "Fitz & Sparrow, Attorneys at Law." They were smiling.

"Your mother took this picture about three weeks before we sat for the Bar exam. We spent hours planning Fitz and Sparrow that summer. We agreed on everything until it came time to pick a practice location. I wanted a big city and Bird, well, Bird insisted he couldn't practice anywhere but Merchants Town." Fitz took the picture back with a laugh.

"We got in a huge fight over it and didn't speak again until he called me about you." Fitz shook his head. "Two stubborn men. We should have never stopped talking."

"I had no idea."

"I thought I was finally going to get my Fitz and Sparrow, even though it wasn't as originally planned," Fitz continued. "But Bird had his heart attack and you told me you were going home for two weeks. Two weeks. You were adamant. I knew the moment you told me you were going home to help your father that your time here was nearing an end. It's honestly why I didn't fight Meredith over making Davidson partner. It should have been you, but that town has some sort of pull. It doesn't matter how hard someone tries to escape it, it always pulls them back."

"I belong there. It just took me longer to realize that than it should have."

"Life is funny that way. It may take some time, but we always end up where we're supposed to be," Fitz mused. "I guess Fitz and Sparrow just wasn't in the cards, but Sparrow and Sparrow is."

"The universe always wins." Paige smiled. "I am grateful for everything you have done for me, for every opportunity you've handed me. I am a better attorney because of you. I hope you know that."

"You are so much like your father. I am going to miss you, Paige Sparrow."

"I can stay for a couple of weeks to help with the transition and hiring. I know I'm putting you in a bind with Antwan leaving as well."

Fitz shook his head. "There's no need for that. We will survive. Go home, Little Bird; your father has waited long enough for this moment. I'm not going to keep you from him any longer."

Paige was packing her office when Miranda stepped in.

"So, Chris got the job?" Miranda's beautiful face twisted into a frown and her bottom lip started to quiver.

"I don't know."

"I'm confused. If you don't know if he got the job, why are you packing up your stuff? Did Meredith fire you? That awful witch!"

Paige laughed. "I haven't been fired. I just decided to follow my heart."

Miranda's face broke into a smile. "You're going home?" she asked.

Paige nodded. "I am."

"Have you told Chris?"

"No. This was a decision I had to make without him." She looked at the ring on her finger. "It's looking like you won't get to be a bridesmaid after all."

"You're calling off the engagement?" Miranda threw herself into the leather chair used for clients. "You should have told me I needed to sit down for this conversation. What happened?"

"Nothing happened. I just realized I don't want to be doctor's wife."

"Any doctor's wife or just Chris's wife?"

Paige didn't answer. "He deserves the type of life he envisioned. We both do. And we just can't have that together."

"Maybe he'll want to follow you to Merchants Town. They could use a doctor."

Paige shook her head. "You're right. They could use a doctor, but Chris isn't the one for the job. I know his heart and it's not there. He might try, for me, but he'd grow to hate me. I'm not doing that to him, so I'm not giving him the choice. I'm not making anyone put their dreams on hold for me."

Paige had most of the boxes packed by the time Chris unlocked the door. He looked from her to the neatly stacked boxes and sadly smiled. "We had a good run, didn't we?" He pulled her tight against him. "I knew two weeks was a lie."

"I'm sorry."

"Don't be. I did the best I could to keep you from that town. You've always loved it most."

"Did you get the job?" she murmured into his shirt.

"I did."

Paige took a step back and wiped her face. "I knew you would. You're brilliant."

"That cheesesteak place isn't there anymore. Philly is going to be cold without it and you."

Paige pulled the ring from her finger and handed it to him. "I'm sorry," she said again, her face still wet with tears.

"I'm proud of you, Paige."

"For what?"

"For doing what I couldn't." Chris took the ring and slipped it into his pocket. "I'm going to miss you."

He kissed her on the top of her head and Paige nearly lost her nerve. "Chris," she started.

"Don't. This doesn't have to be hard. It doesn't have to be sad. Ending this doesn't destroy what we had or make it any less real. We're just moving on in two different directions. We've both seen this coming since even before your father's heart attack. Things happen. Life happens. It doesn't mean the past was a mistake or a waste. You're never going to be a mistake for me and I hope you'll never view me as a mistake, but I know your happiness isn't with me. You deserve to be happy. We both do. Goodbye, sweet Paige." He kissed her forehead again and walked out of the door without looking back.

Chris had never been big on scenes, Paige knew that about him. She had loved that about him. She stared at the closed door and willed him to come back. If he opened the door, she told herself, it was true love. She waited. An hour later, she poured herself a glass of wine and eased herself into the warm tub. He was gone. She thought she'd feel empty, but she just felt whole.

Paige spent the rest of her week reading the books that had been collecting dust on her shelves and indulging in long bubble baths after hours of packing and cleaning. She spoke with her management company and paid a penalty for terminating her lease early. It was a small price to pay for her new life, she thought.

She put in a call to Janison Parks, the only realtor in Merchants Town, and made an offer on Ida Creech's small home just off the river. With the estate already closed, there would be no trouble.

"Eager sellers," Janison said. "They have no desire to come to Merchants Town, and they just want the money as soon as possible. They didn't even go to her funeral. Ungrateful lot."

"The sooner we can close, the better. I don't need a due diligence period or an inspection at this price. Just email me the paperwork and tell me where to wire the earnest money."

"Absolutely, Ms. Sparrow. I see no reason you can't be in that home next week."

"Can we make it any earlier? This weekend maybe?"

"I don't know that I can manage closing by then, but we can make arrangements for you to take possession prior to closing. I'll have it move in ready for you by Friday."

"Thanks, Janison. I plan on being in town Saturday morning."

"No problem. I'm glad to hear you're coming back. I'm sure Julie needs as many hands as possible with her crew."

Paige laughed. "You've got that right."

"Well, it does take a village," the realtor mused. "I'll go ahead and take the home off the market. I'm looking forward to meeting with you and finalizing everything this weekend. Just give me a buzz when you get in. I'm supposed to be at the Little League game in the morning, but I wouldn't mind meeting your movers if you wanted to go watch your nephews play."

"Thank you again, Janison. I truly appreciate that," Paige said, ending the call and immediately calling her mother. If her parents found out she was moving back because it was in the gossip column of the Merchants Town Index, they'd never forgive her.

"Mama, I'm coming home."

"Okay, honey. Well you know you can stay here. Are you coming for Avery's game?"

"No. I'm coming home to stay."

"Oh, Paige. You should have told me to sit down first."

Paige laughed. "Think there might be an opening at Sparrow Law?"

"There's always been an opening at Sparrow Law, honey. You and I both know that."

"Good, because I've already bought a house. Ida Creech's house to be exact. I get the keys on Saturday."

"Honey, are you absolutely sure this is what you want?" Lillian asked, her voice shaking with excitement.

"Yes. I've never been more sure of anything."

"Have you thought it through? It does seem just a bit quick."

"I have, Mom. I've thought about it a lot. I want to come home."

"And Chris? Will he be joining you?"

"No, Mama. I don't think he will." Paige said trying to hide the catch in her voice.

"Oh, honey. I'm sorry. Are you okay?"

"Yes, Mama. I'm more than okay."

CHAPTER TWENTY-THREE

Miranda came over Friday night for one last Charlotte get together. Antwan had already headed to the Triangle, and the two women decided to have a quiet night inside instead of going out on the town. Paige didn't want to make a big show of leaving.

"This is quick, Paige," Miranda said looking at the empty apartment. "Like seriously quick."

"I know. Is it crazy? Am I crazy?"

"I don't think you're crazy," Miranda said slowly. "You might be having a mid-life crisis just a wee bit early, but I don't think you're crazy."

They ordered pizza and sat cross-legged on the floor even though the movers hadn't picked the furniture up yet.

"It seems surreal that I could pack my life up that quick. What if I hate it?"

"Hate what? Merchants Town?"

"Being back home. You've been there. It's a lazy town full of nosy people who know everyone's business. There is no sushi restaurant within a thirty-minute drive and the closest Starbucks is just as far. What if this is a big mistake?"

"Stop it, Paige. You're trying to freak yourself out and convince yourself not to do it."

Miranda was right. Paige took a deep breath. "The house is really cute," she said after a minute. "And there's a pretty nice guest room."

"Is that a hint?" Mir grinned, leaning into her. "You won't be able to keep me away. You father has been promising to take me fishing, and I am going to take him up on it this summer if it's the last thing I do!"

Paige laughed. "My family would adopt you in a heartbeat, Mir. Maybe you should move with me."

"Would they? Would they please adopt me? Surely you know an attorney who can draw up the paperwork?" she said with a wink.

It was late when Miranda left. Paige pulled her into a tight hug. "I'm serious," she said, trying not to cry. "I don't want us to be like my dad and Fitz. Promise me that we will always be friends."

"Don't be silly, Paige. I'm not going anywhere. And when you get too busy to call and let me know what is going on in your life, I can always read Julie's blog."

Miranda headed out with a box of Chris's things that she'd promised to deliver to him. Paige would have done it, but they had been unable to arrange a time. The box was a hodgepodge of things. His toothbrush. The random odds and ends of clothing he kept there. Despite being engaged, he had never really moved in and neither of them had really kept personal items at the others house. They had both liked their personal space too much.

Paige was still laughing when she shut the door behind her closest friend. She realized when she went to the bedroom that she had already boxed up all her blankets and bed linens, so she curled up on the sofa with a blanket her Grandmother Ruth had knitted before she was born. She'd carried that blanket with her everywhere she had lived and had fallen asleep many a night wrapped in it. It had always made her feel safe and warm. She was asleep as soon as her eyes were closed.

The movers were at the apartment as the sun was just beginning to light up the sky. Paige had paid extra for a "before hours" pick up. She met them at the door with coffee and donuts. As they loaded the moving truck, she loaded her new car with the items she wanted with her. The first thing she loaded in the SUV was the box of memories. The last thing she removed from the apartment and put in the SUV was the wooden sign. She wrapped it in the blanket and gently placed it on the back seat. They were both going back where they belonged.

"Please hurry," Paige urged, glancing at her watch. Despite the "before hours" start, she was running out of time.

The movers made quick work of the remaining boxes and headed on their way. Paige did one last pass through the apartment she'd lived in for the past few years. She thought she'd feel some kind of way, that she would at least be sad, but without her items, it didn't even look like she'd ever lived there. Her roots had never been planted firmly in Charlotte. She quickly locked the door and took the keys to the main office.

When Paige reached Merchants Town, she pulled up in front of her father's law office and grabbed the sign and a hammer. That sign had been waiting for years to be hung, and she wanted it up the next time her father walked through those office doors. She wanted her presence announced to the town; Paige Sparrow was back for good.

"Ms. Sparrow! Let me help you with that!" Travis ran up to the porch and took the hammer from her.

"Travis! I didn't expect to see you here. I didn't expect to see anyone here, to be honest. I figured everyone would be at the Little League game."

"We hate we're missing it, but we have orientation starting Monday and we still have a bit of packing to get done today," he said over the pounding. "We took a break to drop something off at your house. Well, your dad's house."

"Hello Ms. Sparrow." Ainsley's bruises had faded but still peaked out from beneath her makeup. She looked happy. There was a basket with a gingham cloth tucked under her arm.

"I don't know what's in that basket, but it sure smells amazing," Paige said getting a whiff.

"Ms. Ciara is teaching me how to cook," Ainsley said, pulling back the cloth and revealing the pastries. She offered them to Paige. "Sweet potato flap jacks. We were bringing them to your dad. Ms. Ursula mentioned they are his favorite."

"Oh, they are his favorite. But you guys didn't have to do that." Paige reached into the basket and grabbed a small flap jack.

"It's the least we can do, Ms. Sparrow." Travis took the sign and hung it. "There," he said, taking a step back. "Perfect."

"Oh, Ainsley. This is delicious," Paige said, wishing she had snagged a larger one. She finished it in four bites.

"I think I'm getting the hang of it. Ms. Ciara's are still better."

"Ainsley is staying with us for a bit," Travis explained. "Her and Mama have become thick as thieves in that kitchen. But I'm

256

not complaining," he said, rubbing his stomach with a smile. "I'm not complaining at all."

"I'm trying to learn as much as I can before we head off for college," Ainsley explained. "I never really baked before. It's fun." The diamond on Ainsley's hand sparkled in the sunlight.

"Did you find the…" Paige started and stopped when she saw Travis shaking his head. "It's lovely," she said after a minute.

"Thank you. Everyone has been so good to us. Some stranger even started an online campaign to raise money for us to have a wedding. Can you believe that?"

"I'd heard about that. You both deserve it. Have you set a date?"

Ainsley shook her head. "We want to wait until after my father has been sentenced." Her mouth formed a hard line. "I want that chapter closed completely before we move on to the next."

"Understandable."

"And we're working on getting Mama to move back here now that it's safe. Once I have my family here and everything settled, we can set the date. I do know for certain it will be in Merchants Town." She smiled at Travis. "Maybe a Christmas wedding?"

"Baby, I'll marry you any day of the week, just say the word."

Ainsley turned to Paige. "Thank you again. To both you and your father. I cannot express how grateful I am. How grateful we all are."

"Just be sure to invite me to the wedding," Paige said with a smile. "And if you need anything, either of you, just give me or my dad a call. You're family now."

"If you're on your way to see your father, do you think you could give him this from us?" Ainsley held the basket out.

"Absolutely." Paige took the basket and thanked them again. She smiled as they headed off arm and arm.

After they rounded the corner, Paige turned to the sign. It looked like it had always been there. She gathered up the old sign to take home to Roger and headed to her car.

"Now that looks perfect," Barb called from the entryway to Henry's Corner Store. She was holding a cup of iced coffee. "Take this and hurry or you'll miss the game," she said with a smile.

The game was in the fifth inning by the time Paige pulled up. She parked near the back, away from the bleachers. No one looked at the black SUV twice. It was the last Little League game of the season, the time before the older leagues took the fields over, and nearly all of Merchants Town had turned out. The bleachers were full, and parents lined the fence. Paige finally spotted her family sitting near the front and made her way over to them. Lillian and Roger each held one of the triplets, and the third was wrapped tightly against Julie's breast. There was an empty seat beside Julie, as if they had been saving it for her.

Avery saw her first from where he stood at third base.

"Aunt Paige! You came!" he yelled over the clink of the bat hitting the ball.

"Run!" she yelled with the rest of the crowd. "Run!"

Avery crossed home plate and immediately ran to Paige. "I told everyone you were coming, and no one believed me!" His face was pink with excitement. "And here you are!" He threw his arms around her waist.

"And here I am," she said, hugging him back. "Now, you better get back in this game before Scotty comes looking for you!"

She pushed him gently toward the dugout and nodded a greeting to Scotty. By his expression, her return had not made front page news.

"Come on, Sis. Have a seat." Julie patted the empty spot beside her. "Avery just tied the game."

"I didn't think they kept score," Paige said, trading the basket of flap jacks for a baby. "They're from Travis and Ainsley."

"Oh man," Roger said, reaching into the basket. "Ciara's flap jacks are some of the best things this side of the Mississippi."

"They're not Ciara's. Ainsley made them. Ciara is teaching her how to cook."

"Oh, really now?" He took a bite. "She's a fast learner," he said, a look of pure contentment on his face.

"One, Roger. Only one," Lillian warned, taking the basket from him and passing it around.

Paige shook her head when Lillian offered it to her. "I've already had two," she confessed. "One while talking to Ainsley and Travis and another on the drive here."

"I don't see your fancy car anywhere," Anderson said, looking out into the parking lot. "Did you park across the street to keep your windshield safe?"

"Isn't your daddy a funny man," she cooed to the baby. "You tell him Auntie Paige got a new car." She pointed to the black SUV. "But I did park as far away as possible. Not going to lie." Paige laughed and turned her attention back to the baby. "And which little angel does Auntie Paige have?"

"That's Ella," Roger said, quite pleased with himself for being able to tell the difference.

"Ella wears pink socks," Anderson explained, revealing a foot.

"What are you going to do when they start removing their socks?" Paige kissed Ella on the head, breathing in the sweet baby smell and marveling in how much they had changed in just a week.

"I voted for tattoos, but Jules shot me down pretty hard. She says I should be able to tell them apart. I don't know how she does it. Must be some superpower mothers get."

Julie leaned over and revealed the bare foot of the baby she held. There was a tiny black "R" scribbled on the heel. "Eliza Ruth," she whispered with a smile.

"He hasn't noticed?"

"Nope."

"That's genius. You really do have superpowers."

"Mom said you bought the honeymoon house."

Paige nodded. "I needed something small and it was available for quick closing. Janison even volunteered to meet the movers there so I could come to the game."

"It's only a mile from our house. We measured."

"Are you telling me this because these babies are screamers and I should get ear plugs?"

"No," Julie grinned. "They're good babies. I just thought it an interesting fact. A mile from us and closer to Scotty's," she said, looking at Paige out of the corner of her eye.

Paige shook her head. "I already told you…"

"You told me some nonsense about Matty."

Paige blushed. "I thought they were together. I mean, she was at his house when I left last week. Are they not an item?"

"Lord, no. I don't know where in the world you got that crazy idea from. She's always at his house. They started treating the large animals there after he built the barn. He'd outgrown the little office he'd first moved into here, so he found a new space but it didn't come equipped with a barn. He decided to just outfit his property and set it up to keep the larger animals there. You've seen the horses and cows. Did you think they were all his pets? You're silly. I can assure you that Scotty and Matty are definitely not an item and they have never been one."

"Hmm," Paige looked for Scotty on the field. He was coaching first base and had knelt, hands on his knees, to talk to the runner.

"I see you're not wearing that engagement ring anymore," Julie said after a minute.

Paige glanced at her naked finger. "No."

Julie squeezed her hand. "Then what are you waiting for?"

Paige handed Ella to Anderson and walked around the fence until she was standing just beyond first.

"Hey, you," she called, her hands shaking.

Scotty gestured to Peter to take his place at first base and jogged over to her. "Hey there! I didn't expect to see you here today. I mean Avery told me you were coming, but I didn't really believe it."

"If you'd have asked me two weeks ago, I'd have said I didn't expect to be here either. The universe had other plans."

"It's true, then? You're back for good?"

Paige nodded.

"And your fiancé? Is he here as well?"

Paige shook her head and held up her ring-less hand. "The universe had different plans about that as well."

Scotty placed his hands on the fence railing and leapt over, pulling Paige into his arms before he'd even landed on the other side. She laughed as he yanked her ballcap off. She was still laughing when his lips met hers and the bleachers erupted in cheers.

Paige Sparrow was finally home.

Acknowledgements

Thank you to my early readers: Cindy Jeffers, Janelle Brienzi, Julie Zuber, Michelle Stallings, Chelsea Armitage, Joni Horton, Elysia P. Jones, Elizabeth Thomas, and Gwen Pendley.

A special thanks to my mother, Shirley Powell, for being my first reader and the voice of reason and encouragement. And to my sister, Sara Turner, for sneaking away from her children to read an early draft.

A huge thanks to my husband, Jack Norton, for his unwavering support.

For all the readers at A Girl Named Tommi, I send you much love.

Josie, Charlotte, Levi – you all have my heart.

www.ingramcontent.com/pod-product-compliance
Lightning Source LLC
Chambersburg PA
CBHW021520240626
47154CB00002B/723